A sweeping and fascinating plot. The author's expertise transforms the fictional story into a reality. An interesting book that sheds a light on the dark and mysterious world of espionage and intelligence...

**General (retired) Danny Yatom,**
**Former Head of the Mossad (Israeli Central**
**Intelligence)**

The plot reveals a gripping angle of the espionage scene and international schemes, which parallel a reality well known to me....

**Hadas Shtaif, Reporter,**
**Galei Tzahal (major radio station in Israel)**

I loved the insight on Iran and the amazing dialogues in this breathtaking thriller...

**Assaf Heffetz, Former Israeli Police**
**Commissioner**

The book brings a set of engaging characters to life in a world of shadows that keeps you hooked. This book could hold it's own as an action movie...

**Aki Avni, Actor (6 time Israeli Oscar winner)**

# Path of Lies
## Thriller

*Moti Shapira*

Some of the events depicted in this book actually occurred. To protect the privacy and safety of his clients, sources and investigators, the author has altered the names, places, times and methods of operation. Any resemblance to actual events, locations or persons, living or dead, is entirely coincidental.

# Translated from Hebrew

Path of Lies
BookSurge Publishing
An Amazon.com Company
7290-B Investment Drive
Charleston, SC 29418

**CREDITS AND SPECIAL THANKS:**

**Editor:** Brad Schreiber

Kim Kiernan

**Graphics:** Revital Eyni Haleva

ISBN: 978-0-692-60152-5

Thanks

To my anonymous friends who helped with the research and collection of intelligence for this book. Countless months were spent gathering facts in the most genuine and authentic way.

# 1

Stephanie stood in the shower, crying. Her legs were spread apart, bleeding, as the hot water rinsed her aching body. She cautiously put a hand on her crotch. The pain was inconceivable. "Fuck you, Tom," she said again, and sat down heavily on the shower's floor. She picked up the scented soap and started to wash her bleeding body, gently. Tears began flowing from her eyes and joined the stream of hot water sweeping down her face. She felt a sudden rage, one that required revenge.

Stark-naked and dripping with water, she got out of the shower and rushed to the first floor, opened the big closet near the kitchen, and pulled out the gun-- a semi-automatic Colt M1911-- that Tom, her husband, kept there. Breathing heavily, she rushed to the second floor and opened the door to the same room she had left minutes earlier. Tom was lying in bed, his eyes closed.

Stephanie, her heart pounding, was unable to think clearly. She grasped the gun with her two small hands, pointed it at Tom and held a steady grip, struggling to pull the trigger.

Tom opened his eyes and stared down the barrel of his own gun in astonishment. With a wide-eyed gaze, barely breathing, he tried to figure out what was going on, wondering if the next few seconds would be his last. Beads of sweat appeared on his face. He tried to say something but was speechless. His astonished look was soon replaced by a pleading one. Stephanie felt her hands beginning to shake. Inside, she told herself to do it, but she couldn't. Breathing heavily, she lowered the gun, then suddenly raised it firmly, as if possessed by a strange, new power.

Instantaneously, everything blurred around her and she collapsed, surprised by the sound of her body hitting the floor.

Tom Holmes normally closed his pharmacy by 2 PM, a habit he had adopted from the days when he assisted his father, who managed the pharmacy with an iron fist. At the beginning of their life together, Stephanie liked the idea of him closing the pharmacy early on Monday afternoons. In the early years of their relationship, and even in their first years of marriage, she cherished any extra amount of time she got to share with Tom. Now, however, Mondays, and most other days, had become an ongoing nightmare.

In the last couple of years, the time they spent together in their home in Moreno Valley had deteriorated. Tom proved to be insensitive and determined to satisfy his own selfish desires. During sex, he didn't care if Stephanie wasn't enjoying herself. He was not dismayed at all by the fact that she wept during intercourse and cried out of pain when he forced himself with great strength. It didn't even trouble him when she wouldn't cooperate and lied there motionless in the bed. She used to mumble, "Come, already, come," not clearly enough for him to hear but loud enough to give herself the ability to bear it. She felt like his body entering hers was like a knife cutting into flesh.

All of her attempts to avoid sex with different pretexts failed. When she tried to refuse him, Tom would insist, "I'm your husband. You can't say no." Twice Stephanie put up a struggle and refused to have sex, claiming she was tired of being his sex slave; it cost her dearly. Tom responded with a vengeance and violence. He hit her, callously, and forced himself on her. His cruelty toward her excited him.

Even in her darkest thoughts, Stephanie never imagined that at thirty-three years old nothing would remain of the hopes that accompanied her youth. A dozen years earlier, life was very promising. When she was young, she felt in her heart and soul that the sky was the only limit, and all she had to do was to reach out and pick what she wanted.

In spite of her mother's objections, she abandoned her law studies at Hastings College in San Francisco during her second year there. She obsessed over the idea of becoming a movie or TV star. She was convinced that her good looks alone would gain her work and love. God had been good to her. She was endowed with lush black hair that fell over her shoulders, a flawlessly pretty, heart-shaped face and bright green eyes. She was tall, had long legs, and the undeniable confidence that came with such attractiveness.

"You could arouse even a Buddhist monk," one of her many suitors at Hastings College used to tease her.

About a year after she left her mother's house in San Francisco and moved to Los Angeles, Stephanie discovered that her good looks were not good enough to guarantee success over the thousands of other young women who flocked to the City of Angels, hoping to make it big in the entertainment industry. In order to give herself the upper hand, she sought help from a friend who was a plastic surgeon, and she underwent surgery for breast enlargement. The additional 350 c.c. of silicone created a most striking appearance, based on the looks she got from men on the street.

Still, days, weeks and then months went by, and nothing significant happened in her career. She lived on Melrose Avenue, in a small studio apartment on the third floor of a building that housed young men and women who, like her, had come to Los Angeles to "make it." Like many of her neighbors, Stephanie earned a living from temporary jobs. She constantly adjusted her schedule to make room for various auditions that her agent would send her on, sometimes with a warning of only a few hours before her required arrival. In between, she studied at a well-known acting school run by a respected coach named David Callahan.

After her first few years of not breaking through in her career, Stephanie traded her temp jobs for a regular position as a waitress at the Urth Café on Melrose, a pilgrimage for major players in the entertainment industry. Day after day, she showed up, hoping one of her connected customers would notice her beauty and make her the offer of a lifetime.

To her dismay, it never happened. Instead, she got countless proposals that had no connection at all to acting. One man offered her a job acting in porno films and another suggested he could help her become a call girl. Hurt, angry and unsure of her future, she rejected the proposals.

Stephanie found the opportunity for her next job in the oddest of places. She met Kevin Shepard, the administrative manager at the Department of Immigration in an exclusive lingerie store, where she worked as a saleswoman. Shepard, a bulky man in his sixties, had gone into the store to buy his wife a pair of panties. Stephanie was hardly surprised when the considerably older man, mummified in an old, dark business suit, flirted with her. She was used to it. Many men, regardless of age or marital status, hit on her. After many attempts, she decided to appease him and agreed to take his business card, even promising to call him.

"What have you got to lose?" encouraged Vicky, her neighbor in the Melrose building and one of the few young people in the building whom she befriended. "You don't do anything in the evenings. Besides, someone of his status, a married man, won't attack you. At worst, you'll be bored, and at best, you'll get a good dinner."

Stephanie had no enthusiasm about her agent, Ross Dalian. Her social life was practically zero. In spite of dozens of men interested in her, she preferred not to tie herself to anyone emotionally. She was not celibate. She had sex on several occasions, but they were casual and singular events. After much thought, Stephanie agreed.

Stephanie was nervous when she arrived to meet Kevin Shepard at a small Chinese restaurant, but Kevin was so kind and polite that she soon felt at ease. As the minutes passed, her fears also vanished. During their conversation, Stephanie talked about her ambitions and told him that she was fed up with her job as a saleswoman and heartbroken about her lack of success as an actress.

"You're a girl with her head screwed on," he said solemnly. "I understand what you're going through and I want to help. My personal assistant is leaving in a couple weeks. Say the word and the job is yours. I would love to see you every day."

A month after the dinner that would change her life, and after extensive investigations into her background, Stephanie began working at the Department of Immigration. Initially she was employed as a junior secretary. However, after a few months of proving her skills, and after even further investigations into her background, Kevin entrusted her with the office management position.

Kevin, the big boss, continued courting her in his own way, but at no point did he try to force himself on her. Still, the fact that many believed the older man and the pretty young woman were having an affair did not bother them at all. Shepard, it turned out, enjoyed the jealous glances of his colleagues when he returned to the office after they had lunch together. And from time to time, they would go out for dinner and he enjoyed introducing her to his friends and acquaintances.

Stephanie realized that it would better suit her to be platonic in regards to her relationship with Shepard. She concluded that even if she was to deny the existence of a relationship, no one at work would believe her. Beyond that, she realized that she was getting preferential treatment from everyone at the office, due to the assumption that she was physically involved with Kevin.

It took Stephanie over six months to figure out exactly why Kevin was willing to settle for entirely platonic meetings. During that time, the friendship deepened. Stephanie became more than just his confidant. She was treated like Shepard's overly protected daughter. And he began to share with her more and more of what was going on, behind the scenes, at the immigration department.

The peak of this trust occurred when, in confidence, he told her about a secret investigation the FBI had been conducting for the past year. They suspected that one of the employees in the department collaborated with a network specializing in providing unlawful entry visas to the United States. Kevin told her that, according to the federal agency, the main "customers" of the network were extremist Muslim elements.

"I do not have to tell you how sensitive this issue is after what happened on September 11," Kevin said, in a low, serious voice.

Then, one evening, as they were dining in a small Italian restaurant not far from the building, Kevin Shepard decided to open up and tell his life story, something Stephanie had consistently avoided asking about since they had met. He started telling her about his wife and two sons. He revealed that the relationship between him and his wife had run aground and that he was considering divorcing her.

A few months later, while enjoying dinner at Nick & Steff's, an upscale steakhouse downtown, Keven sat with a look of anguish on his face and murmured, "I'm gay." It was the last thing she expected to hear from him. "I know that today nobody gets excited about it," he had later continued. "But in the family I come from, it is considered an awful thing. I never had the courage to 'come out' and that's also the reason why I was in a hurry to get married." Kevin spoke quietly. "They'll never admit it but there is a prejudice in the government regarding homosexuals in the Department of Immigration. I'm not sure I would have reached the position I'm in now if I declared I was gay."

Stephanie was completely surprised by Kevin's candor. She looked at the broad-shouldered, outwardly masculine man sitting in front of her and could not believe it.

"Even though we've never talked about it, my wife must suspect something is wrong. We stopped having sex years ago," he almost chuckled. "Funny, but she thinks there are other women."

During this conversation, Kevin revealed that for the past year he had been in a relationship with a Latino man twenty years younger, whom he had met at the gym where he trained. "I feel good with him. I'm happy with him and I wish I could live with him openly. But I know that such a move would badly harm my family." Kevin shook his head.

"It would break their heart."

Tom Holmes came into Stephanie's life just as she experienced the most significant crisis in the four years since she set foot in Los Angeles. Her mood was grim and she often thought of leaving the city to go back to her mother's home in San Francisco.

The term "second year syndrome" was well known to thousands of young women who flocked to Los Angeles from all over the world to make it into the entertainment industry. During their first year in town, the young aspirants did everything humanly possible to fulfill their dream and willingly gave up social life, love, and a steady job. The syndrome was the self-delusion that something was bound to happen in the second year.

Passion and faith continue to follow the majority of these young women during their second and third years in Los Angeles. Stephanie had met and talked to many of them. They went on with "the journey to the dream." The first cracks in their unwavering confidence usually came to light in the fourth year. Doubts and setbacks led them to question their current life and their future.

That's exactly the situation Stephanie was in. She was worn out by her lifestyle, frustrated by the fact that her career didn't take off, and bored stiff by her job at the Department of Immigration, alongside Kevin. The fear of having to "compromise" at some point to find her future in the entertainment business had been with her. She knew she could never fit into the industry of adult movies or, alternatively, make a living as a stripper.

Stephanie thought how fortunate she was to meet Kevin, while Tom Holmes leaned on the front desk at the administrative offices of the Department and gave her some forms. Like Kevin, he was a few years older. There was something reliable and respectable in the tall, gray-haired man, quite different from most of the men she had met during her years in Los Angeles.

As she was handling the papers Tom had submitted (a request to extend the temporary resident visa of a Mexican minor), she learned that he owned a pharmacy in Moreno Valley.

"Where is that? Is it in California?" she asked without looking up.

"You would be surprised, but it's less than an hour drive from here," he replied with a big smile. "You know, Moreno Valley is a small town, nothing exciting. Not something that would interest a city girl like you." He laughed, then added "Can you please tell me how long it will take to get an answer on this application?"

Stephanie shrugged. She liked his courtesy and calm tone. "It's a procedure that takes over a month, if everything is in order. I don't think there should be any problem in your case."

When Tom Holmes appeared once again behind the desk, an entire month had passed. Stephanie's thoughts were troubled by the negative answer she had received, for seemingly the thousandth time, on her last audition a day earlier. She had forgotten all about Tom's existence the moment he had left the office. In fact, Stephanie didn't even recognize him when she saw him.

"How can I help you?" she asked.

"Yesterday, I received a notice from you that the working permit is ready. I hope I'm in the right place," he answered.

Stephanie took a moment to look at the man standing in front of her. She looked at him and liked what she saw. The white pharmacist's coat he wore suited his tanned face. He had dark blue eyes and a look that inspired confidence. Suddenly, she remembered him and flashed one of her professional smiles.

"Moreno Valley, right?" Stephanie spoke, this time looking directly into his eyes. Tom smiled broadly, showing white teeth.

"Still the same," he nodded. "Nothing happens there."

Stephanie pulled a form from the folder in her hand, put it on the desk in front of her and then picked up a big rubber stamp. With a strong, committed hand, she stamped the form and then handed it to him. "Sign both copies, please."

Tom took the form while his eyes searched hers. "Thank you," he said, "I'm gratful."

He had wanted to ask her out, but thinking she would refuse, he gave up. Yet, one week after that, he waited for her at lunchtime, not far from the main entrance of the building. In his hands, he held a bouquet of red roses. His face lit up as Stephanie approached him.

"I didn't know how to thank you for the way you handled my request," he said, a soft and warm quality in his voice. "I thought that a bouquet of flowers might be a good answer."

She took the flowers and smelled them. The gesture touched her. "You shouldn't have done this, really," she said smiling. "I just forwarded the forms. I wasn't involved with the approval and the handling. Really, you shouldn't have."

"But I wanted to," he answered quickly. "Honestly, I just wanted to see you. Sorry, but that's the truth." He looked away nervously.

She came to his rescue. "You don't need to apologize. I'm glad to see you. Really," she held out her hand. "My name is Stephanie."

From there, things evolved naturally. Initially, he called her almost every day to ask how she was. On Monday afternoons, he drove into town in his blue Dodge, and they would spend the day together until nightfall. While Stephanie preferred not to give away too much, except of course the usual details, Tom actually enjoyed telling her about himself. She learned that he was forty-one, single, a pharmacist by profession, and that he lived with his ailing father and looked after him with the help of a Mexican aide hired for that purpose.

Tom also told her that he had given up his childhood dream, to become a doctor. After a year of medical school at UCLA, he returned to Moreno Valley and joined the family pharmacy that his father ran with firm hand. Over the years, he completed his studies in pharmacology and gradually took over the pharmacy management.

Tom surrounded her with great warmth and love and didn't hesitate to repeat, time after time, that he was lucky that such a beautiful, smart, young woman showed any interest in a guy like him. Although she had heard all the superlatives a beautiful woman can hear before, they sounded different coming from Tom.

On one of their Monday afternoons, she got on the train and made her way to Moreno Valley to see Tom. To her great surprise, she was impressed by the small town. She enjoyed the radical change after her long years spent in a big and bustling city. She was attracted by the calmness and the peace of mind of the local residents.

Tom lived in his parents' house. The two story building, large and roomy, was surrounded by a huge yard full of seasonal flowers. His father lived on the first floor with his Mexican nurse, while the top floor was Tom's exclusive domain. The house, built several decades earlier, was well-maintained.

The first, festive dinner Stephanie shared with Tom and his father was enjoyable. His father, who had both legs amputated as a result of diabetes, was very kind to her and obviously tried to add cheer to the meal, despite his health. Stephanie immediately felt at home with them both. She spent the night in Tom's room, where they made love passionately.

Early the next morning, as she boarded the express train to Los Angeles, hoping not to be late, Stephanie did some soul-searching. It was hard to accept, but she was realistic enough to understand that her failure to achieve her goals in show business was not likely to change. She also knew very well what her options were, and none of them were particularly appealing to her. One of the possibilities was resuming school at Hastings College, which now seemed impractical and the thought of going back to live with her mother in San Francisco was depressing.

On the other hand, looking into a possible future with Tom, she found a rare, bright light. She was not in love with Tom, but she concluded that he might be a good and decent husband.

As she sat down in her office, she grabbed the phone and dialed the pharmacy number. "Tom, sweetheart," she said, "I called to tell you how much I enjoyed yesterday. You're a darling and I'm very much looking forward to our next visit."

Six months later, Stephanie Simmons married Tom Holmes in a short civil ceremony at City Hall in Los Angeles, with no family and no friends.

# 2

The crisis in their relationship started during the second year of their marriage. Thirteen weeks into Stephanie's pregnancy, she suffered a miscarriage. Six months later, the devastation of the event began to sink in. The feeling of sadness, guilt and depression had totally broken her spirit, and she couldn't go back to her old self. Without a doubt, the trauma deepened when her doctor broke the bad news that her chances to get pregnant in the future were slim. For a month after the miscarriage, she remained home, spending days and nights in bed, sleeping long hours when not crying over her fate.

Tom did his best to support and cheer her up, showering her with attention.

"It's fine, Stephanie. We will find an answer to this," he would say every time he sat beside her. Darkness would envelope the room as he sat with her on the edge of their double bed. Eventually, Tom mentioned the idea of seeing a specialist at Cedars Sinai Hospital in Beverly Hills, whom Tom had spoken with, but had no guarantees.

One morning, Stephanie got up and after showering, getting dressed and preparing her favorite tea, she sat in the kitchen not far from Tom. "I don't ever want to talk again about the baby we could have had," she said with an icy expression and glassy eyes.

He nodded, hardly believing the sudden change in his wife. "You know, I'll be happy to see you back to being yourself," he said and reached out to caress her face. "God, I just want you to be happy." Stephanie didn't respond.

The next day, early in the morning, she took the train to work as she usually did since moving to Moreno Valley. On the surface, life returned to normal. However, something that neither of them could explain had changed in their relationship. The miscarriage and the expectation of never being able to conceive again led to indifference, and intimacy was gradually replaced by a sense of strangeness and alienation. Stephanie started to avoid their regular walks Monday afternoons. She found that she just couldn't bear the slightest touch from Tom, let alone sex with him.

"Maybe you're just worn out," Kevin Shepard said, when she told him what was going on between them. "Or maybe it's time for you to admit that you simply got married too quickly." Kevin predicted the things to come.

On Tom's birthday, Stephanie decided to surprise him. She left work at one o'clock, bought a sports watch for Tom (one she knew he wanted), and boarded the train to Moreno Valley.

When she reached the pharmacy, she was surprised to find it was closed. Her first thought was that something had happened to Tom's father. She considered calling him, but on second thought, decided to take a cab to his house. Tom's blue Dodge, parked in their driveway, confirmed her concern that something had happened to his father.

Stephanie went into the house, looking for her father-in-law, who used to spend most of the day in an armchair in the living room watching TV. When she didn't find him, she went to his room, where she found him lying in bed, fast asleep. She called out for Tom, but didn't get any response. She was overcome by an uneasy feeling as she called again but didn't receive any answer. She quickly climbed the stairs leading to the top floor, until she heard noises coming from the bedroom. Stephanie faced the closed door of the room, trying to make sense of the sounds. She opened the door abruptly, and froze.

The scene before her took the air out of her lungs. Tom, her husband, was naked, his back to her. He was lying with his full weight on the back of a woman, penetrating her from behind, a position that had always been his favorite. The two were in the fit of passion and didn't notice a thing.

Stephanie felt paralyzed as she stood, staring at Tom's legs and buttocks which continued to undulate wildly. After she recovered, she turned back and left the room, slamming the door and running down the stairs.

From that moment until she boarded the train, her phone didn't stop ringing. At first it was Tom, and then his father's number showed up. She didn't answer. All the way back to Los Angeles she cried bitterly, ignoring the gaze of her fellow passengers. She spent the night in the studio apartment of her friend, Vicky, in her old building.

The next day, Kevin Shepard gave her five thousand dollars in cash. "Consider this an open loan that you can pay back whenever you want," he said, handing her the envelope. She rented a room in the new downtown building, the Loft Pacific, not far from her office.

Tom tried to call her several times, but she refused to talk to him. Days later, she spotted him waiting outside the Department of Immigration, but was able to avoid him by leaving through the back door.

For a week, Stephanie's thoughts tumbled over and over in her mind. She was having trouble facing what she had seen and struggled with deciding what to do about it. Finally, she chose to make the most of the Christmas break and visit her mother in San Francisco, something she had avoided for several years, ever since she had moved in with Tom and decided to marry him.

Heartbroken, Stephanie set out to San Francisco, remembering well the time she told her mother of the decision to leave law school and try to fulfill her dream of becoming a movie actress. She also recalled the visit she took with Tom, when together they told her mother of their intention to get married. Sharon Simmons had not been too pleased with Stephanie's decision to marry.

"I have nothing against Tom," her mother had told her on their private trip to the grocery store. "He is educated, attractive, seems nice… but men always cheat." Her mother shrugged. "And unfortunately, I fear your decisions are going to continue to cause you regret." Her mother had a clear and straightforward perception of the world and did not hesitate to state it. Stephanie's mother continued to speak bluntly.

"If you ask me, I'm going to tell you something we both know you aren't going to do: go back to law school," her mother's eyes held a hint of sadness. "It's still not too late. I hope that now you understand you made a mistake giving up your education and leaving for your silly quest to be an actress. Think about where you would be today if you had continued your studies. Everything would be different if you had a diploma."

Stephanie wasn't surprised by her mother's words then.

Throughout her childhood, when they lived in a small two and half room apartment in the Castro district of San Francisco, she often heard the theory that the ultimate priority for every woman was economic self-sufficiency.

Time after time after time, at every possible chance, her mother insisted that a woman must not depend upon her looks and femininity, but rather, reach a position where she can act independently and without reliance on a man.

"Life is cruel and full of changes, and to survive you have to be ready for all circumstances," she used to tell her. Stephanie knew her mother's words by heart: "Take me for example. I didn't prepare for times of distress. Instead, I lived under the illusion, like millions of women do, that all my life I would be safe. And when turmoil arrived, I was left with nothing." Stephanie didn't understand what her mother meant exactly when she emphasized the word "turmoil." Sharon Simmons never went into details about her past and Stephanie avoided asking questions.

Only once, on a particularly cold and rainy evening, as the two of them were lying huddled up side by side on the bed enjoying hot tea, did Sharon open up a little. Stephanie sensed that her mother was choosing her words carefully, but what she heard that day was engraved in her memory.

"I was about twenty-five," her mother told her, "and you were six months old. Everything changed. We moved to San Francisco but I had nobody: no friends, no family, no husband and I had no profession. I ended up finding work as a kitchen cleaner at one of the restaurants in town. I would work from dusk till dawn on my feet, coming back home feeling sore and broken. We barely had any money after I paid for rent, your babysitter and the groceries. I was lonely and miserable."

Sharon took a long sip from the cup of tea. "The first year, I blamed the entire world for my situation; I blamed my parents, your father, myself, and even you. And then, I remember like it was yesterday, I returned home from work one day at the restaurant, filthy, and went to the bathroom. There, under the flowing hot water of the shower, I cried until I could feel all my frustrations begin to fade away."

Stephanie held on to her mother. Her candor moved her.

"I could hear my own mother's voice saying, 'Enough! This is your life, and you must come to terms with it. You have a little girl who is not to blame for what happened and she needs her mother. Blaming the world for your problems isn't going to help. Take responsibility for yourself and your life.' At that moment, I realized that if I didn't help myself, no one would."

The room fell silent. Stephanie didn't make a move, afraid an unnecessary motion would interrupt her mother's stream of thought. Some time went by before Sharon started to talk again.

"All that time, I was focused on finding a partner. Someone to share life with, who could help me and pull me out of my misery. You know, I didn't look so bad and had no shortage of suitors. But no one stuck around. I really don't know how I managed to take care of you on my own, but I did. Soon enough, I realized that it wouldn't be so easy to find a partner. No one was seriously interested in a divorced woman, although young, with a child. At most, men were looking to spend a couple of pleasant nights with me." She paused yet again, took another sip, and ran her fingers through Stephanie's hair. Their eyes met. "As soon as I realized that my chances to find the right man were slim, I decided to take control of my life and to not rely on anyone and that's exactly what I did and am still doing today. It hasn't been easy, but I try to survive, for you and for me."

Stephanie felt her mother grow a little lighter in the tone

of her voice. "I was very lucky with the jewelry store. A year after I started to work there, the owner decided to retire. I took a chance, kept his lease and became the owner. It's been difficult. I'm not always sure that the revenues justify my investment, but it provides a living. A living I make on my own."

Although her mother worked long hours – often late into the evenings– she used everything she earned to make sure Stephanie was never in need. When Stephanie decided to study law at Hastings and was refused a scholarship, her mother did not hesitate to offer up her savings.

As an adult, Stephanie realized that every human being has a natural need to share feelings with someone. She could sympathize with the pain, the anguish and the frustration that accompanied her mother whenever one of her lovers broke up with her and walked out of their lives. Although Sharon Simmons tried as much as possible to downplay the significance of her romantic relationships, over the years, Stephanie learned to read her true feelings. During her childhood, she found it difficult to accept that strangers shared a place in her mother's heart. As she grew up though, she became the one who encouraged her mother to go out and have fun.

"I bet you can find love," she used to tell her. "I see how men look at you." Stephanie was not exaggerating. Sharon Simmons was indeed an attractive woman, and looked younger than her age. She had a girlish figure and opted for a sporty look (jeans, tee-shirts and sneakers) which added to her youthful look. The lush auburn hair, black eyes and two dimples that showed every time she smiled rounded up her charming appearance.

And now, here they were, face to face with each other once again.

"I missed you," Sharon stood at the doorstep of her house, and reached out for her daughter. "Come on, give me a hug."

They spent the next two days together, at home and walking around in the neighborhood. Stephanie told her mother in detail all she had gone through. She talked about her wedding, her life with Tom in Moreno Valley, her job at the Department of Immigration, the miscarriage and the strong depression she experienced following the loss of the baby, and finally Tom's adultery and her leaving the house. Any reservations between them faded. After long years of emotional estrangement, they once again became mother and daughter.

"I missed you so much. I needed you so much," Stephanie told her mother as they wandered through a big department store. Sharon pulled Stephanie to her and hugged her warmly. The gesture surprised Stephanie. She didn't recall her mother being someone with the habit of hugging. She wanted to say something but decided against it. Instead, she wrapped her arms around her mother's waist in the central aisle of the women's department, ignoring the customers passing by.

"Mom, what am I going to do with my life?" she asked a few hours later, while having a holiday dinner at Mathias, a small fish restaurant where they had often went to in the past. Stephanie had a lump in her throat as tears started to roll from her eyes.

Up until then, Stephanie and her mother were beaming with happiness. The reunion had turned into something joyous. Both were dressed in black. Stephanie wore the black dress her mother had given her as a holiday present and Sharon was wearing black pants and a sweater. A stranger watching the scene would hardly believe that they were mother and daughter.

Sharon looked thoughtful. "I don't want to tell you what to do. It's your decision and only yours, but if I were you, I would go back to Tom. Time is the best healer. Trust me, and not just because of my advanced age. I have seen and heard a lot in my day. There are very few women who haven't gone through a crisis like yours at some point. I know the very thought of him with another woman in your bed is infuriating. But from what you've said, you know he loves you. It seems like he really regrets what he did and is trying to do everything to get you back. Steph, if there was really something special about that girl, he wouldn't be trying to get back together with you so hard. Consider giving him a second chance."

Stephanie struggled with her thoughts. "It's hard. I don't know what I'm feeling anymore. But I do know that I could never love him again after what happened. Even without what happened, things have not been good between us for a long time."

Sharon ignored her daughter's words. "You need to really reflect and think hard about your alternatives. Do you want to get divorced and start an independent life, knowing that there are no great bargains out there? All the best men are married, and the single ones at your age are looking for only one thing, and it is certainly not a relationship. Consider whether you would be able to support yourself after a divorce. If you think that you could handle it both emotionally and financially, go for it. But if not—and now we come to the second alternative—get over your womanly ego, and go back home to Tom. I'm saying this with a sinking heart, but despite his betrayal, I would like you to give yourself another chance to rebuild your marriage. Don't look for the easy solution. Just get up and go. And anyway, just know that your decision will be welcomed by me with a hug and understanding."

Three days after Christmas, right after work, Stephanie boarded the train to Moreno Valley. Tom lingered at the pharmacy as Stephanie took advantage of the time to clean the house, something that had obviously not been done for a long time. Then she prepared dinner with whatever she found in the fridge. Tom was surprised when he walked in to find her there, dinner on the table, and the home spotless.

"I thought I lost you forever and that I wouldn't see you again," he told her and pulled her close to him. "It's the most beautiful Christmas present I ever got. I'm so happy to see you. Really, I'm sorry for what happened. It was stupid and silly and totally meaningless. I'm really sorry."

Two hours later, as she was lying naked on the bed, looking at Tom as he calmly lit the "after sex cigarette," she tried to absorb what she had gone through in the last couple hours. She didn't feel any joy or relief. It was just the opposite. Not only did the anguish that accompanied her all the way from San Francisco to Moreno Valley not vanish during intercourse, it became even more oppressive. Soon after, life resumed and went by as usual, but with the passage of time she knew that her relationship with Tom would never be the same. Frustration and bitterness now became a dominant part of her life.

"Every night, I find myself lying in our bed wondering who is sleeping next to me," she confessed to Kevin Shepard over lunch one day.

Stephanie didn't know how to deal with the betrayal and her overwhelming thoughts. The inability to disconnect from it outweighed her willingness to rebuild their marriage.

Eventually, she stopped pretending and alienated herself entirely from Tom. Once again, she found excuses to avoid spending time together on Monday afternoons, and especially the sex that Tom wanted day after day.

The distance between them grew deeper. While in the past Tom at least tried to talk to her and understand what she was going through, now it seemed he really didn't care.

"We're like two roommates," she confided to Kevin. "We tiptoe so as not to get under each other's skin." This wasn't really accurate.

One evening, after she managed to avoid having sex with him for days, Tom asked to be physically intimate with her. Stephanie curled up in a corner of the bed with her back to him and complained softly of a disturbing headache. This time, unlike the previous couple of attempts, Tom would have none of it.

"Enough. Enough of your lies," he said insistently. "Damn it, what kind of woman are you? I have a right to expect affection from you." He swiftly pulled off her nightgown and clung to her back. She remained stiff and motionless but felt Tom's penis between her legs. Despite all his efforts, he could not penetrate her. "Lie on your stomach," he commanded her in a voice more upset than she had ever heard. He reached out and pulled hard on her shoulder. "I told you to lie on your stomach!"

In silence, she turned over and buried her head into the pillow. She could feel Tom's body clinging to her from the back and his penis penetrating her by force. Excruciating pain pierced her body and she let out a groan. Tom didn't seem to notice what she was going through. If he did, he ignored it. He kept moving fast, indulging in the pleasure that flooded over him.

In the following weeks, he repeatedly had sex with Stephanie without her consent. All her efforts to plead with him were unsuccessful, and when she tried to resist, he reacted violently.

Then, one evening, standing in the shower next to the bedroom, she decided to put an end to his sexual assaults. As the pain pierced her body and a desire for revenge overcame her, she left the shower and picked up the Colt M-1911 that Tom hid in his closet. Then she went back to the bedroom and stood above Tom, who was sprawled on the bed. Balancing her grip on the huge gun, she tried over and over to pull the trigger but she couldn't. The last thing she remembered was the sound of her body hitting the floor.

"Stephanie. Stephanie." She heard a man's voice above her. She opened her eyes slowly and saw Dr. Russell, the long-time family doctor, looking down at her.

"I wanted him to stop," she mumbled softly. "I just wanted him to…Where is he? Did I hurt him? How long have I been here?"

The doctor in his white coat gently put his hand on her cheek. "Shh. Relax. Relax, Stephanie. You're going to be fine. You didn't hurt him. After you fainted, Tom panicked and called me and asked me to come over. All the way over to your house, I kept in touch with him, trying to guide him on how to attend to you. Based on the account he gave me, I was afraid you had a heart attack. When I arrived, I found Tom on his knees, his head buried into his hands and sobbing. Your pulse was unusually weak, your forehead was dripping with sweat and your body was cold. I asked Tom to leave the room after I confirmed that you hadn't suffered a heart attack. I tried to wake you up, but I couldn't. I injected you with a low dose of Valium, which didn't work at first, so I added a bit more to stabilize you. Although the Valium started helping quickly, you didn't stop mumbling. For half an hour, you spoke about details of your life. I couldn't always follow the details, but you shared an intimate account of your pain after the miscarriage, Tom's humiliations and his betrayal. You didn't spare any details about Shepard, your boss, your mother, and how life has played a pretty cruel game with you in recent years. Stephanie, no doubt you need a change of luck."

Stephanie had a throbbing headache and felt very embarrassed about the doctor's new familiarity with her private life. "If you really know everything, you should realize that I need a lot more than luck," she muttered in despair.

"Believe me, I heard quite enough to--"

She interrupted him with a groan and used both hands to cover her face in shame. Stephanie got up from the floor slowly with the doctor's help and sat down on the bed's edge to recount the recent events before fainting. She clearly remembered Tom's sweating and scared face the moment he saw the gun pointed at him.

*I guess he really believed I was going to shoot him,* she thought. *I truly hope that was the last time he tries to touch me.*

"My dear Stephanie," continued the doctor, "I don't want you to worry. Everything you confided to me will be kept confidential. Now, get up, and wash your face. What's important is that you remember I'm here at your disposal for any issue that may arise."

## 3

Professor Yasser Ashraf stood at his podium with his arms crossed. He enjoyed watching the dozens of students fill the auditorium to listen to his lecture.

"Unlike what you hear and read about Islam, the religion is actually more open and liberal than any other religion. Don't be perturbed by the Ayatollahs' fervor. They are extremists who day and night call out for the destruction of those they call infidels, and of all those who don't accept Islam."

Stephanie's eyes were fixed on the professor with the little black beard, who wore blue jeans and a long-sleeved white shirt. She was absorbed by his words. She was really surprised by how good it felt to be back in school, even if it was only a six month seminar, once a week, paid for by the Department of Immigration. Moreover, although she initially feared that the class "Islam: Its Many Faces" would be boring, the lectures fascinated her. She discovered a new world, with unfamiliar complexity, customs, denominations and beliefs.

She devoured the teacher's every word. He was describing the principles of Islam, God, and His prophet,

Mohammed. Ashraf spoke at length on the expansion of Islam in Africa, the renunciation of other gods and total devotion to Allah according to Islamic laws, the holiness of the suicide bombers, and various other topics.

At the office, Stephanie thanked Kevin, who had advised her to specialize in that specific subject, in order to move further up in her career.

"You know, Islamic jihadists are a threat to our security. It will be useful for you to become familiar with their culture and people," Kevin told her.

"To learn, to enjoy and hopefully earn a promotion, what more could I ask for?" she replied. "I can't believe I have such a desire to study after so many years." Kevin Shepard didn't know how right he was when he told her that the course would be a chance to forget about all her problems with Tom for a while. For reasons that she herself didn't really understand, Stephanie refrained from disclosing to Kevin that she had been having a passionate affair with the Muslim professor, Yasser Ashraf, for the last month.

It started two weeks after the beginning of the course. The last lecture had just ended and Stephanie, like her classmates, was on her way to the taxi stand at the entrance of the campus. "Stephanie?" she suddenly heard from a familiar voice beside her. When she turned her head, she recognized Professor Ashraf walking briskly right next to her.

"Hello, professor," she answered quickly, feeling a wave of excitement all over her body. The fact that he recognized her from among the dozens of other students was very flattering.

"I'm also taking a taxi. Where are you heading?"

She turned towards him, her green eyes staring into his. "Out of town. To Moreno Valley. Do you know the place?"

He shook his head. "I have no idea. Do you take a taxi up there?"

Stephanie smiled. "No, no. I take a taxi to the train station and from there a train to Moreno Valley. I--"

"In that case," he said interrupting her, "we can share a taxi to the train station. I take the last train to San Francisco."

"San Francisco? I used to live there," she said.

The chemistry between them was undeniable and the conversation flowed freely. Within the first hour, initially on the ride to the station, then in a nearby café, they felt comfortable enough to talk about their personal lives. Stephanie learned that the professor was forty-five years old, married with two children, and was a regular lecturer at USC. During the school year, he spent the weekdays in his rented apartment not far from the campus, returning to his family in San Francisco on weekends. This week, however, he was going home to San Francisco, mid-week, to celebrate the birthday of his oldest son.

"I really enjoyed your company," he said, as he walked her to the train's platform. "Any chance I'll see you again?"

She looked at him. "Obviously. I'll be attending your lecture next week," she said naively.

"That's not what I meant," he answered with a sheepish smile. "I meant if we can meet for coffee again after class?"

"You're married."

"Well, so are you," he said without thinking twice.

They faced each other silently, but one could sense the excitement and tension between them. Professor Ashraf was the first to break the silence. "I want to see you. I enjoyed your company very much."

"You already told me that once," Stephanie said, flattered.

"I apologize. When I'm nervous I tend to repeat things," he answered, embarrassed.

Professor Ashraf called her at the Department of Immigration the next day and again a day later, but she politely declined his requests to go out again. It wasn't long after their first meeting that she realized, even though she was attracted to his charisma and charm, she did not want to be vulnerable to another man.

"We'll see each other on Tuesday in class," she told him. She was determined to keep their relationship academic.

In spite of her polite rejections, he called her again the next day. "Will you see me tomorrow?" he asked.

"Of course. There's no way I would miss your lecture," replied Stephanie, holding off his advances.

"I meant after school," he probed.

Stephanie indulged him a bit before she answered. "It's possible."

"We could meet at the cafeteria," he suggested.

"I don't think that would be wise. Too many people I know. Too big of a risk."

"There is a small coffee shop in--"

"You said that you have a small apartment," Stephanie spoke coolly and took him by surprise.

"I do," the professor answered, trying to hide his surprise. After he recovered, he continued. "Meet me at the taxi stand. It's a block away from there."

As Stephanie boarded the train home, she felt elated. Her body ached all over, but it was a completely different kind of pain than she was used to feeling after having sex with Tom. Lately, sex with him had repulsed her and led her to believe that something might be wrong with her. Yasser re-awakened her femininity and reminded her what it was like to be intimate without the fear of abuse.

Professor Yasser Ashraf was a wonderful lover, who knew how to stimulate her sexually and take her time after time to peaks she had never experienced. In the hour and half they spent in his apartment, they performed two "rounds," as he liked to call each sexual act. And unlike what she had known from her previous lovers—including Tom, of course--each "round" with Yasser lasted over half an hour. This was not the only difference between the charismatic professor and all the others.

"Wait, I want to understand. You are a Muslim, so why are you circumcised?" she asked, caressing his body.

The professor laughed. "For Islam, circumcision is a commandment, although it is not written in the Quran, but in the Hadid. All Muslims have to circumcise their sons before the age of thirteen. According to Muslim tradition, the Prophet Mohammed was born circumcised."

She could not hold back her shudder. "It must be very painful. What a primitive custom. My God, it gives me the chills just thinking about it."

Yasser shrugged. "Actually, I had no way to object. I was just a few months old when they circumcised me. My mother was opposed, but my father was uncompromising. The meaning of the word circumcision in Islam is 'walking the path of God,' an expression of submission to His will."

Yasser went on to explain circumcision in Islam at length, but Stephanie soon lost her concentration. Her eyes were too focused on her lover's penis, admiring its physical characteristics, another welcomed difference between Yasser and her previous lovers. Passion and arousal took over her as she opened her mouth and eagerly wrapped her lips around his erect penis. She slowly managed to put it into her mouth and started to roll her tongue around it.

Stephanie stared at her lover as he stood at the podium giving his lecture.

"Prophet Mohammed's writings are the basis of Islam. One of his first teachings is the sacred duty to help the needy, elderly, widows, poor and orphans. Prophet Mohammed, according to the Quran, told his followers to learn from all acts of Creation so that they could learn compassion and kindness. The professor left the stand and approached the blackboard behind him. He picked up a piece of chalk and wrote the word "Islam" on the board. He then turned toward the class.

"The word Islam means peace and reconciliation. And contrary to what many of you may believe, you won't find any incitement of hate or war in the Quran. The opposite is true. Please note, the Quran teaches believers that war is always unjustified. The one acceptable cause for it is self-defense against infidels. The purpose of any war should be to restore peace and quiet. Beyond that, the Quran explicitly states that any peace proposal by the enemy should be welcomed by a cease fire, under the condition that the terms are honorable and not shameful." He paused, looking at the dozens of men and women seated before him through his black eyes.

"I believe that what I have just told you is different from what you are used to hearing about Islam. I want to address another prevalent stigma about Islam, common in the West, which is the Islamic attitude toward women. According to the Quran, a man can marry up to four women, but he must act fairly and treat all of his wives equally without preferences for one wife over another in all areas, including, of course, love."

Stephanie, like many of the others, didn't know much about Islam and Muslims beyond what she had heard from the media. And like the rest of the world, she had been stunned by the events of September 11, the terrorist attacks organized by Osama bin Laden on the United States.

She was exposed over many years, one way or another, to the anti-Muslim sentiment common in the news media, influenced by the bloody war waged by the American military in Iraq and Afghanistan. Because she had never been too interested in politics, her opinions on the issue were pretty simple: Islam equals terrorism stemming from extreme religious fanaticism.

As the professor lectured, she began to feel uncomfortable and ashamed. She realized that, like millions of people all over the world, she had been brainwashed in regard to Islam and the Muslims. Even her positive daily contact with dozens of Muslims from every region, who came to the Department of Immigration to get an entry visa to the United States or a working permit, had not changed her opinion on Islam and its believers.

Even if the employees of the Immigration Department were not told to pay extra attention to Muslim applicants, the department followed a standard of "welcome and caution." Stephanie, like most of the department employees, didn't know or understand the reasons behind the unofficial policy, which was to examine applications by Muslims very closely. The employees were to follow the instructions without asking too many questions.

Actually, Stephanie had almost no religious awareness. She vaguely remembered the day in her childhood when she got back home from school and asked her mother what religion they belong to. She also remembered that her mother casually answered, "I'm not connected to any religion. When you grow up, you will decide for yourself the religion you like the best." And with that, the issue was settled and never came up again in their conversations.

Stephanie couldn't remember ever needing to make a decision concerning religion. In the years spent living with her mother, they used to celebrate Christmas without any particular concern for why, like millions of other Americans. As far as Stephanie was concerned, it was the most natural choice. "All my life, my mother and I have celebrated the Christian holidays," she told Yasser one day, as they laid side by side, exhausted, on the bed in his apartment.

"And your father?"

"I have no idea," Stephanie thought for a while after she spoke. "I only know his name was Mario. He died of cancer. In truth, I never asked too many questions. My mother never liked to talk about anything related to him. And apparently, it didn't matter much to me. It's just the reality I grew up with."

Yasser leaned over her and gently kissed her right breast. "I'm actually relieved that my father is no longer alive, either. I mean, I'm relieved that he cannot see how I live today. I'm not exactly the model example of a Muslim. My father would turn over in his grave if he could see me. Islam forbids drinking alcohol, yet I drink. Islam mandates prayer several times a day yet I seldom pray."

"Your father was a pious Muslim?"

Yasser Ashraf considered her words. "He was certainly more devout than me. Even after he left Iran and came to the United States, he managed to observe all of the Muslim traditions. I grew up in America, but I would occasionally go with my father to the mosque near my home and meet his Muslim friends from Iran, who immigrated to the United States like him."

"And your mother?"

"My mother was never devout. She immigrated to the

United States with her parents from Iran when she was a year old, so she was also educated as an American. Unlike my father, who always dreamed of returning to live in Iran, she considered herself an American in every way. Over the years, she began to develop anti-Iranian and anti-Muslim views. She could not stand the religious fundamentalism that has developed in Iran since Khomeini's rise to power."

"I can definitely understand her," Stephanie admitted. "I wouldn't want to live there. I don't think I could live with being forced to cover my entire body. I don't understand how women agree to that."

Yasser Ashraf reached out and gently stroked her hair. "Like many Westerners, your views are shaped by common prejudices. As I explained in my lessons, Islam is much more accommodating and tolerant, even in regards to women, than many people realize. For example, in the West, the *chador* (the piece of cloth that Muslim women wear to cover their body) is seen as a symbol of all women's oppression by men; however, the Quran states the practice is only reserved for Mohammed's wives. It is done in order to separate and protect them from society and is an expression of their honorable status. It's true that Muslim women are required to dress modestly, but they are not required to hide behind a veil and cut themselves off from men in a separate part of the house. These customs, as I have emphasized in my lectures, evolved after Mohammed's death, under the influence of extremist Muslim countries such as Iran.

Stephanie lost her concentration on the "private lecture" that she had been receiving from the professor. She reached for his groin and took his penis. She was delighted to find that her touch aroused him and it started to bulge. Stephanie intensified her hold as she felt a wave of desire rush through her. Now she heard him vaguely.

"Tell me, do all Muslims have such a big thing?" she

asked, holding his penis.

He laughed. "Not necessarily. It's a legend, but I'm not sure it's true. So you like it, huh?"

She nodded, clinging to his body. The manhood of the professor was erect in her hands. Stephanie looked at him adoringly and ran her lips along its entire length, desire running through her body. "It's beautiful," she whispered. "Being with you, Yasser. It's beautiful."

Stephanie looked forward to her after-school Tuesday meetings with Professor Ashraf all week. Even after the seminar ended, she didn't want to stop seeing him. Every Tuesday, she would find an excuse to leave work early and escape to the professor's studio apartment.

Other than their weekly encounters there, Stephanie avoided meeting her lover, despite his repeated pleas. And always, no matter what (even though it was often particularly hard for her) she made sure to board the five thirty train from Los Angeles to Moreno Valley.

The boundaries she used, to limit her relationship with Yasser were, above all, designed to avoid arousing Tom's suspicion. But that wasn't all. Since Yasser was married, she didn't want her feelings for him to deepen. She avoided, as much as possible, asking personal questions about his wife, his children, what he did on the days they weren't together, and, in particular, what he expected from their relationship.

She was satisfied with their little world, not even letting herself think what could be beyond it. "The truth is that I don't really want you," she said half-jokingly, during one of their weekly encounters as she rode him and brought herself to her pleasure. "As long as I have you to myself once a week, I'm satisfied. It does me good."

"You know it is all yours," he said, his hands cupping both her breasts. "I would like to experience other things with you but--"

"You know we can't," she spoke quickly, and to avoid further discussion, she intensified her pelvic thrusts. Her head was now tilted upward, her eyes were closed and her mouth open. Another wave of pleasure began to wash over her. Slowly her breath became more and more pronounced.

A slow groan slipped out of her throat. Yasser reached for her buttocks and continued to move inside her with steady movements. "Don't stop," she muttered in a daze, unable to catch her breath. Despite her request and without warning, Yasser broke away from her and slid his fingers inside her. Gradually, he raised his head and started to lick her all over, gently at first. The professor's tongue movements grew stronger. Then another series of groans escaped her throat and her body was shaking.

When she regained her composure and fell blissfully into his arms, he put his mouth to ear and whispered, "I love you, Stephanie. And I love to make you come."

Stephanie was unable to keep her promise of keeping her relationship with Yasser Ashraf a secret. It happened when she went to visit her mother. She decided to go and see her after she noticed distress in her mother's voice during a phone conversation a few days earlier. Despite the repeated attempts by Sharon Simmons to assure her that business was as usual, Stephanie had a feeling that the abrupt departure of Jean-Paul Benoit, her mother's latest lover, had broken her heart.

"I knew it wouldn't last forever," her mother admitted openly, "and that he would leave at some point. But after you get used to a person, learn to live with him, it's very difficult to go back to being alone. That asshole promised to marry me. In the early days after he left, I simply couldn't be home alone. I couldn't get used to his being gone."

"Why did he leave? Did you two have a fight?"

Sharon lit a cigarette, inhaled and smiled bitterly. "The simplest reason in the world for a man to leave a woman is another woman-- younger, more beautiful, but not necessarily wiser."

"Do you know who?"

Sharon nodded. "A young and dumb girl who had been his girlfriend in the past. He claimed they had separated. Later, I saw her several times on different occasions but I didn't suspect anything. It's just frustrating. I can't deny that I'm sad and I miss him, but I'll get over it. I knew it would end at some point, so sooner is better than later. When it all blew up, he tried to convince me that he hadn't betrayed me. What an idiot. It hurts to live with the thought that he cheated on me with his ex, rather than be a man and tell the truth. I told you before, the best men are married and the single ones want one thing only. There are no good men out there."

She took another drag from the cigarette she was holding. "Since Jean-Paul left, I keep myself busy with all sort of things. I even joined the new gym that opened near the store... It's still hard." There were tears in Sharon's eyes and her voice cracked. "It's difficult to erase his presence in the house, in my life. The small things are the worst. You know, going to bed at night without him, watching television alone, waking up to a silent house. It turns out that I loved him."

Stephanie rose from her seat and sat next to her mother. She placed her hand on her shoulder and gently stroked her mother's hair. "You said that time is the best healer. So, give it some time. I know how difficult that can be since I went through it in a different way with Tom's betrayal. Do you remember what you told me then? You said that we have to believe we are worth loving and be strong."

Sharon rested her head on her daughter's shoulder. Wiping her tears, she said, "I'm so glad you came. You are the only thing I have in this world. Really. I know I wasn't always there when you needed me. I also know that I haven't always been a hugging or kissing kind of mother. But I want you to know that I love you very much. You will always be the most important thing in my life."

Stephanie was touched by her mother's admissions. "I love you, too, Mom," she said softly, as she felt her throat choking and tears filling her eyes. "And I think you are the strongest person I know. I wouldn't want any other mother in the world." This closeness led Stephanie to reveal to her mother that life with Tom had become a living hell and that she intended on leaving him but was just waiting for the right time. More importantly, she told her mother of her extramarital affair. Much to her surprise, her mother wasn't shocked at all to learn about her infidelity. In fact, she even supported it.

"I was sure that, over the years, you had a relationship with your boss Kevin," she said smiling. "I thought that you made him out to be homosexual because it was a cover story. From what you've told me, I understood that he cares for you more than for any other employee in the office."

Stephanie laughed. "No, mother, my relationship with Kevin is strictly platonic. Everything I told you about him is absolutely true."

"So tell me, who is your lover," her mother probed. "And why is he just a lover, and nothing more?"

"Because he's married. His name is Yasser Ashraf and he is a professor. I met him during a seminar at the university. He's forty-five years old and he has two children."

Sharon interrupted her. "Yasser Ashraf?"

"Yes. He's an Iranian who grew up in America. Wait, do you know him?"

"No, of course not," Sharon answered. "But Yasser Ashraf is an Arabic name."

Stephanie nodded. "Right, he is Muslim. He was born in the United States."

Stephanie went on to tell her mother more about her relationship with Yasser. "I feel good with him," she said frankly. "He stimulates me intellectually, he is interesting, tolerant and, well, actually, an incredible lover."

"I can understand that. That's how I felt about Jean-Paul," Sharon mentioned begrudgingly as she sipped from the glass of wine she was holding.

At the mention of Jean-Paul, Stephanie stopped smiling and quickly changed the subject. "You know, you never told me how you met my father or where we lived before we moved to San Francisco. Come to think of it, I really don't know anything about your relationship with him or your life together, except for the fact that I was born in New York and that we moved to San Francisco when I was six months old."

Sharon Simmons kept silent. She busied herself pouring another half glass of wine and inhaled deeply. "What's the difference? You should be more concerned with your future. Your father is a dead chapter in our lives. Where is digging into the past going to get you?"

Unlike previous attempts at conversations on the same subject, this time, Stephanie persisted. "Why can't I know about you and my father? I never even asked questions when you told me that he had died. I don't take pleasure in saying this, but I have a feeling that you are hiding something."

"You're wrong, Stephanie," Sharon replied. "I have nothing to hide. I just think that there is nothing to be gained from--"

"For example," Stephanie interrupted, "I want to know why you don't have any pictures of him and why you never talk about him. Don't you think that I deserve to know more? I'm not a child anymore."

Sharon remained silent. She studied the bottom of her wine glass, trying to hide from the stream of questions. Stephanie wasn't willing to give up. She knew that now was the time to take advantage of the recent intimacy between her and her mother. She insisted and pushed ahead.

"So, mother, tell me. Why are you so reluctant? You should know that whatever you are going to say won't hurt me. I'm ready to hear it."

"It won't affect you? I'm not so sure about that," she murmured softly. Her face turned pale and took on an anguished look. "I'm not feeling well. Maybe it's the alcohol. Maybe I should eat something."

Stephanie wasn't leaving without answers. "Mother, no excuses. This time, I'm not going to leave the house without you telling me. Maybe you'll feel a better if you tell me. You always say that sharing makes life easier."

Sharon, feeling light-headed, sat down, and started to mumble. "Sometimes we are in situations, situations that are different and strange, when we don't know what… how…"

"Mother," interrupted Stephanie. "You've had too much to drink. I'm going to make us some tea and toast. When I return, I want answers. Do you hear me? I want to know it all."

After Sharon took her first bite of the toast, she realized that there was no way around the subject. She decided that the time had come to tell her daughter the whole story for the first time in thirty three years. "I don't know where to start," Sharon began. "It will be hard for you to hear what I have to say, but please listen to me until the end. I was born in London to parents of Persian origin. My name was Faida. My father, your grandfather, was the economic attaché for the Iranian embassy in England. We moved to Iran when I was thirteen."

"Mother, is that the booze talking or is this the truth? You grew up in Iran?" Stephanie's mouth was opened in shock. "I don't understand. How? How is it possible and how did you get to the United States?"

Sharon waited to answer and continued. "I understand much of this will be hard for you to believe. Be patient. I don't know how well you know history and the chain of events, but in 1979, a revolution took place in Iran. The Ayatollah Khomeini overthrew the Shah and rose to power, which meant I had to leave the country, or escape to be more exact."

"I cannot believe what I'm hearing. Where was I born?" Stephanie asked. Sharon tried to say something but Stephanie continued her barrage of questions. "Wait, so I was born a Muslim?"

Sharon finally answered. "I took on the name Sharon Simmons when I arrived in the United States. We had to start a new life. There was no choice. Enough Steph, please. Enough for today."

Stephanie raised her voice. "No! I won't stop. You've keep secrets from me for decades. And how stupid I've been all these years for giving up every time you wouldn't talk about it. Do you have any idea what a shock it is for me to hear this? What is our original family name?"

"Motaki."

"Motaki," she repeated, as if trying to get used to the sound of the name.

They both remained silent. Thoughts circled around in

Stephanie's mind as she tried to absorb every detail. Stephanie said suddenly, "I'm thirty-three years old. You said you came to the States in 1979. So, how come I was born in New York?"

Sharon's face turned pale once more. "Stephanie, leave it please," she said softly. "It's more complicated than you think. Let it be. I'm begging you."

She looked at her mother for a long time. The fury spilled out of Stephanie. She stood up in front of her mother, and shouted. "You're driving me crazy! When will you understand that I'm mature enough to know who and what I am? Are there other things you are hiding from me? You erased my past. You erased everything. Why can't I know where I was born?"

"According to your birth certificate, you were born in New York," Sharon quickly replied. "Let's take a break. We can talk more about it tomorrow."

Stephanie couldn't calm down. "According to my birth certificate? Where was I was really born, mother? I was born in Iran, wasn't I? What's so awful about being born in Iran? You're hiding something else. Maybe my father didn't even die of cancer. Maybe he's not even dead. I wouldn't be surprised if you tell me he's a mobster or a serial killer… what else are you hiding from me?!"

Sharon closed her eyes and leaned her head back on the couch. Her breath was heavy. Stephanie took a long look at the woman sitting in front of her, wondering if she even knew her at all.

"I'm waiting," she finally insisted.

A long while went by before Sharon responded. At first her words were timid and her voice low. "I'm not proud of any of this. I wanted to spare you all the pain and confusion, as well as risks associated with the truth." With tears in her eyes, she carefully took out a cigarette and lit it. Stephanie noticed her trembling hand.

"Stephanie, you were born in Teheran," she said as she exhaled cigarette smoke. "Six months later, the revolution started. Ayatollah Khomeini put Iran in a state of turmoil. Many who worked for government institutions, like me, had to leave, to run away. We feared that Khomeini's ruthless followers would seek revenge." She dried her eyes, her voice becoming more stable.

"I worked for the Shah's secret police, SAVAK. It's an organization similar to the CIA. Your father served in the police department but wound up supporting the unfolding revolution. He couldn't bear the corruption of the Shah regime and believed that Khomeini's revolution would be good for the country. Despite being tough and sharp as a policeman, he was also naïve."

Stephanie put her arm on her mother's shoulder, pulled her and kissed her gently on the head. After a few seconds, Sharon resumed talking.

"Your father wasn't ready to leave Iran and I was afraid they would kill us. I tried to persuade him to run away with us, but he wouldn't listen. 'I'm Iranian and this is my home,' he repeated. I had to decide, in just a matter of hours. Khomeini's people had started to arrest anyone who had worked for the Shah. Dozens from the secret police were caught. We had no choice but to run away. I left everything and didn't say goodbye to anyone, not even to my parents and the rest of my family."

Sharon's hand holding the cigarette was shaking. "I picked you up at home. You were sleeping like an angel. When I lifted you from the bed, you woke up with a broad smile on your lovely face. I'm telling you this because in the three months before the flight, you used to cry every time I woke you up. Your cry would break our hearts. We didn't know what you were going through so we took you to specialists. They did comprehensive tests. But the tests led nowhere. Then, as if by miracle, on that morning of our escape, something different happened. You woke up glowing, with a smile that you didn't have before. I believe you sensed something. I remember like it was yesterday, that smile, the look in the eyes of my innocent baby. It fueled me with strength and I knew I was doing the right thing."

She put out the cigarette and dried her tears. "It was the hardest day of my life. The separation from your father was unbearable. He kissed you repeatedly and held you tightly, not wanting to let you go. It was awful. That's how we left home, you and me with a small bag. And I never saw him again."

"How did you escape?" asked Stephanie. "How did you get to New York? How did you manage to register me as a New York citizen?"

"I had good friends who took care of everything. They destroyed any trace of our former identities. They obtained passports for us with the name Simmons. I thought it would be better for you if we start all over again, without the burden of the past. Trust me, it wasn't easy to decide to leave everything behind. If I had insisted on staying in Teheran, it would have been our end. It was clear as daylight."

"Then you are not divorced or a widow."

Sharon shrugged. "I told customs in New York that your father had died."

"And what about my father?"

"Some good friends advised us that it would be best not to keep in touch. For his safety and ours."

"Is he really dead like you told me?" Stephanie dreaded the answer but had to ask.

"A year and half after the escape," Sharon began, very slowly, trying to hold her emotions in check, "I got a phone call from Mahmoud Sharkaawi. He was your father's best friend. Mahmoud was one of the toughest in the unit where your father served. He was under your father's command. It turned out that your father had saved his life in the course of duty. Since then, Mahmoud felt an obligation to him. Mahmoud became an officer in the intelligence unit of SAVAK. He was the mastermind behind our disappearance. He was the only one to know our phone number in New York. We agreed that he was going to call me only in an emergency case."

She paused here and took a deep breath. "And one day, Mahmoud called. He was sobbing when he said to me, 'My dear, you are really alone now. They got him. He didn't survive...'"Sharon looked up at her daughter. "Your father was killed, Stephanie."

# 4

Even though her mother's story had been a shock to her, Stephanie was not surprised by Tom's indifference to her retelling it. He slowly finished the dinner she had prepared and then showered, changed clothes and left to watch a football game at a friend's house. Their relationship in recent months had been a "mind your own business" type of relationship. Although they shared the same apartment and the same bed, they lived separately in practice. Tom stopped asking what she was doing during the day, while she lost interest in what he was going through. Some days they barely spoke to each other.

Tom sought other diversions. From time to time, he would leave the house in the early evening only to return in the early morning hours. Stephanie decided not to make an issue out of this despite her suspicions.

On one hand, for practical reasons, she didn't want to start an argument that could break the already thin ice that their marriage was on. On the other hand, she was avoiding having sex with him. She could barely even stand the touch of his hand. If it turned out that Tom was having an affair with another woman again, she decided she would accept it, especially since she was guilty of the same thing with Yasser Ashraf.

Unlike Tom, Yasser not only understood Stephanie's excitement in learning about her family's past, but also, he was eager to draw parallels with his own story.

To her surprise, Yasser completely understood why her mother kept, for all of those years, the information about her identity and her past a secret.

"I can understand your anger and bitterness," he told her. "But you are judging her from your own perspective, based on the parameters of a very Western, parent-child relationship. From what you've told me, I think your mother had good reasons to erase any connection to Iran, Islam and your father."

"What do you mean?"

"I also lived in the home of Iranian refugees. For my parents, my father in particular, the longing for Iran was always mixed with an irrational fear of what they called the long hand of the Ayatollahs. When I was a child, I didn't understand what they meant, but as I grew up, I figured it out well enough. Do you know how many refugees from Iran, especially opponents to the Ayatollah regime, were assassinated over the years?"

Stephanie stared at Yasser Ashraf, trying to understand what he was implying. "Are you telling me that they are still looking for people from that period?"

"I don't think so. But there is no doubt that what your mother did took courage and determination. She had to totally change her life. Escaping and leaving her husband, that takes a special kind of woman."

"Amazing," Stephanie agreed. "Maybe she feared that my father would start looking for me?"

"It's a fair assumption. After all, she made it clear that your father couldn't bear to let you go. Maybe he agreed with your mother escaping, but didn't want you to leave. Who knows what really happened there?"

Stephanie thought about the fact that, unlike every other encounter, they were dressed and talking in his apartment. It wasn't more than a few minutes after stepping into his apartment that she would usually be naked and drifting into a fit of passion, forgetting the outside world.

Yasser reached out and lovingly stroked her hair.

"I feel like there's more to this than what she told me," she said a bit frustrated. "I have a million questions that I didn't manage to ask."

"Now that you've started talking about it, it will be a lot easier."

Stephanie shrugged. "You don't know my mother," she countered. "If she really wants to keep something to herself, she retreats and won't say a word. I'm surprised she told me this much."

"You know what I would do in your place?" he offered. "It may sound weird to you, in your current circumstances, but I would visit Iran. Aren't you curious to know where your parents lived? Where you were born?"

Stephanie nodded. "I've thought about it several times these last few days. Have you been there often?"

"Twice," he replied. "Five years ago and eleven years ago, on work-related trips. I didn't have any privacy because I was being escorted by a student from the University of Teheran. I wasn't able to explore freely."

"Maybe we could go there together?"

He thought for a moment. "It's not a bad idea at all. I do have an open invitation from the University of Teheran. I'm not sure what sounds more exciting though, you're going back to your birthplace or the fact that it would be our first time spending a week or two together?"

Stephanie reached out and gently played with her lover's

goatee. "It could be so nice. You really think we could do it?"

"First, I need to check dates. If everything works out, I would love to travel to Teheran with you. I don't want to promise anything yet, but I promise to check."

Stephanie playfully covered his mouth with her hand. "Now, don't you think that we've done enough talking?" she asked, smiling.

Yasser laughed and pulled her to him. His lips gently brushed her mouth while his hands explored her body. "It's a gift," he whispered, "you're learning about Iran."

Stephanie closed her eyes, hoping he was right, and let the sensations she felt take over.

In the following weeks, Stephanie used every free moment to collect more and more information on Iran. Late at night, mainly when Tom went out to his secret appointments, Stephanie browsed websites related to the country, focusing mainly on Iransos.com.

Unsatisfied with what she could find online and following Yasser's advice, she bought a bunch of books about the Islamic Republic and Islam. Stephanie was fascinated by this world she had only seen in Yasser's classes. Soon, she could quote from the so-called "Five Pillars of Islam," the five central precepts every Muslim must observe. She knew how to define various concepts of Islam, like *shaaria*, *al-abada*, *majal* and *halal*. She could differentiate between the schools *shaaria* and *halam* that exist inside the religion, talk about the various factions, like Sunni, Shia and Hawarji, and name the central figures who had shaped Islam, and the cities holy to Muslims.

Unlike the lectures she had been to on Islam, she easily absorbed and memorized the extensive material. "I don't know what I'm going to do with everything I've learned," she said jokingly to Kevin. "But it feels good. It gives more meaning to my life."

From then on, she used every meeting with Yasser to discuss the various issues she had read about. He was as enthusiastic about it as she was and always contributed a new point of view to the subject. If Stephanie previously admired the professor, that admiration grew by several times. She loved exploring his huge knowledge, and appreciated how open he was to share it and involve her.

"Why don't you go to study in a more orderly way?" he asked. "At USC, there are dozens of courses on this subject."

"I don't think it suits me," she answered. "After all, I'm not going to make a career of it. All I want is to know a little more, and I don't intend to do anything in particular with it."

Yasser draped himself across her on the bed and kissed her bare back. "You never know. There are thousands who convert to Islam every year. I personally know many Americans and Germans who started studying Islam out of curiosity and ended up becoming devout Muslims. Most even grew a thick beard and began praying five times a day."

"I will never grow a beard," she said, laughing loudly. "While I don't see myself wearing a *chador* and covering my face, I wouldn't mind visiting a mosque or talking to a priest."

"*Mullah*," Yasser interrupted, "is the term for a Muslim priest. A *mullah* knows the Quran by heart and is well versed in the *hadit*, Islamic law. I will gladly join you to visit a mosque. I haven't been to one in a long time."

As she was leaving the apartment, she reminded him of his promise to look into the possibility of traveling to Iran.

"I'm sorry. I won't be able to go this year," he said as he hugged her. "But next year, in March, I will have a two-week vacation. Do you think you can wait until then?"

She returned his hug. "Yes, of course, I'll wait. Frankly, it's hard to believe that it'll ever really happen."

Just a few months later, Yasser waited for her in his apartment. When she arrived, he stood in the middle of the room, his black eyes staring at her with a strained look she had never seen before.

"Is something wrong?" she asked as she kissed him.

"We need to talk," Yasser replied in a serious tone.

She sank into a leather armchair, staring at him. "What happened?" She felt her heart sink. "Yasser, you're scaring me with that look. Say something."

"Stephanie, I think it's time for us to go our separate ways."

The words came at her like a blow.

"We've had a wonderful time and I'm sorry it has to end like this," he continued.

Her body shivered and her vision began to blur. "Why? What happened?" she said, barely able to catch her breath.

Yasser lowered his head, unable to withstand her gaze. "Judy, my wife, is four months pregnant. It wasn't planned, but we've decided to keep it. The semester ends in two months and we decided it would be best for me to go on a sabbatical and for us to spend time together back in San Francisco."

Stephanie didn't grasp what he was saying at first. In all the time they were together, as per the "rules" she had set for herself, she refrained from asking her lover about his wife, his family, and especially his plans for the future. She vaguely remembered now that on one of their first encounters, he had said that his wife's name was Judy.

"Congratulations," she said sarcastically. She felt her

stomach turning over. She took a deep breath at the same time that her green eyes met his. "You should have called me and said this all over the phone. You could have spared me this embarrassment," she said, trying to keep a steady tone despite her choking up.

"This is not a conversation for the phone," Yasser said sadly, "and it's not easy. This is something I could only tell you face-to-face. I'm sorry, really. There are still things I can't tell you, that are beyond just you and me, but believe me when I say that it's tearing me apart. Someday in the future I will be able to tell you everything. If there's one thing I want you to know now about our relationship is that it wasn't just a fling to me. You are the most important woman in my life."

Stephanie winced, hearing him say the words. "While this is a complete shock to me, I have to admit you never misled me." She tried to keep her voice from shaking as she spoke. "I knew you had another life beyond the two or three hours a week that you were with me. I knew you had a family. I knew that our relationship couldn't last forever. But…" she struggled to hold in her tears. "I was dreaming of at least going to Iran with you."

Yasser Ashraf squirmed uncomfortably in the silence. He took a few quick steps toward her, knelt at her feet and held her hands. "I'm really sorry. There will always be a soft spot for you in my heart." Yasser kissed her fingertips warmly. "I think it's also the best thing for you. You deserve a new love, one not held back by Tom or by me. You are an extraordinary woman, sensitive, beautiful and smart. You deserve so much better."

Stephanie sat still, finally letting the tears flow. Now his voice was barely audible.

"I've told you before and I'll tell you again, you have to get out of the trap you are in today. I really mean it,

Stephanie. You must make the difficult decision and leave Tom. I know that if I stayed in the picture, you would remain stuck, never fully having either of us." He squeezed her hand. "This is for the best."

She left the apartment completely drained, emotionally and physically. She didn't know if she was in love with Yasser, but the time spent with him made her life more interesting, gave her satisfaction and sexual excitement and, more than anything, an intimate setting where she felt feminine and loved. They had forged a strong emotional connection. She felt comfortable in his company and never hesitated to openly tell him about her work and her relationship with Tom. Despite their differences and what it would have taken to get there, she felt that Professor Yasser Ashraf could have been a good and trusted partner in life.

"The sex wasn't the main bond between us, even if that's how it started," she told her mother as they walked under the summer sun in San Francisco. "I loved his wisdom, his humor, his gentleness and sensitivity. And comparing him to Tom makes it so clear to me what I want and what I don't want."

They sat in one of the cafés at Pier 39, ignoring the groups of Japanese tourists passing by on their way to the old shipping pier, one of the most popular attractions on Fishermen's Wharf. Despite the chilly weather, the area was crowded.

Sharon put her hand on Stephanie's shoulder. "At least you have a place to call home, someone you can talk to occasionally and to share your expenses with. Women sometimes don't appreciate the things they have right in front of them."

Stephanie shrugged. "Mother, there has been more than one occasion that I found myself standing on the station platform in Los Angeles, wanting more than anything to not get on the train home. With all my heart, I think I was ready to swap places with you. You're free. You do whatever you like. You know how to manage."

A skinny waitress approached the table. They ordered a pot of jasmine tea and two slices of cheese cake. Stephanie waited for the waitress to leave before continuing. "Ending the relationship with Yasser has left me empty. Those two to three hours together somehow kept my life in balance. You know what I mean, right?"

A few months later, it all changed again. One evening, Tom left the house as usual, right after dinner. Stephanie had gotten used to not even asking where he was going and just saw it as an excuse to surf sites that dealt with Iran and Islam.

It was nearly midnight when she heard a heavy knock on the door. When she opened the door, she saw two policemen, a man and a woman, standing in front of her with a serious look on their faces.

"Mrs. Stephanie Holmes?" asked the policewoman.

Stephanie nodded. "Yes. What happened?"

On the way to the hospital, the policewoman informed her that Tom had been in a car accident an hour earlier. "He was on his way home and apparently he had been drinking. He collided head-on with a truck in the opposite lane. He has been seriously injured, and the doctors are doing their best to save his life as we speak."

Tom didn't survive his injuries and died that same night. Stephanie dealt with Tom's death with mixed feelings. She could never forgive him for what he had done to her and she suddenly felt freer than she could ever remember. But she also felt tormented by the possibility that she was the cause for Tom's emotional state and may have had a role in his death.

Based on the advice of Tom's father, she sold the pharmacy. Since the pharmacy was under Tom's name, she was legally entitled to collect all of the money. She chose instead, in a generous act, to transfer half of it to Tom's disabled father. Despite her attempts to go through the motions of being a heartbroken widow, she could not stand living in that house any longer. It didn't take long for her to finally decide that she had had enough. With money she had inherited from the sale of the pharmacy, and with the help of Kevin, she rented a small studio apartment back in Los Angeles.

On the first night at her new studio apartment, she laid alone on her bed, feeling invigorated with freedom. She thought of the irony of how, just a few years earlier, she had wanted to get out of her small studio apartment. Now, as she lie in bed, she felt more excited than ever.

"It was thrilling. I felt like a student on her first day at the dorms," she told Kevin the next day. "It's like anything is possible now. I forgot what it felt like to live a life without constant fear and anxiety."

"Now, you can understand what I've been trying to tell you," he said, suppressing a smile. Kevin had never hidden his dislike of Tom. "You should send flowers to his grave to thank him for making the decision for you," he joked. "If he hadn't died, you would still be stuck with him for who knows how many years."

"I know," she said. "I was terrified of being alone. I think seeing my mother suffer from her loneliness brainwashed me into fearing the same thing... Thank goodness that's far behind me now."

Stephanie thoroughly enjoyed her new independent life. Knowing that she didn't have to rush to the station to make the evening train anymore, she relished being able to just get home quickly, sprawl out on her bed and relax instead.

One of her first decisions as an independent woman was to go on a strict diet, to shed the ten pounds she had put on during her marriage. She signed up for a gym not far from her apartment and worked out there for at least two hours every day. She completed her "transformation" with a new haircut. Based on her stylist's advice, she gave up her lush, flowing hair and adopted a short, symmetrical bob, with straight bangs across her forehead.

Although she began making new friends, Stephanie also revisited an old one, Vicky, from her first apartment on Melrose. They set out on a shopping spree, during which Stephanie bought herself new clothes, elegant yet revealing, that she wouldn't have worn when she was married. Stephanie and Vicky even ventured out a few times to "Macho," a club where Latin pop music played seemingly non-stop.

"You need to loosen up and go with the flow," Vicky repeated each time Stephanie tried to make an early escape from the place. "Have fun! Nothing bad will happen if you let go a bit."

Stephanie was aware that Vicky wasn't exactly the ideal companion for her. Over the years, Vicky's career had not advanced in the slightest. Eventually, just to make ends meet, she went to work as a dancer at one of the strip clubs downtown. She had also accepted a financially appealing offer by the owner of one of the strip clubs to appear in several porn movies produced by one of his friends. And when in financial distress, Vicky didn't think twice about going out on a "mission" for one of the escort offices popular in the city.

"I'm not exactly proud of what I'm doing," Vicky confessed to Stephanie. They were watching a colorful gay pride parade on Santa Monica Boulevard in West Hollywood. "But unlike other girls without a career or anything, at least I had the good sense to buy myself an apartment and put some money in the bank." She shrugged and smiled. "I've always thanked God that he gave me the strength to stay strong and not fall into something like drugs. With all of the pills, crack and heroin I've seen around, I don't know how I've come out all right. But I have."

# 5

Mona Hussein was an employee in the administrative division of the Department of Immigration. She was twenty-seven, petite, dark-haired and full-figured. Over the years, Stephanie had encountered her several times, usually in the elevator, but she never stopped to say anything beyond a passing "good morning."

One morning, they were standing next to each other in the elevator on their way to the upper floors. Mona's eyes were fixed on the elevator's control panel, following the rapidly switching floor numbers on the display. Stephanie seized the opportunity to take a look at the young woman standing next to her. She wore a turquoise tunic that covered her blue jeans.

"Beautiful tunic," she said.

Mona turned toward her, a shy smile on her face. "Thank you," she replied softly. They both walked down the long corridor on the fifth floor that led to the administrative wing.

"I noticed that you wear tunics a lot. You have a very particular style," Stephanie said with a smile. "Where do you buy them?"

Slightly surprised, Mona answered. "There's a small store downtown. They sell tunics in every color. It's not far from here."

"And you must have all the colors," Stephanie smiled again.

"This is perhaps the only way that I can compromise between modern life and my faith," Mona responded.

Stephanie should have recognized the reason for Mona's unusual style of dress sooner, a blend of modern Western style with the conservative Islamic culture. In recent months, she had read dozens of articles on the dilemmas facing Muslim women living in the West. "You're Muslim?" she asked.

Mona nodded. "That's right. The tunics help me feel like I can live harmoniously in two different worlds."

Stephanie slowed down and looked at her. "It's probably not so simple."

"It's a constant struggle," Mona agreed. "But someone who really believes and cares about it will find a middle ground. Some women are not willing to compromise, but I believe that you have to respect and adapt to the environment you're in. I think it's possible to find clothes which are modest and chaste, as my religion requires, but at the same time are fashionable."

"How come you don't wear a *chador*? I was under the impression that devout Muslim women tend to cover their hair, necks and shoulders," Stephanie inquired.

Mona came to a halt, an embarrassed smile on her face. "I don't think I need one, but it's an issue that I discussed with our *mullah* at the mosque. He is a believer who isn't cut off from reality. I explained that I can be a devout Muslim without a *chador*."

In the following weeks, Stephanie found herself seeking out Mona Hussein. Something about the young Muslim woman intrigued her. She had a gut feeling that Mona could become the close friend she was missing, someone she could share feelings and emotions toward religion with.

At first, Mona was suspicious of Stephanie's attempts to approach her. Her persistence won out though, and Mona became more and more relaxed and outspoken with each meeting. On several occasions, they had lunch together, and Mona agreed to join Stephanie for coffee after work. Their relationship really deepened when Mona accepted Stephanie's invitation to visit her house over a weekend.

Stephanie found Mona to be an intelligent and realistic woman with a surprising, cynical sense of humor, especially toward herself. During the time they spent together, Stephanie learned that she had emigrated from Iraq to the States with her family shortly after U.S. military forces occupied the country.

From Mona's story, Stephanie understood that the relocation of her family to the United States was part of a deal her father had made with the American military. Mona didn't elaborate on the nature of the deal so Stephanie didn't pry, choosing to respect her privacy. According to Mona, she and her family had a difficult time integrating into the United States, particularly during the first two years, despite the fact that they spoke English.

"The problem was mostly a mental one," Mona said with the same shy smile that popped up every time she felt embarrassed. "Although Iraq is a modern and progressive country, contrary to what many in the States believe, we suffered from culture shock. There were many Western characteristics that we were not familiar with: the social promiscuity, degradation of family values, exhibitionism."

"This may be the melting pot," Stephanie agreed, "but there's a lot of ignorance here about other cultures. It makes sense that someone raised in the Muslim world would struggle to adapt to the American mentality."

Mona smiled broadly. "You'd be surprised to know that I became more religious only after we came to the States," she shared. "In Iraq, we maintained the traditions, but without strict adherence. I even used to wear tight tee-shirts."

"And what led to the turnaround," Stephanie wondered.

Mona took a sip of her coffee. "America." Mona spoke matter-of-factly. "It wasn't exactly my idea. My father and brother were the ones who pushed me to it. For us, as Sunnis, a woman's conduct is very important. Modesty is of supreme value, more so than education and beauty. It is clearly written in our Holy Scriptures: A pious woman should lower her eyes. She should wear a head cover. She should not display jewelry or ornaments, except the ones seen by her husband, her father, her father-in-law and her children.

"My oldest brother has always been religious, but he became especially pious here in the States. He is the one who convinced me that the one and only way to uphold the values I was raised on—to preserve my chastity and avoid any temptations that the United States offers--is to follow the ways of Islam."

Stephanie looked at Mona, disconcertingly. "He pressured you into it? And what about your own will?"

Mona smiled at her. "In our Holy Scriptures, it is explicitly written that the man is the guardian of the woman. Therefore, a good woman is a compliant woman. It's written: 'Good women are obedient. They guard their unseen parts because Allah has guarded them. As for those from whom you fear disobedience, admonish them and forsake them in beds apart, and beat them. Then if they obey you, take no further action against them.' "

It seemed like Mona was enjoying the attention Stephanie showered upon her. She was flattered that the secular American was so interested in her life, not just her friendship. They sat on the black leather couch in Stephanie's living room, now enjoying a cinnamon flavored tea.

"I live with it. The trick is finding a middle ground," Mona said, philosophically. "I'm mature enough to realize that life is one big compromise. There is a saying in Arabic: 'He who operates with constraint gets his wish.' I try to do the same. I'm not a fanatic. I will never do anything that would create anger." She paused for a moment and then asked Stephanie, "Tell me, why are you so interested in the subject?"

"Lately, I have been trying to learn about Islam," she said hesitantly. "It started with a training course I was enrolled in, but it became a whole different story when I found out I was born a Muslim."

Mona was amazed. "I'm surprised to hear you're a Muslim." She was trying to wrap her head around the new revelation. "It doesn't fit. I mean, no offence, but you don't act or dress like it." Mona thought for a moment. "Though, I have met quite a few women of Muslim descent who, after moving to here to the United States, gave up their religion, and completely assimilated to Western culture."

"It was shocking for me to learn as well," Stephanie continued. "It wasn't that long ago that my mother told me about it. I admit, I have yet to come to terms with it fully." Stephanie avoided going into the details.

Mona gently touched Stephanie's hand. "I believe it's not a coincidence that you became interested in Islam. You are looking for your roots. I think I would do exactly the same if I discovered that I'm Christian or Jewish."

Stephanie chose her following words carefully. "You know what I would like," she said slowly. "One day, I'd like to come with you to the mosque. I read about mosques and clerics all the time."

"With pleasure!" Mona smiled. "No problem! I would love for you to join me." She paused for a moment and then continued. "I think it'd be best to come during the week, though, when there are not so many people."

Stephanie shuddered. She stood frozen, grasping Kevin's phone in her hands, trying not to drop it. She stared at the small screen, unable to comprehend the words she was reading. He had pulled up an article on his smartphone, and asked Stephanie to take a look at it. The headline read: *Faculty, Staff and Student of USC Mourn the Passing of Professor Yasser Ashraf, Head of the Department of Middle Eastern Studies.*

Stephanie frantically read the rest of the article, which was too short, and left out any details of how he had passed, or what sort of funeral services would be held.

"I remember you told me you he was your professor," Kevin spoke gently "and that you were very impressed by him. Do you know if he was ill or anything?"

It was a few seconds before Stephanie faintly managed to speak. "No, no, not that I know of." She shook her head, handing the phone back to Kevin. "I'm in shock. It can't be."

She tried to keep calm, but failed. Her throat tightened and tears filled her eyes. Kevin put his hand on her arm. "I'm sorry," he spoke with compassion. "I didn't know it would affect you so greatly." He eased her towards a chair. "Come sit down. Do you want some water?"

Since their separation, Stephanie had been having a hard

time keeping Yasser Ashraf off her mind. Time after time, she would end up in bed recalling the time spent in his company, barely resisting calling him, longing to just hear his voice. The break up, especially after such an intimate relationship, left a great void in her heart.

Since moving back to Los Angeles, Stephanie Simmons tried to move on and had dated several men she had met through Vicky or online via Facebook. None of the relationships lasted long. Sometimes, it seemed like she was only looking for flaws in her suitors, especially sexually. Quite a few of them revolted her.

"Nobody touched me like Yasser used to," she remembered telling Vicky.

"You don't give anybody a chance," Vicky protested.

Stephanie shrugged. "I don't care. Maybe I'm not yet ready for a new relationship." She couldn't believe that Yasser Ashraf, the man she had opened up her heart and soul to, was now dead. As soon as she got home, she called the University.

"Hello, my name is Stephanie Simmons. I was a student of Professor Yasser Ashraf," she choked up as she spoke his name. She took a breath and then continued. "I saw the obituary today and I would like to get some information."

"Yes, ma'am," the voice came through the phone, "How can I help you?"

"I-I would like some information." She was fumbling with her words. "Do you know how he died? Or when the funeral is going to be held?"

The answer was swift. "The funeral was yesterday, in San Francisco. I don't know exactly what happened, but I heard he was involved in a car accident on his walk home from the university."

Stephanie hung up the phone, her mind spinning with questions. She decided to take a taxi to Yasser's apartment, their old secret meeting grounds. The street was relatively quiet. The only people around were two workers from a cable company talking loudly by their car.

Stephanie stood in front of the main entrance, unable to decide whether or not to ring the intercom. Suddenly she heard a female voice behind her. "Can I help you?" Stephanie turned her head. She saw a slender woman with cropped black hair, walking toward her.

"You're a friend of the professor, right," the woman asked. "I've seen you several times when you came to visit him." Stephanie did recall seeing this woman a number of times when she visited the apartment. The woman stretched out her hand.

"I'm Professor Nelly Auerbuch. I was a colleague of Professor Ashraf. I live in the same building."

Tears filled Stephanie's eyes. "I saw the obituary in the newspaper today," Stephanie choked up. "We separated a few months ago and I haven't been in touch with him since." Stephanie suddenly felt dizzy and sat down on the cement sidewalk. The slender woman rushed toward her.

"Do you want a glass of water?"

Stephanie shook her head. "It's okay. I just feel dizzy. I'll be fine."

Nelly began to rummage through a big bag she had been carrying. "I saw what happened. It was an awful sight." She shuddered at the thought. "He was just crossing the road when a car suddenly appeared out of nowhere and hit him… Just like that… The image… it's still fresh in my mind… I was standing right here."

Stephanie didn't say a word.

Nelly pulled a bunch of keys out of her bag. "Everything happened so fast," she continued. "Seconds, really." She began shaking her head. "He died on the spot. The woman who was driving didn't even stop to see what happened. She hit him and took off."

"A woman?"

"Yes, yes, an older woman was driving. I'm sure of it. I told the police, too."

As soon as Stephanie was back in her apartment, she threw herself onto the bed and burst into tears, ignoring the ringing phone. It was only when she saw Kevin's number on the display that she quickly grabbed it and answered. He was calling to invite her to dinner.

At first, she refused his offer. However, after his third phone call, she relented. "If I keep staying home alone, nothing good will come out of it," she said, reluctantly.

A little later, as she sat next to him in his elegant Mercedes, she confessed to him the real reason why she agreed to join him. "Honestly, I was afraid to stay home alone with the stock of pills I have in the medicine cabinet. I'm scared of how bad I feel."

Kevin studied the traffic in front of him silently, then he spoke. "I know you're a sensitive woman, but it looks like the professor's death has hit you pretty hard. You must have been very good friends."

"Much more than that," she contemplated how much she was willing to share with Kevin. Finally, Stephanie decided to just tell him everything.

"I had an affair with him," she admitted.

His lips curled into a small smile that quickly disappeared. "I'm not exactly surprised," he said solemnly.

Stephanie talked at length about Yasser, his personality, his character and their relationship which began with sex but became a great love. She told him of how hurt she had been the day he decided to break it off, even though she had done her best to keep herself emotionally uninvolved.

"Stephanie, you fell in love with the right person, but at the wrong time," he spoke soothingly.

Stephanie stared out the window of the car, trying to sort out her thoughts. "You know, even though it was just an affair, I have amazing memories of him. Every time we met, I learned something new about myself, about life or the world. The affair helped me survive my broken marriage with Tom. I wanted to leave Tom, but I was afraid that if I left, it would pressure Yasser."

She turned to Kevin, a new thought suddenly occurring to her. He quickly glanced at her and then back to the road in front of him. "Maybe I really was in love with Yasser and didn't want to accept it. I don't know. I remember every moment with him, every sentence we said. We even planned a visit to Iran together."

Kevin was puzzled. "Iran?" he questioned. "Why Iran, of all countries?"

Something stopped Stephanie from replying. Although it felt deceitful not to tell him that she was Muslim and of Iranian origins, she finally spoke. "It was because of the class," she lied. "He told me about Iran and its beauty. He wanted to show me where he had his roots."

Stephanie was excited as she walked beside Mona on the way to the mosque *Al-Aksa* in the outskirts of Los Angeles. Stephanie wore a flowered tunic, her head and shoulders covered by a light floral veil that she purchased a few days earlier in the city center.

She looked at the dozens of women and men walking beside her toward the imposing structure that towered over all other surrounding buildings. Beards of various lengths adorned the men's faces. Most of them wore black pants and white shirts. Others had on white *sharwals*, which are flowing pieces of cloth that is tied around the waist.

To her great surprise, many of the women she saw were wearing Western clothes, high-heeled shoes, long skirts, and blouses. However, all of them, whether young or old, made sure to cover up with a long coat and a head scarf. Stephanie looked up and examined the tall structure topped with a dome and minaret.

"The tower is called *maadina*," Mona whispered, pointing to the dome and minaret. "The *muezzin* calls to prayer the faithful from up there."

They stopped and looked up at the Hipustili Mosque.

"It has pillars like the prophet Mohammed's home in Medina," Mona continued to explain, as men and women silently split into two groups and disappeared into the mosque. They ended up in a large yard, open to the sun. The yard was partially paved. There were several fountains in the center and water flowed continuously.

"It's the purification area," Mona told Stephanie, cupping water with her hands from one of the fountains and washing her face. "This area is called *midaa*."

Stephanie watched Mona and carefully imitated her. She collected some water in her hands, and with a quick movement, washed her face.

They continued into the prayer hall, which was spacious and had no furniture. The floor was covered with colorful carpets. All the women then proceeded to the corner of the hall to each pick up a Quran. Mona took two books and then gave one to Stephanie. Stephanie examined the lamps, the chandeliers and the calligraphic decorations that decorated the walls and ceiling of the mosque.

"Verses from the Quran," Mona whispered, pointing to the writing. On the walls, in between the Quran verses, she noticed different geometric shapes, leaves and colorful flower motifs. Without a word, the women knelt on the carpets, forming rows parallel to the *qiblah* wall, the one in the direction of Mecca. Stephanie noticed a niche in the center of the wall, which Mona briefly explained to be the *mihrab*.

"It is intended for the faithful," Mona whispered, "to easily identify the *qiblah* wall."

An hour later, even as she sat in Mona's house sipping hot tea, Stephanie couldn't relax. She was fascinated by the visit to the mosque and was eager to know more. Mona was delighted to share her knowledge. "Friday is the sacred day for Muslims, like Sunday for Christians," Mona told her. "If you'd like, you can come with me to mass prayer in the mosque on a weekend sometime. In Arabic, it's called *al-juna*, which means day of assembly. The cleric, the *mullah* or *kady*, will deliver a sermon to the congregation, the *khutbah*."

"It's a day of rest," Stephanie interrupted, attempting to show off her knowledge.

"No," Mona explained. "Friday is not a day of rest for the Muslims—"

A male voice interrupted Mona. "In the Quran," he spoke, "Friday is the holy day because man was created on that day."

Stephanie turned her eyes to the man standing in the doorway. His black eyes were fixed on her and a slight smile appeared at the corners of his mouth. "The Quran states that when, on Friday, the call to prayer is being heard, hurry to the place to mention the name of God. And at the end of the prayer, ask for support from God and invoke the name of God for strength."

Mona quickly rose from her seat. "Stephanie, please meet my brother, Halid."

Stephanie got up. She was surprised by the physical appearance of the man standing in front of her. She remembered that in one of their conversations, Mona described her oldest brother as a devout Muslim. She was expecting to meet a dignified, bearded adult who dressed in traditional clothes. On the contrary, Halid was in his mid-forties, short and pot-bellied, with a black goatee, which was neat and tidy. There was nothing to indicate that he was a devout Muslim. Stephanie thought that his look was absolutely Western and secular. He was wearing a white shirt, neatly pressed, and high-cut black pants, which were tight on his body and stressed his belly. Stephanie couldn't help but notice the gold Rolex watch on his right wrist as well as the gold cuffs that adorned his white shirt.They shook hands. His were wet with sweat.

"I'm glad to meet you," he said in perfect English. "Mona told me about you. I understand that today you went to the mosque."

Slightly embarrassed, Stephanie nodded as she felt the man's black eyes examining her body.

"And what do you think?" he questioned.

"It was quite an experience," she replied.

"You should come with us on a Friday, as Mona suggested," he said. "You know, on Fridays, our mosque is bustling with people. You'll be very impressed, especially by our mullah's sermon. He is a wise man of great stature-charismatic, intelligent, and he has an enviable knowledge of the Holy Scriptures."

Stephanie smiled uncomfortably, unable to look directly at the man seated across from her, while his eyes stared openly at her breasts.

"I would love to come, really. Like I told your sister, the visit to the mosque was an exciting experience for me."

"If in the future you would like to deepen your knowledge, I will be happy to teach you." Halid smiled.

"Maybe. I still don't know what I'm going to do with all this, but thank you for the offer."

Stephanie spent that weekend visiting her mother in San Francisco, something she started to do once a month since becoming a widow. As usual, they spent their first hours together updating each other on what was going on in their lives.

Sharon's health was the main issue. She had been feeling generally weak and had gone through extensive medical tests to find out the cause. Despite this, the doctors didn't find the source of the problem.

"It's not just the physical weakness," Sharon said as she arranged the jewelry display cases, part of her morning routine after she opened her store. "I feel like my mental energy is being drained too. I don't care about anything. Nothing makes me feel good."

"Mother, you need some passion in your life. Maybe a relationship or a new job." As she stood next to her, Stephanie couldn't help but be impressed by her mother's slender figure. "Did you lose weight or am I just imagining things?"

Sharon stood up facing her. "That's what scares me most. I haven't checked my weight, but I think that in the last two months I've lost at least fifteen pounds." She looked down at her body. "I think that's a bad sign."

"You're talking nonsense," Stephanie replied. "What I think is that you need a vacation. Not one or two days, but at least two or three weeks."

Sharon laughed wryly. "I really do feel like I need a holiday. I wouldn't mind a week or two of complete relaxation, without anything to do. You could do with a holiday, too. Come on, we'll plan something together.'

Stephanie was overwhelmed with joy. She held her

mother's hand. "Actually, I was planning on taking advantage of my annual vacation to take a trip to Iran" Stephanie's eyes lit up with excitement. "Why don't you join me? It could be very nice. I read that the country has impressive tourist sites."

"Iran?" Sharon asked, without concealing her astonishment. "Of all places in the world, it's one of the worst! Don't you know what happens there? Are you aware of their hatred for Americans? It's the last country in the world that I want to visit."

"I thought of returning to our roots. You and me. I don't know. Maybe it's not really a good idea."

"Not a good idea at all."

Stephanie shrugged. "Okay, let's think of somewhere else. Haiti? Or Italy is overflowing with handsome men to pick up."

"Sure. Haiti sounds nice. Maybe we could do some sailing and visit some of the nearby islands. Start looking into it."

Later in the evening, Stephanie told her mother of the sudden death of Yasser Ashraf and of the deep sorrow she had been experiencing from it. "You know that I don't usually dream, and if I do, I don't remember my dreams. The other night, though, I dreamed of him and I remembered every detail of it. Since we split up, not one day goes by that I don't remember or think of him."

"He must have given you the idea of the trip," Sharon said softly.

Stephanie nodded. "The idea of a visit came a few weeks before we separated. We planned to go to Iran together." Stephanie let her mind wonder for a moment, then brought herself back. "Don't you have any interest in Iran? Don't you feel nostalgic? Aren't you curious to see the places you grew up with again?"

A few seconds passed before Sharon answered. "I have no desire to go back there." Her voice was stern. "To me, Iran is dead. I made a new life for myself here and I don't feel the need to look back."

"And you're not interested in reuniting with friends, people you worked with? Going to Dad's grave?"

"You're as naïve as a child," Sharon scoffed. "What are you talking about? Don't you understand that they will kill me as soon as I set foot there? You think that Iran is America, where anyone can do whatever they want? That anyone can say what they want?"

Outwardly, Sharon Simmons maintained restraint, but clearly, she was troubled by the idea of her daughter's trip to Iran. She sat down on the bed and looked at her daughter with concern. Stephanie took her clothes from the closet and put them in a bag for her trip back to Los Angeles.

"Are you really thinking of a trip to Iran?" Sharon asked.

Stephanie pulled out a new short-sleeved floral dress and placed it on the bed.

"I would love to go." She spoke with certainty. "I'm curious to see where we lived. It's part of my life, whether I like it or not. Obviously if I was going with Yasser, it would all have been easier."

"I can't tell you what to do, but if you ask me, I really think you should give up on the whole thing. I'm afraid that it's dangerous for you." Stephanie was surprised at how serious her mother's tone had become.

"What can they do to me? Besides, my passport says I'm Stephanie Simmons," she reasoned. "I would really like to visit my father's grave, at least to see it."

Sharon shook her head. "I want you to promise me something," she spoke with concern. "I want you to promise me that you won't go there."

"What's going on with you?" Stephanie dismissed her

mother's worries. "Why are you panicking? I really don't understand. Is there something you're not telling me?"

Sharon sighed. "You are an amazingly beautiful woman. You will be easy prey for the locals. I'm afraid of them and I don't trust them. They can be cruel and I want you to promise me—"

"No, I don't want to promise. It doesn't mean that I have decided to go but I'm thinking about it." Stephanie stood up to her mother. "Just so you know, I've spoken with several Americans of Persian origin lately who went there and came back. That's right, they looked past the difficult political and economic situation and saw a rich history and interesting sites. So stop acting like everyone in Iran is a terrorist or a rapist."

Stephanie left shortly thereafter, quickly hugging her mother goodbye, resentful of her lack of support.

# 6

Stephanie kept playing around with the idea of visiting Iran on her annual holiday but didn't think about it too seriously. It was just added to the list of many ways she could spend her time off.

At one point, she debated between accepting Kevin's offer to join him on a week-long cruise to the Caribbean islands or Vicky's idea of an adventurous trip to India.

One day, without any notice, her mother paid Stephanie a surprise visit at her apartment. "To what do I owe this honor?" Stephanie asked, rushing to hug her mother. "You look a bit pale."

It was obvious that Sharon was very upset. "I'm fine," she said, "but we need to talk. Since your last visit, something has been bothering me, nonstop."

"What happened? Did the doctors find something?" Stephanie grew concerned.

"No, no. It's not about my health," Sharon hurriedly answered. "I'm fine. The doctors said it was anxiety and they believe that it can be solved with some pills. That's not why I came."

Stephanie sighed in relief. "You scared me," she said. "I

was expecting the worst for a second there."

"No, absolutely not," Sharon said, still uncomfortable. "I really am sorry. I really came because I wanted to talk about your plans to visit Iran."

Stephanie smiled in surprise. "Oh, really, don't be so serious about it. The whole thing about a trip to Iran was just an idea. I'm not at all sure that–"

"It's not just the trip to Iran," her mother interrupted. She reached into her large bag and pulled out a pack of cigarettes. She sat, lit up and confessed as she smoked.

"I was thinking about the conversation we had, you know. I swore to myself I would protect you and do whatever is humanly possible so you could start a new life here in the United States. It's one of the reasons why I have never told you anything about Iran or our past. They were looking for me then, and I believe that even today they would be more than happy to get their hands on me."

Stephanie noticed her mother's hands were shaking.

"Do you have an ashtray?" asked Sharon.

Stephanie got up and silently made her way to the kitchen. She returned a minute later holding an ashtray and placed it on the round table. Then she sat down on the couch next to her mother.

Sharon's voice was trembling. "You know, Steph, you are more precious to me than anything. I just want to see you happy. I know I wasn't the best mother, but I did my best."

Stephanie couldn't stop herself from rushing her mother to get to the point. "Mother, tell me. What's happened?"

Sharon took a long drag from her cigarette. Her breath became heavy and tears began flowing from her eyes. Her voice was calm, though, when she finally spoke.

"After our last talk, I couldn't sleep for nights on end. I think you have the right to know." Sharon paused. Searching for the right words to say, her eyes darted around the room. Finally, when she could no longer avoid it, she spoke. "Your father is alive. He lives in Iran."

Stephanie suddenly felt dizzy. The words were like a slap in the face. She opened her mouth, but couldn't manage to say one word.

"I wanted you to know the truth, but I just couldn't do it," her mother pleaded. "Steph, I know you probably hate me for it. I thought it would be better if you didn't know. I was concerned for your safety. I believed that not knowing would spare you a great deal of grief."

Stephanie sat motionless, staring at her mother, a strange feeling bubbling up inside her. Sharon nervously avoided her gaze and put out her cigarette in the ashtray, as she let out the remaining smoke from her lungs. "Like I've already told you, during the Shah's rule, I worked at SAVAK. I was one of the women who was a liaison between Iranian intelligence and the British intelligence agency, the MI-6. MI-6 and other organizations worked together to thwart Khomeini's rise to power and supported the Shah's rule. After Khomeini's people took power, we were viewed as spies. Everyone in my department had to get out of Iran. Some of my best friends, who had worked with me in the same department, were hanged in the main square of Teheran. Those who did manage to get a trial were given brief ones for show, without the option of being represented by a lawyer. Most of them also ended up hanged in the main square."

Sharon paused and pulled out another cigarette. "Your father was a police officer but, unlike me, he supported the revolution. He believed that Khomeini would improve the living conditions of the people. He wasn't willing to leave Iran with us. He just trusted them." She lowered her head. It was obvious to Stephanie that she was emotionally distraught.

"You and I managed to leave Iran at the last moment, thanks to MI-6 contacts I had. They got us to England and a few weeks later, we were transferred to the United States. My friends from the MI-6 made sure we had all the documents needed to start a new life: a new identity, employment, everything."

"What happened to my father?" Stephanie asked anxiously. "How do you know he's alive?"

"Like many others, your father was arrested a few days after Khomeini took over the country. He was questioned, tortured and thrown into prison. I told you about your father's loyal friend, Mahmoud Sharkaawi. He saved him. In spite of the fact that Mahmoud was also in the police during the Shah's period, Khomeini's people accepted him. It turned out that he was smart enough to become connected with Khomeini's men well before they came to power in Teheran. I have no idea what price your father paid for his naiveté. I don't want to think of how they must have tortured him. Anyway, Mahmoud managed to have your father released after a few weeks."

"Were you in contact with him?"

Sharon nodded. "I spoke with him twice over the years. He wanted to know all about you. He went back to the police force and is now deputy chief of a police station in Teheran. He admitted that he had made a mistake not leaving Teheran with us, but his life is much better now. He remarried and has three daughters."

The words echoed in Stephanie's head. She could feel her heart beating furiously. "How could he do that? Aren't you technically still married?" Stephanie was surprised at how jealous she felt of this man she had never even met.

Sharon Simmons shut her eyes and laid her head on the back of the couch. "Steph, neither of us officially exist anymore. The British had to fake our death in order to ward off Iranian intelligence. They staged the crash of a light plane, which we were supposedly on. Our friends in intelligence knew it was the best way for us to start a new future."

Sharon was staring off into space as she continued to huff on her cigarette, confronting a past she wanted to forget. "Your father knew that it was off-limits to contact us. He knew they were listening to his phone calls. He feared, rightly so, that contacting us could expose the fact that we were alive and living in the United States."

Stephanie interrupted her. "It sounds like a movie, a horror movie. What did you do in Iran that got them so obsessed with finding you? Why are you so scared?"

Sharon grabbed Stephanie's hand. "Other than having worked for the Shah, your father and I are also Sunni. In the West, people can't understand the bitter hatred that Shiites and Sunnis have for each other. When the Ayatollahs rose to power, they didn't stop at persecuting the Shah's people. They also targeted the remaining Sunnis in the country."

Stephanie shrugged. "Mother, after a six month course on Islam, I somewhat understand the differences. I just don't understand why they are looking for you in particular? What kind of work were you doing that made you such a big target? You said that the British intelligence staged a plane crash and that everyone believes we're dead. Why would they put so much effort into helping us? And why would they try so hard to find us?"

Sharon laughed bitterly. "It's not just me they're looking for. They're searching for dozens of other men and women who had positions during the Shah's era. I told you, they consider us traitors. Too bad Ashraf didn't tell you about the hundreds of Iranian expatriates who have died around the world over the years, under strange circumstances. I'm not paranoid. Your father knew the risks as well as I did."

"When was the last time you spoke with him?"

"About five years ago, while he was in Yemen, training their special police forces. He finally found a way to contact me safely. Despite all the precautions he took, it was still a stressful conversation for him, so we were only able to speak briefly. The first thing he wanted to know was all about you. I told him that we live in the United States, that you live and work in California and that you are happy."

"Ladies and gentlemen, this is your captain speaking. In about ten minutes, we are going to land in Teheran. Please fasten your seat belts and remain seated until the seat belt lights go out. Thank you for flying Iran Air. We hope to see you again on one of our flights." The captain's voice gave Stephanie chills, as she pushed her face up against the window, excitedly surveying the city appearing before her eyes.

The words of her mother, talking about her father now having three children, echoed in Stephanie's head. She stood in front of the customs counter and handed over her passport. The clerk on the other side of the counter opened the passport with a practiced hand.

"Hello, Ms.-" the clerk looked at her passport, "Regine Damir. May I ask for the purpose of your visit? Vacation? Business?" The clerk spoke in perfect English.

"Family visit," she answered, trying not to show the nervousness she felt inside. "I'm supposed to visit my uncle."

After what felt like an eternity to Stephanie, the clerk picked up the big seal beside her and stamped her passport. "Welcome to the Islamic Republic of Iran. Have a pleasant vacation, Ms. Damir."

Stephanie took back the passport and walked forward. She was overwhelmed with relief. "God, thank you," she whispered to herself, as she walked toward the arrivals area of the airport. Stephanie was well aware that the decision to obtain a fake passport was dangerous. On top of risking immediate dismissal from her job, she would have likely been sent to jail for several years.

The idea for a fake passport actually stemmed from her mother's vehement opposition to a vacation in Iran. Sharon persistently reminded Stephanie of the chain of dangers she could encounter on her visit to Iran, more so if she planned on meeting her father and family. "Chances are that they will arrest you right at the airport," she told Stephanie. "It would be months, before they released you, if at all. You don't know how they can be."

To try and further make a point about the dangers in Iran, Sharon brought someone over to Stephanie's apartment who introduced himself as "a friend" of her mother, and an expert on Iran. He depicted a bleak picture of Iran, attributing it to growing religion fanaticism and turmoil.

"The hatred the Iranian public feels often gets turned against visitors in the streets. It's not safe for Americans to walk around."

Stephanie listened to her mother's friend but the words of Yasser were louder in her mind: "There are so many wonderful people in Iran…"

At one point during the meeting, the friend laid out his reasoning.

"The best argument for you not going to Iran is sitting right next to you." He turned his eyes to Sharon, who sat expressionless. "Even now, we don't know if one hundred percent of Iranian officials believed the plane crash story."

"I'm asking you to promise me that you won't go," her mother begged her, soon after the friend had left.

"I promise," she murmured slowly. At the time, she had meant it. Her mother had gone through such great lengths to keep her from Iran that she had begun to doubt her ability to make the trip. Additionally, she figured the safest way to go would be obtaining a fake passport, but was not sure she'd be able to pull it off.

The suggestion from her friend Vicky to travel to India started looking more reasonable and she even called her to set a date. That all changed again when Stephanie happened to find a passport a few days later in one of the lower drawers of her desk at work. She had forgotten about the passport she was asked to issue for a woman named Regine Damir. When she searched the main computer for the details of the applicant, she was surprised to find out that the passport had been issued six months earlier. For some reason, the applicant never turned up to collect it.

Even though she tried to push the thought from her mind, Stephanie couldn't help but see an opportunity, albeit a risky one, in the passport. Using the passport to enter Iran would be a safe way to "bypass" the dangers against which her mother and her mother's "friend" had warned her of.

The only problem was the photo. Having experience with passport issuance, though, Stephanie knew how she could get it replaced. First, she purposely damaged some parts of the passport, including a significant portion of the picture. Then, following the usual procedure, she filled in a request to replace a damaged passport. She attached two photos of herself, and finished the form by signing her new name at the bottom, Regine Damir.

A few days later, she was excited to find "her" passport among the dozens of usual entry visas and passports in the mailbag. She opened it and sighed in relief when she saw her photo attached to Regine Damir's passport. She immediately put the passport in her bag.

"I have decided not to travel with you," she told Vicky as they sat at Kyoto, a luxury Japanese restaurant in downtown Los Angeles that had become a favorite of theirs.

Vicky took the news with indifference. "Suit yourself," she replied with a shrug. "You are going to end up marrying that Kevin Shepard one of these days. It's probably your fate."

Stephanie smiled at her. "Relax, I'm not going with him either."

Vicky looked at her with amusement. "Is there someone or something that you're hiding from me?"

"I don't want to go into it." Stephanie was adamant that of all people, she would not share the details of her trip with Vicky. "The problem is that my mother knows him and she is not exactly crazy about him."

Vicky stared at her. "Aren't you a bit old for your mother to be deciding that for you? You should do what's best for you."

"That's precisely what I'm doing, but I don't  want to I told my  .d like to to use you as an excuse'So I .upset her Stephani ".m going with you on a trip to India'mother that Ie was smirking. "I just need you to go along with it."

"Sure, it's fine." Vicky shrugged. "I have no problem with it."

Stephanie quickly crossed the arrivals terminal of

Teheran Airport, dragging a big blue suitcase. Her eyes wandered around the spacious terminal as she walked through it, admiring the new scenery and taking in the dozens of new faces around her. Once outside, she raised her hand and waved at the line of taxis waiting nearby. One of the taxis rushed to her.

"Where to, Ms.?" the driver asked in English, as he put her blue suitcase in the trunk.

"The Northern Police Station," she said avoiding the bald man's eyes that were too obviously admiring her curves.

"No problem, Ms."

A strong smell of onions hit Stephanie as she settled into the back seat. She hurried to open her window and stick out her head.

"Lady, what you are doing is dangerous," she heard the driver's voice. "I suggest you put your head back in."

"Sorry," she whispered, trying her best not to breathe in the smell. "When will we get to the police station?" she asked.

"In approximately a half hour, depending on the traffic."

Stephanie was captivated by the sights passing by her taxi window. There was something magical about the bustling streets they passed. She had never seen such a unique mix of modern and old, of wealth and poverty. The taxi drove past a shopping mall that displayed fashionable clothing. A minute later though, they passed through a neglected and rundown neighborhood, pictures of Ayatollah Khomeini emblazoned on every corner.

The voice of the taxi driver interrupted her thoughts. "It's your first time in Teheran?"

"Yes," she replied succinctly.

The driver didn't give up. "Where are you from?"

Stephanie was prepared for the question. "London," she

answered quickly, a feeling of nausea rising in her stomach from the potent smell of onions.

"I hope you will enjoy it here. You will see Iranians are nice people."

"Yes, I know," she said, holding back the vomit.

The taxi finally stopped at a large office building. "We are here, Ms."

Stephanie knew she was taking a chance by visiting the police station without prior notice and then requesting a meeting with the deputy commander of the station. "I'm a relative," she told the desk officer, a thin man with a thick moustache and an indifferent look, who sat behind a long counter at the entrance to the station. She leaned against the counter, ignoring the suspicious glares from other parts of the room. "Tell him my name is Regine Damir."

Twenty minutes went by. She sat on a small stool in front of the counter, until a side door was opened and a young man wearing civilian clothes came out.

"You are Regine Damir?" he looked at her suspiciously. "You are asking for Colonel Motaki?"

Stephanie got up from her seat. "Yes," she said, "I'm a relative of his. I arrived this morning from London."

"Follow me, please."

Amir Motaki, deputy commander of the police station, was a tall and portly man, with a thick mane of black hair. He looked very impressive in his carefully pressed uniform. She swelled with pride as she reviewed the many decorations hanging neatly on his chest.

Colonel Amir Motaki, her father, needed only a couple of moments to understand what was going on. As soon as they were left alone in his spacious office, his expression suddenly changed, and a broad smile replaced the grim look.

"Some time ago, your mother told me that you wanted very much to come see me. I know that it was risky for you to come here, but here you are," he whispered in English, hugging her. He didn't wait for her approval. "I'm so happy to see you."

She hesitated for a moment, but it didn't take long for her to fully lay her head on his chest, careful not to touch the decorations. "You can't understand how my life has changed since I heard you were alive," she said with a faltering voice.

"I can't believe how beautiful you are. You look so much like your mother," he noted with a big smile, as he motioned toward a leather armchair. "Please sit down. How was your flight? Are you tired?"

She shook her head. Colonel Motaki was unreserved with his emotions and his broad smile never left his face.

"I have so many questions to ask you," he spoke heavily. "I just don't know where to start."

Stephanie sat down. "Believe me when I say that I have a lot to ask you as well. Luckily, we have time. I will be in Iran for quite a while."

The conversation seemed tense at first, mixed with fear and excitement and nervousness. After some time, everything became much more natural. Her father really showed his comfort when he opposed to her plans to stay at a hotel.

"I really hope you haven't paid for the hotel in advance," he stated. "I'll take you back to my home."

"It's fine," Stephanie answered. "I don't want to bother you. I got a room at the Olympic Hotel. Maybe it would be better if I come to your house later."

"Absolutely not. I don't want to hear about a hotel. I will call home to tell the family that I'm coming with a surprise." His voice was insistent. "I want you to meet them."

A few minutes later, she was sitting in the back of a

white Mercedes. The word "police," in Farsi, was written in huge letters on both sides of the car. Her father sat beside her in the back as two policemen manned the front. Stephanie fixed the blue scarf on her head and straightened the tunic she was wearing. The car leapt forward and into the flowing traffic.

Teheran never stopped surprising Stephanie. From what she could see, the information she had about the city from reading various websites was largely unfounded. Although it wasn't a modern city by Western standards, it also wasn't a city of poverty and misery. Her attention was especially drawn to the many children playing in the streets near the huge mosques scattered across the city.

As if he was reading her thoughts, Amir Motaki said, smiling, "You came on a good day. Today, the haze is less noticeable. I don't know if you were told that we have an air pollution problem in Teheran."

The city had endless traffic jams. Vehicles of every make and year, including some she had never seen before, surrounded their own. The traffic was stressful, made no better by the aggressive drivers who were unfazed by the fact that they were driving in a police car and honked loudly at them.

From time to time, her father said something to the young driver who would then eagerly push the siren button on the dashboard. The ear-piercing screech, which at first caused Stephanie to freeze in her seat, cleared the lanes and allowed them to drive quickly.

"You see," she heard her father jokingly say to the driver, this time in English so she could understand, "there are some advantages to being a cop in Iran."

To her surprise, Stephanie felt quite connected to the hustle and bustle of the city. It was as if the streets, buildings and thousands of people that passed her window filled her with a warmth, a warmth she had never experienced before. Many policemen, carrying batons, were stationed at key intersections and corners they passed. In spite of the warnings by her mother and others, Stephanie felt quite safe beside her father.

"There is a student demonstration today, which is why you see so many police in the streets," Amir Motaki interrupted her thoughts. "We had to close some streets to allow for the demonstration, which created these traffic jams. Anyway, the demonstration is supposed to start in half an hour, so we will manage to get home before it all starts."

"Why are they demonstrating?" Stephanie asked.

"You know young students," Amir smiled. "They want more freedom, more liberalism. Same as all the young people in the world, no? It's nothing serious."

At the same moment, the young policeman driving the car spoke in heavily accented English. "I suggest you open the windows. The air conditioning just stopped working." He spoke apologetically. "I really don't know what happened."

"No problem. It's fine," she responded smiling, and opened the window on her side. "It's not that hot. I expected it to be much hotter."

"How is your mother?" Amir asked. The sudden question caught her off guard, and she couldn't decide on how to answer.

"She works all week long and sometimes even into the weekends. She owns a jewelry shop." Stephanie thought for a moment before continuing. "She had a boyfriend for a long time, but it didn't work out. Lately, she has not been feeling very well."

"What do you mean she is not feeling well?" Amir straightened up. "I remember your mother being a strong woman. What's going on with her?"

Stephanie chose her words carefully. "I don't think it's anything serious. She did do some tests and there was nothing they could see. I think it's more psychological than physical."

Amir relaxed back into his seat. "Do you meet often? Are you in good terms?"

Stephanie nodded. "There was a time when we drifted apart a bit." Stephanie recalled the time she had distanced herself from her mother. "But more recently, we have become very close. Sometimes, I go to San Francisco. Sometimes, she comes to visit me in Los Angeles."

Amir Motaki decided to change the subject. "How long will you be staying?"

Stephanie shrugged. "I don't really have a set plan. I have a month off from work, so I'm just letting things happen..."

Amir reached out and touched her hand. "I'm very glad you came, Stephanie. You look so much like your mother. She was a very beautiful woman." Stephanie grabbed his hand as he held her chin, and ignoring the gaze of the nosy policeman sitting in the front, she leaned forward and softly kissed her father's cheek.

"I'm sorry," she said, immediately moving back from the kiss. Besides the fact that the intimate gesture was against the laws of Islam, Amir was really a total stranger to her.

"What are you sorry for?" her father asked, obviously amused. "I wish my daughters were that affectionate. When they were young, they smothered me with hugs and kisses. Now that they are all grown up, they barely allow me to kiss them on the forehead."

\* \* \*

Her welcome into Amir's home was warm and affectionate, and it wasn't long before her nervousness faded away. Amir introduced Stephanie first to his wife, Dalram, who was in her late fifties. The pale, skinny woman wore a black, wide tunic with a white scarf around her neck. They embraced warmly.

"Welcome to our home," Stephanie heard Dalram say in English. "I'm happy to meet you. We have thought about you a lot. We fixed you a place to sleep. Feel at home."

Next, the three girls were introduced: Zaher, Tahara and Lily. The three girls were also slender. Lily, the youngest, was fourteen. Unlike her two older sisters, who were wearing jeans and a short sleeve tee-shirts, she wore a green tunic over her jeans with a matching scarf around her neck.

Tahara was the tallest and Stephanie judged her to be about twenty. Unlike her sisters who had small noses and black hair, Tahara had an aquiline nose and golden hair. Stephanie decided that she dyed it.

Stephanie scanned Zaher with curiosity until Dalram said aloud what they both had been thinking. "It's amazing how much the two of you look alike. Not just the eyes and nose, but the forehead, the lips and the physique."

"It really is interesting," said Stephanie, looking at Zaher. "I have a picture of myself from about six years ago and I look exactly like her. Unbelievable."

Zaher smiled in embarrassment. "Stephanie is much more beautiful, mother. How can you compare? She looks like a Hollywood movie star."

"Don't be so modest," Stephanie insisted. "You are stunning. Look at yourself. I once tried to be an actress in Hollywood, but I didn't make it. I'm convinced that if you were to try, you would pass the first audition you go to."

Amir's home was on the third floor of a luxurious residential building located in the northern part of the city, an area considered to be among the most exclusive. A red sofa stood in the living room beside two matching armchairs. A large painting and a spectacular photograph of a snowy mountain hung above the sofa. A long, antique chest supported a large, modern TV, the kind you would expect to find in an LA home.

All the rooms had vibrantly colorful carpets. Stephanie noted all the standard household appliances you would find in the Western world. The stories she had heard from her mother about what a backwards and impoverished country Iran was were quickly being challenged.

Zaher was supposed to give up her room to Stephanie and join her two younger sisters in their room, but Stephanie insisted on sharing the room with her. "In fact, you are my little sister," she told Zaher. "I have no problem at all sleeping in the same bed with you. It would be a nice change to not be alone at night."

In the following days, Stephanie had a chance to learn much more about her family. The most striking thing about the family's relationship was her father's strong hold on the women of the house, including every day, mundane issues. Nothing was done without notifying him first.

Amir left the house early in the morning, before everyone else was awake, but not before prayer. The long hours spent working at the northern police station of Teheran, which oversaw one-fifth of the city's vast territory, were only part of the cost he paid to be deputy commander. He returned home late in the evening, only to continue working. He reviewed documents and frequently gave orders to his aides by phone or the radio transmitter, which he usually kept on him.

Even on the day that Stephanie arrived in his home, Amir didn't stray from that routine. Shortly after he had helped Stephanie settle in, he left again for the police station and only came home around midnight.

"He must love his job. It seems he is always working," Stephanie told Dalram as they sat on the living room couch watching TV.

Dalram shrugged. "I don't know if he likes what he is doing, but it's a respectable job that has to be done. It's the way of life he chose. I guess there are good and bad days. I'm not sure that what he is doing today, but I know lately he has been confronting the student demonstrations quite a lot."

"How is that going?" Stephanie asked.

The slender woman thought about the question for a moment. "He would rather focus on the fight against crime," she looked at Stephanie. "Thieves, murderers and rapists. He believes the main role of the police is to guarantee the safety of the city's citizens in their daily life. Of course, he cannot choose what he does and doesn't do. I believe that, all in all, he has faith in his job, and that's what matters."

Stephanie found out very quickly that Dalram was a shy woman who spoke very little and focused on housekeeping. According to her, she learned her fluent English during her studies at an American school that used to be active in Teheran. She was also the one who took it upon herself to teach her three daughters the language.

In recent years, Dalram had strengthened her connection to Islam. She practiced all the precepts, which included praying five times a day.

"It's all because of my little sister, Lily," Tahara told Stephanie with a smile, hugging her sister. "Lily influences mother on everything religious. Everyone knows that Lily will soon replace one of the *mullahs*." Tahara and Zaher burst out laughing. Lily furiously freed herself from her sister's arm.

"I have no idea what kind of brainwashing she is going through at school," Tahara teased, trying to avoid her little sister's fists. "This little girl is really scary. You know what we call her at home? Her nickname is Khomeniti."

Lily faced her sister with a serious look. "It's better than your way of life," she snapped. "You think it's better to dress like you do? Dye your hair like some slut? You should be ashamed."

Zaher stepped in, attempting to diffuse the heated conversation. "Actually, I think that mother's religiousness began when she was diagnosed with breast cancer." She looked at Stephanie. "All the medical procedures she went through, first the surgery and then the chemotherapy, affected her deeply. It's totally natural for people in distress to look for something to hold on to."

Stephanie learned that Tahara was a second year political science student at the prestigious Teheran University. She was an opinionated and temperamental young woman, full of energy. Unlike her two sisters, who were modest in their appearance, Tahara was both aware of her natural gifts and knew how to highlight them with her makeup and clothing. Aside from her studies, she spent a good deal of time socializing outside of the university.

After pledging to keep it a secret, Stephanie learned that Tahara was part of a secret discussion group composed of a few dozen male and female students. "The group discusses topics banned by the government," Tahara explained. "Tonight, the discussion is going to be on a book about what is really going on in Iran, *Lolita in Teheran*. Do you know the book?"

"No," Stephanie answered. "I never heard of it."

"I think you should read it," Tahara chimed. "It will give you a new perspective on what's going on in Iran and will help you understand the forces at work here. The book tells the story of a university professor who got some students together at her home to read and discuss classic books, both foreign and Iranian. Eventually, she fled Iran because she couldn't bear the widespread brainwashing and the infiltration of religion into everyday life." Tahara became more and more excited as she spoke. "Like them, we get together, each time in a different place, to discuss and analyze classical books that the Iranian authorities, under instructions from the religious leaders, are forbidden to put out."

Tahara's voice was now steady. "What's going on here is just absurd," she said, her eyes flashing. "They are taking this country backwards; they forbid the distribution of certain books, they block websites, they force traditional clothing on us. It's unbelievable. And people just submit to it. It's really hard for us, the younger generation, to come to terms with the situation. It's disgraceful."

"I'm guessing you must have been at the student demonstration," Stephanie speculated.

Little Lily was quick to answer for her. "She was too busy with her boyfriend," she blurted. "She went to hug and kiss him. She is an infidel. Tahara infidel!"

Tahara grabbed her sister. "Who are you calling infidel? You know very well I promised father I wouldn't attend the demonstration." Tahara released her grip on Lily and regained her composure. She looked at Stephanie. "I would have been in the front line," she spoke calmly. "Despite my opinions, I respect my father."

Lily was unfazed by Tahara's lashing out. "Too bad you didn't participate and too bad they didn't arrest you. You might have learned something if you had spent a couple of days in jail," Lily sneered.

In spite of her young age, Lily was without a doubt an extraordinary and feisty girl. In spite of strong opinions and the fact that she adhered strictly to religious dogma, she still managed to gain the love of everyone, including Tahara, as the temperamental center of attention.

Zaher, the eldest who looked the most like Stephanie, was administrative manager at Giamran Hospital. Giamran was located north of the city and specialized mainly in heart diseases. According to Zaher, the hospital was considered to be one of the top medical facilities in the country despite its small size, partially due to sophisticated cardiac equipment from Germany.

Over the following days, as they shared one small bed, Stephanie found out that Zaher had been engaged to one of the senior doctors at the hospital for two years. The families had even met and set a date for the wedding.

"As the date approached, I started to get cold feet," Zaher said frankly. "Imad, that's his name, didn't hide his wish to leave Iran and try his luck in Europe. Things weren't bad here, but he thought he would be able to earn more in Europe. At first, I was quite excited by the idea. I thought that it might be nice to work a few years in Germany, earn good money and then return to Iran. When he began the actual groundwork to leave the country though, I realized I didn't want to go." Zaher had a certain sadness written on her face.

"I can't see myself living away from my family, away from the sights I grew up with. I strongly disapprove of what has been going on in Iran in recent years, but I love my family, the people, and my country; most importantly, I love what I'm doing here."

# 7

Stephanie's first few days in Teheran were quiet, except for a phone call to her mother which she made from a booth at a market on the outskirts of town. Little Lily explained how to use the booth and gave her the right coins.

"I'm fine, Mom, really," she said repeatedly over the phone. This was a time when her acting skills really came in handy. "India is amazing. It's filthy though, and they haven't even heard of toilet paper in some places. Mom, you won't believe it; it's just amazing to see millions of people living in such low standards, without basic necessities, who can still make ends meet."

Throughout the conversation Stephanie couldn't stop picturing Blondie, the CIA agent she had met at her mother's request, nearly two weeks before flying to Teheran. At that time, Sharon didn't seem to believe that Stephanie had actually shelved her plans to travel to Iran.

"I want you to meet someone," her mother told her one day.

"Who do you want me to meet?" Stephanie was skeptical.

"Steph, it's someone who has known me a long time. It's very important to me that you meet him," her mother had insisted. "I'm really concerned. You don't understand the risk involved in going to Iran. They tortured and killed scores of the Shah's former intelligence personnel, chasing them to the corners of the world to find them. They have connections all over, with the Russians, the Hezbollah. You just don't understand how far their arms reach."

Sharon told her about a close colleague she had worked with in Iran, who was successful in tricking the Revolutionary Guard, and with the help of his family was able to leave the country. Somehow, he had reached Amsterdam, where he was able to get a job as a production manager with a candy manufacturer. Over the years, he even married a local girl and had children. "But then, one morning, twenty years after he left Iran, he vanished. All attempts to locate him were unsuccessful, as if he had been swallowed by the Earth."

Sharon paused for effect. "Our close friends have no doubt that he was kidnapped by the Iranian government. In my opinion, he is either dead or lying bruised and beaten in a small detention cell somewhere in Qum."

"I've heard the stories," Stephanie answered coldly. "Who do you want me to meet with?"

"His name is Dan Aniston, but everyone knows him by his alias: 'Blondie.' He told me he can meet with you this coming Thursday at 5 PM."

Stephanie looked at her mother, confused. "Who is he? What does he have to do with me?"

"Dan Aniston is in charge of the 'Rehab Department,' a special unit within the CIA. They have endless resources: money, assets, and companies. The 'business men' running these companies are all CIA agents. They specialize in handling, aiding and closely monitoring people on the intelligence team who are facing problems while serving the agency in hostile countries. The unit is capable of burying old identities and building new ones, and they've even been known to buy up small businesses around the world for people in trouble. They are not above the law, but they have no boundaries; everything goes. They will do whatever it takes to ensure their own interests take complete precedence," Sharon insisted. "Blondie has been with us many years and I want you to know that I have complete trust in him. I would have no problem walking with him on the edge of a cliff in pitch darkness with my eyes closed and hands tied behind my back."

Despite all Sharon said, Stephanie was unconvinced that she needed to meet with Blondie.

"Stephanie," Sharon's voice grew stern. "I'm not asking you, anymore. I thought you would go because I asked you to. But I see you are being stubborn. The truth is, you don't have a choice. Meeting Blondie is a part of protocol, and you must follow it.

"Protocol?" Stephanie asked.

"We are done discussing it." Sharon continued. "You will meet with him, and you will abide by whatever he tells you.

Stephanie started to protest, but could hear the seriousness in her mother's tone. She begrudgingly took the address and went to an office building on Main Street in Santa Monica. She paused for a long moment outside the building, enjoying the unique atmosphere of the bustling area. Crowds of young people walked, biked and jogged alongside the beautiful avenue, just a block from the Pacific Ocean.

She took the elevator to the tenth floor, showed her I.D. to the stern-looking guard, and walked through the checkpoint. Moments later, she faced a locked glass door.

She rang the intercom gently. The response was a faint buzz. Stephanie pushed open the door and stepped into a large lobby.

A young secretary, blonde and blue-eyed, welcomed her with a smile. "Thank you for coming to TD Limited Strategy and Public Relations. You must be Stephanie. Please have a seat. Our representative will be with you shortly."

She wasn't surprised that the office appeared to be a P.R. firm. "It's all a cover for a branch of the CIA," Stephanie remembered her mother explaining.

Dan Aniston definitely lived up to his nickname. He was a man in his fifties, tall and muscular. But his most noticeable feature was his flowing, bright golden hair that came down past his shoulders. Stephanie found herself staring at the blonde locks that framed his face.

"Your mother was right," he said, after they shook hands in his office. "You're very pretty." Stephanie did not respond. She was in a rush to get this meeting over with. She sat on one of the chairs and anxiously spoke.

"I'm in a rush," she said coldly. "Let's start. My mother told me that you have important stuff to tell me."

Blondie smiled at her. "It's important to all of us that you don't travel to Iran, Stephanie. We are talking national security here," he said with a serious expression. "Here at the CIA, we have rules of conduct for 'cobras,' slang for new recruits. It's been decades since your mother joined the program. Usually, support and aid are given for fifteen years. Because of the sensitivity of the operations your mother took part in, we assume that the danger is not over and that this trip is highly risky." Stephanie didn't even flinch. She had expected him to say those exact words to her.

"Sorry," he went on, "but this is how things stand. The moment that your mother told you about Iran and the escape and your new identity, your status with us changed. It was easy keeping you safe before because you knew nothing. Now that all that information has been disclosed, your risk level has gone way up. For years, your mother has been trying to convince us to authorize the disclosure of her life story. Despite her efforts, we had national security issues to consider, and decided to delay your exposure to this reality as long as possible."

Stephanie sat staring at Blondie for a long time. She did not like his cocky attitude. "You can imagine that without our help, you wouldn't have gotten the position with the Department of Immigration so easily," he said with a smile. "We noticed that you were getting a bit lost in L.A. and we decided to help."

Suddenly, her mother's voice broke through her memory, and Stephanie found herself still standing in the phone booth. Stephanie could feel the anger and resentment building up inside of her as she recalled that meeting with Blondie. She brought her attention back to her mother.

"Take care of yourself! Don't drink tap water and don't--"

Stephanie cut her short. "I know, Mom, I'm being careful. I'm feeling fine. You don't have to worry. I'm getting off now. There's a long line of people waiting to use the phone."

Stephanie put down the phone. Oddly enough, she felt quite comfortable with the fact that she was lying to her mother. She had been lied to her whole life, and felt no guilt in returning the favor. Walking slowly, she left the phone booth and made her way back towards her host's house, ignoring the stares of a nearby group of men.

Stephanie tried to keep a low profile as she explored the city but was mostly unsuccessful. Even though she took extra care to dress modestly, her looks attracted attention everywhere she went. She decided it was better to just ignore the interested glances she received on every street and tried to avoid any unnecessary conversations.

Stephanie was genuinely enjoying her stay in Iran. She got used to her host family's way of life quite quickly, as well as to the city of Teheran. She fully embraced the dry and humid climate, the richness and diversity of food. There was a mixture of the religious and the secular and that interested her as well.

She hardly ever had a chance to talk to her father, especially in private, aside from the few moments in the late evening when he returned home from work. The high-ranking police officer was very busy, in "over his head," as his apologetic wife would say.

"These days, the entire police force of Teheran is being deployed because of the student demonstrations. I don't know how much you know, but the young people are being very critical to the outcome of the recent election." Dalram spoke with remorse. "He did plan to take a few days off to spend with you. I hope you understand."

The truth was that Stephanie didn't really feel his absence. The women of the house lavished upon her with warmth and attention. She felt at ease in their company. Stephanie got used to waking up very early when the *muezzin*'s voice, calling the believers to pray at the mosque, penetrated into the house. It was hard to fall back asleep after that, so Stephanie soon gave up trying to do so.

Dalram would get up to pray on the small carpet beside her bed and then start the housework. When Amir woke up every morning, about an hour later than Dalram, the house was already clean and breakfast was waiting on the kitchen table. He left for work right after eating. Every day, Dalram accompanied him to the door and kissed him goodbye on the cheek.

Tahara and Zaher would quickly finish their prayers and then hurry to the kitchen, but not before kissing their mother on the cheek and wishing her a good morning. Little Lily, who never skipped any prayer, was the last one to come to the kitchen.

Stephanie began joining Zaher for a quick morning prayer and would walk with her down to the kitchen. Breakfast was modest; it was made up of sheep cheese, butter, jam and sliced bread. Stephanie, who wasn't used to eating until noon, made do with two cups of hot sweet tea.

She spent the mornings touring the city alone, one of Tahara's ideas. Amir approved, but not before providing Stephanie with an official police document, signed by him, confirming that she was an American citizen visiting relatives in Teheran.

"I suggest," he said with a serious expression as he handed her the document, "that when going out, you dress modestly. I don't want you to attract too much attention. I know you want to explore, but it is not the custom here for girls to be hanging out on their own. So take extra cautions."

Every night, the three girls would gather in the living room to prepare Stephanie a detailed itinerary. It usually turned into a nonstop hour-long argument, as they all disagreed on where she should go, where she should avoid and how she should get there.

During the first week, Stephanie got to see a few of Teheran's main museums, such as the Museum of Modern Art and the Glass and Ceramic Museum. Much of what she learned came from wandering the streets and using public transportation to get there. Her encounters with the local population, despite her lack of fluency in the language, provided her with the tools necessary to better understand what was taking place around her.

Teheran intrigued Stephanie. She was fascinated by the bustling street life, the colorful markets and even the endless traffic jams. She relished the images that appeared in front of her, a unique blend of the ugliness and breathtaking beauty. Teheran was a city of extreme contrasts, an unlikely mosaic of Eastern and Western life.

One did not have to venture far from the opulent mosques, the vast and manicured parks or the charming little streets to find entire neighborhoods characterized by filth and neglect. Stuck between the modern malls, high-rise buildings and markets overflowing with goods, there were dilapidated houses and poverty that cried out to heaven.

One of Stephanie's most lasting memories was of young children splashing water at each other in the canals dug along some of the roads. Tahara later told her that the water in the ditches came from nearby rivers. She claimed the ditches were meant to supply water to the trees.

"In many neighborhoods, the water ditches are the biggest attraction during the summer months, and not just for kids," she told her. "Dad forbids us from approaching the ditches. He claims that some people are using them as toilets. According to him, it is life-threatening to bathe in the ditches since the water is filthy and carries diseases."

There was always a strong presence of military and police personnel in the city streets. Initially, she thought that it was in response to the student demonstrations, but she soon realized that it was just another part of their environment.

The men and women Stephanie encountered during her wanderings were mostly friendly. Despite only knowing some broken English, they usually tried to answer her questions and help her as best as they could. Still, there were also those who responded in a hostile way or who completely withdrew from contact with her. Stephanie had a hard time accepting this behavior, especially because she took extra care to follow closely to the customs of the country. She dressed modestly, usually wearing white sneakers, jeans, a long tunic on top of it all and a large kerchief over her head.

Little Lily often tried to clarify things for Stephanie. "Here, women don't hang out alone in the streets. You must have run into devout Muslims, the type who assume that a woman on her own in the street is a sinner. Apart from that, some people here are not exactly crazy about the United States. I don't have to explain to you why, right?"

Tahara joined the conversation. "You should be thankful you didn't run into the 'Modesty Patrol.' Those guys are real fanatics. They are above the law. If you're lucky, they'll arrest you, but they can just as easily beat the hell out of you. It could be in the middle of the street in broad daylight."

Lily used the opportunity to tease her sister. "Tahara was arrested six months ago," she said quickly while she distanced herself from her older sister. "She would still be in jail today if Dad hadn't helped get her out."

Tahara rushed towards her little sister. "Come here, you little Khomeini," she hissed. "Wait until I catch you. I'll lock you up in the bathroom, just like I did last time you got on my nerves." Lily escaped her sister's grasp. Tahara continued. "Tell Stephanie what you want to be when you grow up. Tell her. Little Khomeini here wants to join the Revolutionary Guard."

One night, during one of the many heated discussions around the dinner table, the topic became about the thick smog covering Teheren which had been significantly powerful that day. Stephanie admitted having a hard time breathing. She learned that the smog was due largely to the more than a million vehicles going through the city on a daily basis.

"Not long ago, I read that over half the cars in Iran don't conform to international fuel standards, and they burn double the amount of gas than the average European car," Tahara explained to her. "It said that the Iranians have no intention of investing in fuel efficiency because we don't have a fuel problem."

Lily contributed her knowledge on the topic in her characteristic, serious voice. "You were lucky to get here in the summer," Lily offered. "The conditions in winter are even worse. In winter, the smog builds up under a layer of cold air. On some days, it is practically impossible to breathe; schools are closed and students are forced to stay home all day. Last year, we lost four school days because of heavy smog."

In the first couple of days, Stephanie decided that the best way to get a feel for the city's rhythm was to use public transportation to get from her hosts' home to the museums. There were several occasions, though, where she could no longer tolerate the crowded busses which had no air conditioning, so she turned to taxis.

Traffic in Teheran, whether by public transport or private cars, crawled slowly. The traffic jams were unavoidable and even the police standing in the main intersections were unable to bring any order.

One day in particular, Stephanie hailed a taxi. The driver was a young man in his thirties whose most noticeable feature was a pair of Ray-Ban glasses two sizes too large for his small face. He was also very good at cursing in English.

The ride quickly turned into a nightmare for Stephanie, who felt like a captive in the back seat. Her fearful eyes carefully watched the driver maneuver recklessly among the lanes, as he tried to force his way through the thousands of vehicles surrounding them.

At one point, he wanted to turn right but instead of waiting for the green light, he overtook the car in front him by moving left into opposing traffic while the light was still red. It was a miracle they were not hit by an oncoming car.

Soon after finishing her visit to a museum or after spending the day wandering the streets, Stephanie would often meet with one of her sisters. They usually coordinated the meetings the evening before, making sure Stephanie knew exactly where to go. She met with Zaher twice a week at Giamran Hospital, and the two of them would go out for lunch.

Once, they ate at a large restaurant in a shopping center not far from the hospital. The restaurant's specialty was fish and chips. The place, decorated in a sleek and modern style, was packed with men and women, young and old, all professionally dressed.

"Most of the people you see here work for commercial companies or in nearby government offices," Zaher explained. "These people can afford to dress well and eat out. They are not the ones you see on the streets." Stephanie liked the food. The local version of fish and chips was a pleasant surprise. The fish was well-smoked, the fries were thinly sliced and soft and the vegetables on the large plate were very fresh.

The second time they went out, Zaher convinced her to try the local food. They walked up one of the main streets in the area until they arrived at a small restaurant called *Stars*. "Dad loves to come here. The owner is a childhood friend," Zaher told Stephanie. "According to him, the food in this restaurant is the best in Teheran."

A tall, heavy man, dressed in black trousers and a white shirt, welcomed them with a broad smile. "This is Hussein, the owner and one of Dad's close friends," said Zaher. "I'm sorry, but he doesn't speak English. He only understands a little bit."

Hussein escorted them to one of the side tables as he enthusiastically conversed with Zaher. Stephanie, who understood nothing, gathered that she was the topic of the conversation. Zaher later confirmed that, after Hussein went back to running the restaurant.

"He said that we look alike," she said smiling. "He was sure that you are my long lost sister."

Stephanie had never seen most of the dishes that soon filled their table. Zaher described each one. The appetizer was kebab, a meatball dish with assorted vegetables and stuffed vine leaves, soaked in pomegranate juice. She encouraged Stephanie.

"Don't be afraid to taste it. I promise you will enjoy it. But don't stuff yourself. There's still the main course," Zaher warned. Both of them also got a large drink of goat yogurt mixed with water. The cool and slightly tart drink was very refreshing, and Stephanie quickly found herself on her second.

For the main course, Zaher ordered two types of meat, minced kebab skewers and a skewer of veal, cut in strips. Both dishes were succulent and nicely seasoned, served with barbequed tomatoes and onions. For their dessert, which

Hussein did not charge them for, they got a delicious cake that tasted slightly of rose water.

Stephanie loved spending time with Zaher. She felt like she could talk to her about the most personal subjects, which they had indeed done late at night in the room they shared. Unlike her younger sisters, who never hesitated to express their feelings and share their knowledge, Zaher was reserved in a modest kind of way. "Even though I'm the oldest, I'm like the sandwich girl," Zaher said jokingly. "I'm in the middle, stuck between Mom's conservative religious beliefs and Dad's more lenient beliefs. I'm also in the middle between Lily's fundamentalist school education and Tahara's almost radical world view that she gets from the university."

Zaher, feeling comfortable enough to share her thoughts with her stepsister, continued. "I think extremism, at any level, leads nowhere. Still, I believe the proverb that says, 'Don't cut the branch you're sitting on.' After all, I live here, I make a decent living and respect my mother's and Lily's way. I truly think there is a beauty to them wanting to maintain our traditional religious values. But I don't want any misunderstandings. I strongly believe that the regime, under the influence of the Ayatollahs, is leading Iran towards a collapse, one that could look like what happened in Iraq. On the other hand, I don't think Iran should become an extension of America. I'd rather not see another McDonald's in Iran again. No offense, of course."

"It's okay," Stephanie assured her. "I'm not too crazy about what's been happening with American society for the past few decades either. I don't know what an ideal society even looks like."

"Don't get me wrong," Zaher said. "I think it's very important to understand other cultures. I can understand why Americans love McDonald's and Disneyland, but I don't agree with that life style. There are some basic qualities which I admire about the States and the West, like gender equality and a democratic vote, which technically we have here, but we know the truth. In the end, we know who makes the decisions. And it's certainly not the people. I'm not an anarchist. I think laws should be in place. But when the alternative is more oppression, then I'm not so sure."

Stephanie loved that she had an opinion on everything, even if it didn't sound like a popular Teheran point of view.

Using a tone of polite defiance, she explained to Stephanie, "People here are influenced to not argue. They are scared to express their opinions. The more they withdraw into themselves, the more restrictions the authorities can place on them."

Tahara, the middle-aged sister, was able to meet with Stephanie according to her university schedule. On their first outing, they spent an hour in a very unusual tea house, located on one of the side streets by the university. Stephanie and Tahara were the only women. They were surrounded by dozens of older men smoking hookah pipes ( *kalion* as it was called locally) who stared at them quite often. Tahara noticed Stephanie's discomfort and tried to put her at ease. "It's okay. We're not breaking any laws. You can relax. They can't do anything." But it was only after some of Tahara's schoolmates walked in that Stephanie relaxed.

Soon, a large urn, decorated with flowers, was placed at the center of the table. Next to it was a kettle containing tea leaves. Each one at the table, in turn, poured hot water into a glass and then added some tea leaves, according to his or her preference. The scent was intoxicating. Stephanie drank eagerly from her glass, but flinched at the surprisingly bitter taste in her mouth.

One of the students showed her that in order to enjoy the tea, she should suck on a sugar cube while sipping.

"That's how the two flavors, the bitter and the sweet, blend but still keep their own character," he said.

The conversation of the table focused on an Iranian film called *Café Transit*. Stephanie realized that this was the group Tahara told her about previously, the group which discussed topics that challenged the current government's oppressive laws and exposed themselves to materials that were banned. One of the young women had watched the film at home a day earlier and shared her impressions with the others.

"Have you at least heard of it?" Tahara asked her.

Stephanie shook her head. "Actually, I don't think I've ever watched an Iranian film," Stephanie admitted.

Tahara explained that the movie followed the story of the struggle of an Iranian woman, a mother of two girls, who is widowed and left to the whims of her brother-in-law. "Completely against the instructions of her late husband's family," Tahara passionately stated, "the woman decides to reopen the coffee shop her husband had managed and tries to succeed where most business owners are men. The problem is that very few women in Iran even dare to think that way. They live in constant fear of society's conventions."

One of the young women interrupted Tahara. "Or if they go into business for themselves, they work as prostitutes for wealthy Arabs in Dubai. I know a woman like that: my mother's cousin. They kidnapped her as a girl, in the dead of night, and no one has heard from her since. It's so sad."

Stephanie told the students about one of the auditions she once did for an Iranian-American co-production. The character she was supposed to play in the movie was an Iranian woman trying out her luck in horse racing.

This revelation attracted the entire group's attention, and they showered her with questions about the film industry in Hollywood. Her attempts to explain that she was never really part of it didn't stop them.

Stephanie soon realized that they wanted her to share her knowledge of Hollywood more than they wanted her to share about herself. "The only star that I met personally is George Clooney," Stephanie told them, amused by the sudden attention that she was getting. "It was at a party I was invited to. He was very nice, a real charmer and a ladies' man. According to rumors though, he's also quite naughty."

"Does he look as good in real life as on screen?" asked one of the young women, barely containing her curiosity.

"He looks good," she answered grinning. "Not really my type, but I can see why women go crazy over him. He's got a dazzling smile and a very impressive tone in his voice."

On another occasion, Tahara and Stephanie met at a mall called *Kaam*.

The seven-floor shopping center, designed like the ones Stephanie was used to in the States, was spacious, clean and well kept.

Stephanie was surprised to find dozens of shops stocked with a large variety of merchandise, although no Western brands were to be seen. Tahara read her mind. "This is the area for the general public. The rich have their hidden mall, underground, where you can find all the brands, including American ones. There's so much hypocrisy here. A couple of months ago, one of the Ayatollahs made a motion to force the shop owners to cover the mannequin's heads in the shop windows. Can you believe that?"

Stephanie watched the women walking by. Her mind flashed back to the first time she had learned about the Ayatollahs. She remembered sitting in the classroom, watching Professor Yasser standing there, his arms crossed, giving his lecture explaining how the extremist groups of Ayatollahs were one of the main causes to the bad reputation that the Muslim religion and Islamic culture in general had adopted. She suddenly felt a sadness welling up inside of her, longing to see him. She had done really well distracting herself from her sadness. Suddenly, she was flooded with all of the memories.

"It's incredible," Tahara's voice woke her from her daydream. "You see modest clothing and head covers everywhere. Yet, you find revealing dresses, short skirts on sale, behind closed doors," Tahara smiled, whispering.

Stephanie observed the women, covered from head to toe.

"Women here lead double lives. Don't be misled by what you see on the streets. Most Iranian women are up to date on fashion. When they go out, due to restrictions, they dress modestly. At home though, far from the eyes of the 'Modesty Patrol,' they sometimes dress differently, depending upon their husbands. The only way to buy those clothes here is in secret. You have to know someone in order to purchase them."

An hour later, when they left the rows of colorful shop windows, Tahara continued talking about her beliefs. "Fashion is one of the things that the current regime struggles with the most. This is especially true because Western fashion and style, which they consider to be opposing to the teachings of Islam, has been on the rise since Ahmadinejad came in 2005.

"A citizen who breaks the law in regards to clothing for the first time gets off with a warning. A repeat offender could stand on trial and be sent to a special guidance course. The shop owners complain that these measures by the regime are bad for business, but it doesn't help. When the Ayatollahs make a new ruling, even the president himself won't dare to challenge it. All in all, I think that the clerics are more powerful than this president."

Tahara recalled the parties her parents used to host from time to time when she was a child. "Dad was already a high-ranking officer in the police force, and Mom was still secular. They had many friends who used to hold dance parties. The Ayatollahs were already ruling Iran though, and they considered gatherings where women and men met to dance to be extremely dangerous. I remember the evening gowns the women used to wear. It looked like a fashion show by the best Italian designers."

Tahara smiled, her mind going back to a happier time. "I remember the guests arriving at our house dressed very modestly, as they would on the street. Once inside though, they would change clothes to reveal the latest European fashions. This situation hasn't changed, but it has become harder to do. When I go out to a party, I take a second outfit in a bag and change. I think that even my parents haven't seen some of my clothes."

Stephanie was amazed that Tahara had to dress like she was two different people. "When did your parents stop holding those parties?

Tahara sighed. "After Dad was promoted to colonel, he couldn't risk it anymore. Mom started getting closer to Islam at the same time. That was just one of the results."

"I can't imagine your mother in an evening gown," Stephanie giggled.

Tahara smiled. "Yes. Today, you can hardly imagine the way she used to be. She is a totally different person. As you already know, she became very ill the last few years. It brought her closer to religion. She also stopped taking care of herself. She was once a beautiful woman. I still remember her all made up, wearing tight jeans. Dad used to tell her she was the most beautiful woman in Teheran."

"She's still very pretty," Stephanie insisted. "And she seems to be at peace with her decision to live according to Islam. It must be good for her."

"Perhaps," Tahara shrugged. "I don't know. I respect her way of life but find it hard to accept all this madness. That's not the type of Islam I want. It's also not the Islam that I know. Trust me when I say that I have read the Quran many times over. You won't find the extreme ideas the Ayatollahs preach there. You won't find anything suggesting oppression of women, which you get from the Revolutionary Guard."

One day, Tahara invited Stephanie to join her at the home of one of her girlfriends. Only when they were standing in the doorway did Tahara disclose that it was the location where Tahara attended a weekly meeting of a secret group.

"I'm asking you not to tell anybody," Tahara said.

Stephanie was not pleased, in part because she was concerned about getting in trouble. She also did not feel comfortable being the center of attention in a meeting that was held secretly. There was a lot of excitement over Stephanie among the four male and three female students. One after the other, they approached her, shaking her hand and introducing themselves. Stephanie tried to answer their barrage of questions. Where was she from in the States? How long would she be staying in Iran? What was her impression of Teheran?

Compared to them, the teacher of modern Iranian history introduced to her as Ali Hijhazi seemed reserved. He was tall and broad shouldered, and he wore black trousers with a white shirt. Stephanie noticed that his hand shake was short and weak, and his eyes lowered when he faced her.

Unlike the group of young students who eagerly gathered around Stephanie, listening to her answers, the teacher, whom Stephanie estimated was in his late thirties, disappeared into the next room. She could not make up her mind up about whether the attitude he showed towards her was the result of shyness or because he disapproved of her presence there.

The group, when not talking to Stephanie, conducted conversation in Farsi, meaning Stephanie could not understand a word. She paid the most attention to Ali's voice, mediating the discussion amidst the medley of voices. Ali had a melodious, deep voice, pleasant and relaxed.

Stephanie turned on the television, hoping to find something to keep her busy. Since it was around noon, though, most TV programs were meant for a younger audience. She flipped through the channels to find something of interest. Finally, she paused on a channel showing an episode of a children's series she used to watch as a kid. The dubbing in Farsi brought a smile to her face.

Once in a while, Tahara left her friends and came over to make sure Stephanie was alright. She felt uncomfortable because of the situation she had put Stephanie in.

"I'm sorry," she kept on saying, "I didn't think you would be stuck here. We won't stay too long."

Stephanie didn't want Tahara to feel guilty. "It's fine," she said. "Go back to your discussion. I'm just fine. Don't you worry about me."

The hostess, a short girl with full lips, also felt uncomfortable because Stephanie was sitting alone in the living room. A few times, she left her discussion group to make sure all was well with Stephanie. "I see you're bored. Are you sure you don't want to join us? At least, you'll be sitting with us and not here all alone."

The girl pointed at the two bowls on a long, wooden table. There were dried fruits in one of them and pistachios in the other. "How is it that you haven't even touched the world's best pistachios?" she asked, smiling. "Did you know that Iran is the biggest pistachio producer in the world? It's the second largest source of income for the country, after oil."

Stephanie grabbed a handful of pistachios. The hostess was still not satisfied.

"And try the fruits. You really don't know what you are missing. This one is wonderful. Very sweet. It's a hybrid of watermelon and melon. We call it *harbuza*. It's cold and sweet. Do you want something to drink?"

"It's okay. I'm not thirsty. I will try the fruit though" she said.

Stephanie watched TV until the meeting ended. Ali approached her and her stepsister at the end of the meeting. "Tahara, do you want me to drive you home? If so, we better leave right away."

Tahara's eyes lit up. "Come on, Stephanie. Ali offered us a ride home. We won't have to bother with public transport. I just hope we don't run into the Modesty Patrol. A month ago, my girlfriend got arrested for riding in a car with a fellow student."

During the ride, Stephanie sat in the back and listened to their conversation. The two spoke Farsi again, so she soon lost interest and chose to focus on the view from her window. To her surprise, she noticed that Ali's shining, dark eyes often looked back at her with interest in his rear view mirror.

# 8

When Stephanie wasn't with Zaher or Tahara, she accompanied little Lily around town. Since Dalram, who mostly cared for the house, hardly went out, Lily ended up purchasing necessities.

The market was a fifteen minute walk from the house. Every time they went, Lily would take a different route to impress Stephanie with her knowledge of the area. Thus, Stephanie, even as she explored all of the popular sights, could get a sense of the streets and areas that most tourists would never see.

The main market especially fascinated her. Though she had visited several others, none were as colorful, vibrant, and busy with the bustle of vendors and customers making deals than this main one. The market was divided in several sections, each one centered on a different product, like spices, cereals, coffee, herbs and tea blends. One could also find varieties of dried fruits, from lychee to guava, cranberries, raspberries and dried apricot paste. Stephanie asked about what looked like paper eggs in a jar at one of the stalls. Lily explained they were jasmine bulbs that, when covered with hot water, opened up into a flower.

Pistachios were sold in one of the market's largest sections, where crates and bags of different kinds were stacked side by side. "You see," Lily boasted, "We sell these all over the world, as well as to you Americans."

Lily wandered the market like it was her private property. Many of the vendors knew her. Those who were familiar with her family showed respect. From time to time, she would pause to acknowledge the shout of a vendor asking to give his regards to her father.

Stephanie soon became familiar with the vendors Lily frequented. They bought vegetables from Abu-Hassan, a man who advertised his merchandise to everyone by loudly yelling that there isn't, has never been and never will be a place in the whole market where vegetables are cheaper. She bought fruit from Munir and Samir, twins who both boasted identical, small black beards. Not far from the fruit shop, they purchased spices and dried fruit from the "The Refrigerator" (a sixty- something-year-old man who was nicknamed that for his size).

They bought fish from Rabah, and meat from Yussouf the butcher, who was called "The Crazy" in the market because of his frequent seizures. The last stop in their shopping spree was always at Ahmed's sweets stall. Stephanie took her time at his shop, tasting bits of confection before buying.

The vendors gave her the bill on a piece of paper which Dalram consulted at the end of each month. Lily never carried the goods home from the market. As soon as she arrived at the market, she would be surrounded by young kids looking to offer their services in exchange for a fee. She would choose one of them to join her in the stalls and carry everything home.

Stephanie really enjoyed her time with Lily. The girl was so full of energy and always had something to say. Family members joked that she was a "hopeless chatterbox" and had scores of questions for her American stepsister. Stephanie didn't always reply to Lily though, and was careful to avoid answering personal questions. When Lily couldn't get an answer, the young girl would make an angry face, put her hands on her hips, and confront Stephanie. "You don't answer. You are trying to deceive me. I may be young but I'm not stupid."

When she wasn't questioning her about boyfriends and her mother, Lily tried to teach Stephanie Farsi. At first, she focused on simple words like *cha* (what), *choja* (where), *zitor* (how), *ki* (when) and so on. To Lily's surprise, Stephanie was quick to pick up the language. As days went by and they made more trips to the market, her vocabulary expanded.

"To tell you the truth," Stephanie told Tahara late one evening, "I'm afraid that Lily will scold me in the middle of the street in front of people if I don't learn Farsi, so I'm studying hard. Our little sister's willpower scares me a little."

Tahara burst into laughter. "I believe you. After father, she seems to have the most power in this family."

On her second weekend there, Stephanie joined her father on a work-related trip to the town of Qum. "I have an important meeting that will probably last several hours, so you will have an opportunity to visit one of Islam's holiest towns," he told her.

"Do you think I will have a chance to visit the house where I was born?"

Amir smiled. "You ruined the surprise I had prepared for you. Grandmother is preparing lunch, where you will also meet your cousins, two brothers and three sisters. They remember you as a crying, but cute baby and are excited to meet you."

"Isn't that a bit risky?" Stephanie asked.

Her father leaned toward her and spoke in a confidential

tone. "They know who you are. We do have to be careful about who knows, but I have no doubts when it comes to our family. They have proven their trustworthiness before and I'm sure this will be no different. They are flesh and blood. Who can I trust if not them?"

Stephanie didn't react.

"My meeting starts at 8 AM, and the drive to Qum is about 140 kilometers. We will have to get up very early," he said.

"I have no problem getting up early. I used to get up at 6 AM. every day in order to catch the train to Los Angeles," Stephanie explained.

In the morning, after they hurriedly drank the hot tea Dalram had prepared, Stephanie and her father left the house. Her father's personal driver was waiting for them outside in a police car. There were no traffic jams that early, so they were soon through Teheran and on the main road to Qum. They stopped in Dalijian, a small, working class town, for a quick breakfast.

"I know you are not a big fan of breakfast," her father said as he spread a thick layer of butter on a slice of bread. "But experts say that it's the most important meal of the day. If I have a good breakfast, I can go all day without any food."

"Back when I lived with mother," Stephanie recalled, "I would eat breakfast every day before leaving for school. But I stopped making time for it in college. It was the same during my marriage since I always had to leave so early."

Amir's eyebrows raised with interest. "Actually, I barely know anything about you. How long have you been married? What does he do?"

Stephanie felt a tightness grow in her stomach but she took a deep breath and plunged ahead. "I was married to a guy named Tom Holmes. He had a big drugstore in a town not far from Los Angeles. It wasn't the most successful marriage, but I tried to make it work. Unfortunately, he was killed in a car accident."

Amir was confused. "A car accident? Stephanie, I'm so sorry-"

Stephanie interrupted. "I was preparing to divorce him before it happened. It was shocking more than anything. I felt guilty for the relief it gave me," Stephanie spoke as she looked out the window. "It's all over now anyways." She lowered her eyes awaiting what she knew was the next question.

"I'm not sure it's appropriate for me to ask, but how come you didn't have children?"

Stephanie shrugged and searched for a polite way to avoid going deeper into the pain of her past. "You can ask as many questions as you'd like," Stephanie told him, "But some answers, I'm not ready to share."

Her father nodded. "One thing I really regret though is that I was unable to get in touch with you some time ago. But isn't there a saying for that? 'Don't cry over the spilled milk?' I want to tell you that over the years, I've thought about you a lot. Even though I made a new home for myself, with my wife and three beautiful daughters, you were always in my heart. I don't know if your mother told you how much I loved you. I was crazy about you."

Stephanie looked at the man beside her and thought back to Tahara's description of her father. On one of their trips to the mall, Tahara had opened up a bit about their father's experience with the Revolutionary Guards.

"They destroyed his emotions," Tahara had explained, a hint of sadness in her eyes. "I've been told some stories from other family members about his life before he met my mother, around the time you and your mother left to go to the States. When he was arrested, they tortured him until he became a machine. It's like, they pulled out his heart."

Stephanie, having learned that information, became aware of the distance her father had been keeping from her, absorbing himself in his work. She would see glimpses of a fatherly connection with him, but felt like there was a wall between them for the most part. He had been doing a very good job of remaining stoic, and free of any signs of weak emotions. But now, Stephanie saw a film of moisture in his eyes as he spoke about how much he had thought about and loved Stephanie in her absence. He blinked it away and turned back to look out the window. Stephanie now realized that Tahara was wrong. He was in no way like a machine.

Stephanie and her father talked all the way to Qum. There was a sealed window between them and the driver so they could talk freely. Amir Mutaki asked many questions, wanting to know as much as possible, even subjects Stephanie would have rather not recalled.

She told him about her studies at the university, life in Los Angeles as an aspiring movie star, her job at the Department of Immigration and even a little about her most difficult times with Tom. With a candor that surprised herself, she found herself going into depth.

"Today, when I think of my marriage, I understand that I was actually trying to fix my life. Mother used to say that a woman has two choices in life, either to build a career or marry. I chose the second one."

Amir hadn't forgotten his earlier question. "It's a pity you didn't have any children. A child would have given a purpose to your life and connected the two of you," he said.

Stephanie shook her head. "We tried. Today, I can say that it's better I don't have any."

Her father probed. "Better? How can you say that?" he asked.

Stephanie paused, trying to decide how much she was willing to share. She took a deep breath, and it all came bursting forth. "Tom, my husband, wasn't a decent man. After the miscarriage, I had a nervous breakdown. I wanted a child more than anything, so I was totally heartbroken by the miscarriage." Her voice broke and her father put his hand on her arm. "I think that the crisis in our relationship began after the miscarriage. It wasn't the same after that. He started to believe that I wasn't a good wife."

Amir sighed at the thought of his daughter having to go through such emotional torment. "I'm very sorry to hear that you had to go through all of that. I have no doubt that you will find the right man. The future will be better. *Inshallah*," he said.

"I'm fine, really," she insisted. "After Tom passed, I got a nice apartment, started going out and having fun again. Since I've been alone, I've also become much closer to my mother. We take turns visiting each other."

Amir clearly had something else on his mind. He asked his next question with difficulty. "How is your mother? Does she still have the store?" his eyes searched outside at the passers-by, trying to look indifferent to the answer.

"I think she is doing well. She supports herself. She is always worried about things that are beyond her control, but I think she will manage. "

"I understand she hasn't mentioned me often." She could hear a sense of sadness in his voice.

"It's clear to me she only mentioned you when I forced her to," she replied.

Total silence fell on the car. Amir's eyes were fixed on the road. After a couple of minutes, Stephanie couldn't bear the silence any longer. "How come you didn't try to contact me?" In spite of her efforts, the pain she had been carrying for all these years began to surface.

It was obvious that Amir didn't know what to say. "You may never know all of the answers," Amir said, turning to her. Stephanie could see the passion in his eyes, the regret he had been feeling for the lost time. "I didn't have any other choice," he continued. "The year your mother took you to the United States was very difficult. I was released after a month-long investigation, but the government kept checking on me all the time. They were just waiting for me to make a mistake, for an excuse to take me in. They were watching so closely, that I couldn't risk contacting you for fear they would come for you. It was years before I was able to clear my name."

"Mother told me," Stephanie nodded.

"I don't know what she told you, but some people here in the government still consider her a traitor. I didn't want to cause you any harm so I did not try and communicate with you both. Then, I turned a new page in my life. I got married, raised a family and went back to serving the police."

"You have a beautiful family," Stephanie forced a smile. She really was happy with the life he had built for himself, and she loved the time she had been spending with her sisters, but she couldn't help but feel a sense of longing for the relationship they could have had, the memories they could have shared.

Amir gave her a look of gratitude, and took her hand. "Thank you. I really do have a wonderful family, and I thank God for that. Never in my wildest dreams did I imagine that one day, after destiny shattered one family, that I would be able to raise a new one. I loved your mother very much and you were really the joy of my life. On your birthday, I was the happiest man in the whole world. I walked through town, strutting proudly like a peacock," he beamed. Then a look of seriousness came over his face. "I don't want you to judge me. Life has led me down this path, for better or for worse. Nobody is to blame for this fate."

Stephanie felt the weight of the moment with her father, in the car. He was unburdening himself and she decided it was safe to really talk about things she never did with her mother. "I was disappointed, confused," she said. "I wasn't angry. Actually, I did get mad at mom because she hid so many things about you and my past. Up until a few months ago, I didn't know anything. Mother, a spy? Me, a Persian? My father, alive and well? Can you imagine how devastating that is? To get up one day and find out that your life was one big lie?"

"Don't be angry at her," Amir spoke delicately. "She wanted to protect you."

"If," Stephanie challenged him, "you loved my mother as you said, how come you let her go? Why did you give up on us?"

Amir's eyes looked pained again. "Today, looking back, I know that your mother's decision to leave and disappear was right. Your mother is a brave and smart woman. I prayed that the separation would be temporary, that someday, one way or another, we would be reunited. But at least, we are reunited, Stephanie."

"Do you wish you had come with us?"

Amir chose his words very carefully. "It wasn't an option," he said. I couldn't imagine leaving my home. It was so different with your mother. She had a highly sensitive job and was very active with two intelligence agencies. There is speculation that your mother, together with British intelligence, ran an operation that installed sophisticated listening devices in the homes and offices of the opposition leaders. In fact, your mother got an agent to plant a listening device into the bedroom of then-exiled Ayatollah Khomeini, who had temporarily moved his residence from Iraq to Paris. Now you may understand why they wanted her head at any price."

Stephanie gasped. "My mother? In charge of planting listening devices? I can't believe it," she exclaimed. "Father, she doesn't even know how to use her smartphone."

He smiled for a second and continued. "Don't misunderstand. Despite all the pain I went through, I don't regret having stayed behind in Teheran. I love my job, my family, and this country. I believe in Iran, and I can't see myself living in any other country in the world. While I don't agree with what's been going on here in recent years, we still have a strong country and a wonderful people. Even if it doesn't happen in my time, things will get better."

The car slowed down.

"What's going on?" Amir asked the driver.

Jamal, the driver, sounded amused as he spoke. "We are approaching Qum," said Jamal, "which means we are getting to the checkpoints."

Indeed, until the car reached Qum's main street, they had to stop at several checkpoints where armed soldiers thoroughly searched the car. Given the presence of Amir, though, who wore the Iranian police uniform, the soldiers saluted and spent little time searching.

"As you may already know, security is a very important issue in Iran," Amir explained, "and you can understand why. All kinds of sensitive facilities, including the Iranian Space Agency, are located in this area. That's why there are so many check-points."

The car entered the large parking lot of the police headquarters in Qum.

"I believe that I will be busy for about two hours," said Amir, as he opened the car door. "I will leave you with the Jamal. He is a trusted driver. He will take you around town, wherever you wish. I suggested that he take you first to the temple of Fatma Maasuma, the sister temple of Imam Ali al-

Rida. It would be a shame to be in Qum and not to visit one of the most sacred Shiite shrines."

After the touring, they picked her father up and Stephanie was warmly welcomed in his family's home in Qum. The spacious apartment, located on the third floor of a new building, was spotless, and it was clear that the family worked hard to get it ready for her visit.

Her father introduced Stephanie to his mother, Margin, and his two younger brothers, Mohasin and Daoud, in their forties. Standing behind them waited their wives, Fatma and Zeema, alongside Mohasin's four children and Daoud's three.

"Nice to meet you," she said over and over warmly, shaking their hands and kissing them. She was quickly impressed by her grandmother, Margin. The slender woman, despite her white hair and wrinkled face, was clear-headed and full of energy and excitement. She hugged Stephanie, kissed her warmly on the cheek, and grabbed her hand without letting go, as she persistently attempted to converse with Stephanie in Farsi, which of course, Stephanie didn't understand.

Amir started translating his mother's words. "She said that God has been good to her," he translated, "because God brought back her beloved granddaughter before her death. She says that now she can die in peace." Amir looked at Stephanie. "No doubt," Amir said quietly to Stephanie, "if things keep going on like this though, she'll outlive all of us."

It was difficult for Stephanie to take in the fact that the woman in front of her was her grandmother and to fully accept that all of the people in the house were her family. Her heartbeat quickened as a wave of warmth swept through her. The old woman gently stroked Stephanie's face and said something again to her in Farsi. Amir translated. "She says that you were the most beautiful girl in Iran, when you were born," he smiled. Margin left the room and returned with some pictures, one of them of a baby girl in a crib wrapped in a floral blanket.

"This is me?" Stephanie said in amazement, as she held the picture. "I have never seen a picture of myself at that age."

"You were about two months old." Her father noted, peering over her shoulder. "I think your grandmother bought that dress for you."

Margin took back the pictures and spoke while Amir translated. "I will make copies of the pictures and send them to you in Teheran. You can show them to your friends in the States," she told Stephanie.

Amir checked his watch. "*Maman*, I suggest we start eating," he said. "It's already late and we still have a long journey to Teheran. I promise you they will visit again."

They sat down around the table. Mouthwatering aromas soon filled the room as the women came out of the kitchen carrying trays loaded with food. Stephanie looked at the dishes with great interest. Noticing this, her grandmother encouraged her. "Eat my daughter, eat! Don't be embarrassed. Come on."

Stephanie looked at the dishes with bright eyes. She ate excitedly, and constantly thanked them all in Farsi, as Lily had taught her, for the delicious food. Fatma, the younger of the two wives, described the dishes on the table.

"This is *asha rashta*, a noodle dish," she spoke proudly. "The secret to why it's so good is in the way your grandmother makes the noodles. You can buy them at the store, but trust me, your grandmother's is the best." Fatma pointed at the rice bowl. "There are several different kinds of rice. This one prepared by Zaama is white rice with saffron. We call it *pulau*. I cooked the rice with an herb called *sabzi pulau*. I really hope you'll like it." Fatma spoke as she gave Stephanie a serving.

"And what is this?" Stephanie pointed at a deep dish with brown meat. "It looks really tasty and has such an amazing aroma."

"This is *horesh gurma shibez*," Fatma continued, "It's a beef stew with herbs, prepared by Zeema. It really is tasty. And this is *avgoshta lap*, beef stew with lemon, grandmother's specialty. Everyone in the family knows that if she prepares *avgoshta lap* without us begging her for months, it means she loves her guests." Stephanie smiled.

After the sumptuous meal, Stephanie and her father hugged and kissed the family members, and set off on their way.

"I'm glad you met your grandmother and your uncles," said her father, on the ride back to Teheran. "It's been a long time since I have seen my mother so excited. You can't imagine how much she loves you. Soon after you were born, she moved in with us. Since both your mother and I were usually busy working, it was actually your grandmother who took care of you. She would wheel you around the neighborhood in your stroller and show you off to her friends. Sometimes, it looked like you were her daughter, not her grandchild. She also used to call you 'Princess' and buy you beautiful dresses. You really were a very pretty baby."

"Not anymore," laughed Stephanie.

"Not at all," he joked.

Stephanie shrugged. "I had no idea," she said. "Now, I feel bad that I can't spend more time with her."

"We have a saying here: 'He whose heart was revived by love will never die.' A person doesn't have to stop loving," her father explained. "The love you shared with your grandmother will never go away. I believe love is our lifeblood. It's the emotion that drives us as human beings. And when I say love I don't just mean the love between a man and a woman; love can be between father and his son or daughter, between mother and her daughter, towards something or somebody. Love for me means cherishing life. Time and distance can't change that."

"I love that saying," Stephanie said thoughtfully. "I think it means a lot."

"Would you ever consider getting married again?" her father asked.

Stephanie nodded. "Sure. I know it would be hard after my last marriage. I've gotten used to being alone… but I believe in relationships. I would happily be with someone who was good for me."

"And children?" he continued. Stephanie chose not to share her fears that, following her miscarriage, doctors had told her she could not get pregnant again.

"Do you mean if I would like to have children?" she asked. "Of course. Recently I've thought a lot of adopting, or even using artificial insemination."

Amir Mutaki interrupted her. "I am not against single mothers and I know that it's become quite common in the Western world, but I believe a child needs both parents. You are still young, you can still give birth, there's no reason to think of such alternatives at your age."

"They are just things to think about," Stephanie replied. "It's not like I am going to do it tomorrow morning. I know how serious a decision that would be."

"I think a child should be born to parents. It's the most natural thing," he insisted.

"I think my mother is a good example," Stephanie offered. "She raised me on her own, even though she was never financially comfortable. She never even said a word about it. But as I got older, I was able to see the struggle."

"It's odd that in all these years she didn't remarry," Amir spoke, shaking his head.

"Her problem is- and she admits it- that she usually meets the wrong men. I mean, she won't let herself fall in love. She is too rational. Being rational always comes first," Stephanie said.

"Your mother has always been rational," said Amir. "The problem is that love, which we all need, is not a rational thing." Amir and his daughter rode in silence, thinking about the meaning of his last statement.

# 9

Stephanie was beginning to fall in love with Teheran. She adapted to the city, its climate, the traffic jams, the way of life, the people in the street, and of course her family. She also got used to the sight of women wearing veils and even to the armed soldiers standing at almost every corner. Her stay in Iran was supposed to last three weeks but, she knew after just a few days, she wanted to lengthen it.

"What's the hurry to go back?" little Lily asked her one day as they sat at the kitchen table eating breakfast. "You haven't seen anything yet."

Zaher entered the conversation. "I really don't understand what the rush to go back so early is," Zaher added. "This is the first time in your life you are able to meet your family, to see where are you from. Three weeks is very little time. Will you have any problem at work, if you stay longer?"

"I don't think so," Stephanie replied. "I have a very understanding boss. But I feel a bit uncomfortable. I don't want to interfere with your life at home."

Dalram suddenly grew angry. "That is too much," she interjected as she slammed down one of the dishes she had been putting away. "This is your father's home, just as it's my home or Zaher's and Tahara's and Lily's. Don't you dare ever think like that! You are family. Do not insult us."

Stephanie was embarrassed, and shocked to see this temper come from Dalram, who had been so quiet and passive up until now. "*Babhshid*," Stephanie said in Farsi. "I'm really sorry. The last thing I want is to hurt or insult you. I thought after all this time that I might be a burden to you all."

"You are not a burden," little Lily insisted. "We want you to stay as much as you like."

Stephanie stroked the young girl's head. "Thank you, thank you," Stephanie could feel the tears in her eyes. "You are all so incredible. I have not felt this good in a long time. I really do want to stay, and so I will stay."

She called the airline and asked to change the date of her flight, paid the fee for the change and booked a new date for the return flight for ten additional days. As soon as she put down the phone, the three girls rushed to kiss and hug her. Then, Dalram came over with no sense of the anger she had expressed, and she hugged and kissed Stephanie.

"Our house is your house," she said affectionately.

Together with Zaher and Tahara, Stephanie went to the Azadi movie theater in the city center, in a new and modern complex. Tahara explained it had opened a year and a half earlier and included, on top of the plush seats, a bar in the lobby of the main entrance. *This beautiful shopping center could be in America,* Stephanie thought. She didn't tell her sisters but, for the first time, she found herself feeling homesick.

The girls watched a film called *Baaran*. Stephanie, who had never seen an Iranian movie, let herself get carried away by the simple and touching plot. The movie was about the working class, as seen through the eyes of a teenage boy named Latif. Latif worked at a construction site where Iranians and illegal Afghanis work side by side. Despite the squalor and poverty, Latif falls in love with Labaran, an illegal Afghani worker employed in the kitchen of the construction site. Despite cultural differences, they wind up together, living in Iran.

As they left the movie theatre, Tahara spoke excitedly. "You must try *fallodeh*," she said. "In this area, there is a vendor who makes *fallodeh* in an old-fashioned way. It's been at least half a year since I went there last time. I hope he hasn't closed down."

A few minutes later, each one was holding a glass of the refreshingly frozen dessert. Gradually, the area in front of the store was filled with young people drinking and chatting as Tahara described the drink to Stephanie. "*Fallodeh* is a mixture of rose water, sugar, and lemon," she said, taking a bite.

"It's very tasty, really delicious. We say, 'It really hits the spot,'" Stephanie answered.

Tahara smiled. "Father used to take me here when I was little. I think that's the only one in Teheran where they prepare the *fallodeh* according to tradition."

Tahara suddenly sat up as she noticed someone walking toward them. "What a surprise," Tahara exclaimed. "Ali Hijazi. What are you doing here with us common folks?"

Stephanie remembered Ali Hijazi, the tall, broad-shouldered man, who drove her and Tahara home at the end of the literary meeting. Once again, he was wearing black pants and a white shirt and this time, too, he rushed to withdraw his hand after shaking hers warmly. The only thing different this time was that he had an older man with him.

Ali, very seriously, introduced his companion. "Please meet my friend, Dr. Said Mugabi, a colleague at the university." Tahara introduced Zaher and Stephanie. They soon discovered that Ali and Dr. Mugabi had also seen Baraan.

"It's very weird," Ali said. "Paradoxically, the revolution of 1979 was good for the Iranian film industry. Lately, there's a new generation of young film makers with social consciousness who want to show the reality as it is without ending up in the realm of fantasy and kitsch. I mean, film makers like Farouiz Said, Mohsan Sheahid Sals--"

"Where did you get all this knowledge?" Tahara interrupted.

The young man smiled, embarrassed. "I love movies in general, but particularly Iranian movies. I think that movies, like literature, are an integral part of the local culture," he stated.

Tahara tried to challenge him. "I read on the internet that since the Revolution, the Iranian movie industry has lost its worldwide prestige," she argued. "I mean, look at the fact that screenwriters have to present their scripts to the censor and also rely totally on government funding. It's like the Ayatollahs have control in movie content. And I'm not even talking about the ban on showing Western movies."

"As I just said, it's a paradox," Ali repeated. "It's true what you say about censorship. And also, it's the reason why recent Iranian movies don't bring up the subject of love. But the filmmakers can find ways to overstep the bounds. They refrain from denouncing the regime, but definitely show an honest picture of the situation. A good example is the movie 'Baharan.' My opinion is that Majid Majigi, the director, did a wonderful job of pushing boundaries in a smart way."

Zaher turned to her stepsister. "I suggest we start back. Tomorrow, I have to get up early," she said.

Ali was very quick to offer. "I will be more than happy to take you home."

Tahara smirked. "I hope we can all squeeze into your wreck of a car," she teased. They all laughed and set out for the car. Stephanie walked alongside Ali Hijazi. The two were silent until Ali broke the ice.

"Did you like the movie?" he asked. "I'm curious to know how it seems to someone who doesn't live in Iran." A little surprised that he had addressed her, she answered quickly,

"Actually, I was very impressed," she managed to fumble out. "I don't understand that much about Iranian movies, but I thought it was well made, stimulating, and very touching. A lot of American movies are about effects and are kind of trivial."

"I heard you have worked in the American movie industry," he said.

Stephanie giggled. "I was young and believed I could fit into that industry," she felt a little foolish as she spoke. "It took me several years to realize there were others prettier than me, more talented or more willing to do anything to get a job. Apparently, I didn't want it bad enough."

"But you are very pretty," he stated, in his very matter-of-fact tone. It was so nonchalant that for a second, Stephanie thought she had imagined it. She looked up to see if he had meant it, when he continued. "I have to say," he resumed, "when I saw you the first time, I thought you were an actress because of how beautiful you are. And you have a great personality. I'd honestly rather see you in a movie than anyone else."

That night, Stephanie couldn't stop thinking of Ali

Hijazi. During the few minutes they had walked side by side, he managed to really impress her. She felt caught up in emotion, an overwhelming attraction to him. She liked his confidence and the genuine interest he showed in her. There was something solid about the young man with bright black eyes, something she had never come across in a man, not even in the late Professor Yasser. Ali Hijazi projected manhood and reliability that gave Stephanie a feeling of confidence as she had never sensed before.

The nice guy, however, was shrouded in mystery. Despite all her efforts, Stephanie was unable to assess this Ali Hijazi; she was unable to make up her mind about who he really is and what it is that he seemed to want from her. Questions began to circle through her mind. Was it by chance that he walked with her that night, or had he planned it? Was his admiration sincere or merely a result of courtesy?

A few days later, as soon as she got home from the university, Tahara asked Stephanie if she would like to watch the movie Suntori, which had been banned in Iran.

"The director is well known and I heard it's a good movie," Tahara claimed.

Stephanie was puzzled. "If the movie has been banned, how can it be seen at a movie theatre?"

Tahara smiled. "It's on DVD. Ali invited us. He said he'd be very pleased if you come."

Stephanie was excited by hearing Ali's name. He had asked for her. She suddenly became aware of Tahara's stare and tried to cover her excitement. "So, how did he get a copy of the movie?" she spoke with as much disinterest as she could.

Tahara laughed. "He must have purchased a pirate copy at some stall in the market," she said. "The fact that there is a ban doesn't mean you can't find a DVD or CD of a movie or group that you like. You can buy a pirate copy of a lot of things, and it's relatively cheap."

Zaher, who sat on the couch in the living room watching TV, joined the conversation. "Once, I brought home a few DVDs I purchased from a dealer. Mother almost fainted. Not to mention Lily, who went absolutely wild," Zaher said with a giggle.

"Well, are you coming or not?" Tahara asked Stephanie. "Besides, I have a feeling that Ali likes you,"

Stephanie smiled. "Why do you say that?" she asked.

"Trust me, the guy is in love with you," Tahara blurted. "He asked me questions about you for almost a half hour. Really, a cross-examination that would shame the Revolutionary Guard. I never had such a long, private talk with him."

"What did he ask?" Tahara now had Stephanie's complete attention.

Tahara shrugged. "All sorts of questions," Tahara continued, "Like how long will you stay in Iran, if you have a boyfriend back home. That kind of stuff. He really is obsessed with you, I know it. I have known him for two years, and he has never spoken that much, certainly not with students."

Zaher offered her opinion. "He is handsome and seems like a nice guy," Zaher chimed in. "Do you like him?"

Stephanie acted as casual as she could under the circumstances, trying to process this new information. "Ah…yea…a bit… but," Stephanie was frantically trying to find the words that would make her seem unaffected. "Yeah, he's nice. I just never thought about him as, you know. I'm not going to be here very long… so… I don't know." Stephanie could feel her face getting hot.

Tahara stood in front of her, a big smile on her face. "Look, she's blushing," Tahara became giddy with delight. "Zaher, come see Stephanie." Zaher rushed over and both sisters stood there laughing, trying to cover their faces so as not to embarrass her too much. Stephanie shook her head and rolled her eyes, still trying to deny it.

"My dear sister," Tahara giggled, "you won't convince me. It's pretty obvious. Don't be embarrassed. I think Ali is a handsome man. Last year, we ran a poll among the female students on who was the most popular teacher. Ali won. Don't say you don't like him."

That night, as she went to bed, and after much soul-searching about Ali Hijazi, Stephanie decided that, despite the strong attraction she felt, it would be wrong to get emotionally involved with him. She was due back in the States soon. On top of that, she felt that her father and his wife would not approve of her getting involved with Ali and then leaving. It was going to be difficult enough saying goodbye to her family in Teheran, let alone a new lover.

As soon as she and Tahara arrived at Ali's apartment, in one of the most exclusive suburbs of the city, she felt confused and excited. When Ali opened the door, her heartbeat increased wildly. She was amazed at how much he was affecting her.

At the end of the screening, Ali found a moment alone with Stephanie. "I hope you don't mind if I invite you to lunch tomorrow?" he posed it as a question, and his hint of nervousness made Stephanie smile.

"Lunch? Tomorrow?" she answered, trying to keep her voice even and cool. "Actually, I have no plans for tomorrow. Sure, why not?"

From that moment on, Stephanie didn't try to stop herself; thrilled and excited by the feelings and emotions that overwhelmed her, she grew closer to Ali. *I don't have the strength to fight my feelings about him. But God, please, don't get me into trouble with another heartbreak,* she thought. From then on, Ali Hijazi and Stephanie met every day, usually early in the evening. They sat at small cafes, visited the mosque Shahid Natahari with its eight minarets, went to restaurants or strolled in the large city park.

As if by unspoken agreement, they opted not to address the subject of the time; as they both knew, Stephanie would be returning soon to America. Stephanie was happy and didn't try to hide it. For the first time in a while, she felt alive and beautiful.

When they were together in public, they obviously avoided any physical contact. But as soon as they were alone, they hurried to hug and kiss with abandon, having trouble holding back their growing desire. One day, when she was getting into his car, Stephanie decided to suggest a new plan.

"I had a busy day," she said. "Doing some chores for my family. I'd prefer a quiet evening… just you and me." Ali looked at her, picking up on her underlying motives.

"Me too," he smiled. "I don't want to be around a crowd. You want to go to my place?"

"With pleasure," she said, without thinking twice.

"I wasn't sure how you would react if I suggested you come to my place," he admitted. "I'm warning you, though, the apartment is in a big mess."

Ali didn't have much sexual experience and was naturally shy. Stephanie realized soon enough she would have to guide Ali in the ways of lovemaking. At first, she worried about Ali's reaction to her sexual confidence. But finally, when merely kissing him was not enough, Stephanie gently pushed Ali back on the bed, lay on top of him and began moving against his groin. The movement of her hips intensified both of their passions. As she began to verbally encourage him, she placed his hands on her body. Ali, proving to be a fast learner, soon began to explore her body.

Although Ali didn't have much sexual experience, she couldn't complain about his sexual appetite. After they rested, their naked, sweaty bodies intertwined, it was Ali who began to take the initiative for the second round.

In their initial meetings, Stephanie and Ali talked a lot about a variety of subjects. But knowing that soon they would part, she wasn't entirely open with him. She told him about her marriage to Tom and his death, talked at length on her trying to get into the movies and also about her course on Islam. But she chose not to talk of her relationship with Yasser Ashraf, and certainly didn't elaborate about her mother or that Amir was really her father.

Ali didn't make it easy for Stephanie, though, asking pointed questions. While they were having dinner at a small fish restaurant not far from his house, Ali began to probe. "Why is it that, suddenly, after so many years, you have decided to visit your family in Iran?"

"Actually," Stephanie began, "I was thinking about visiting Iran for a while. But I decided to actually do it only when I learned that I have family in Teheran. Now that I've met them and you, I'm sorry I didn't come earlier."

Ali smiled and took her hand from across the table. "The loss is all mine," he said, gently. "These days, few Americans visit Iran." Ali paused, unsure about something, and then plodded ahead. "I don't want to invade your privacy," he said, "but how come you have no children?"

Stephanie rolled her eyes but decided there was no reason not to share. She quickly told him about the miscarriage and the pain she suffered in the following days. "Today, looking back, I'm not sure if I'm sorry or glad about the miscarriage. Sooner or later, we would have divorced," she said."

"You have all your life in front of you. You are young,"

he offered.

Stephanie smiled and nodded. "I don't think about it too much," she said. "There is a saying: 'People make plans and God laughs.' Look at us. Who could have predicted we would be together, here, in Teheran."

"I, too, didn't believe that someday I'd feel what I'm feeling now," he added. "You have no idea how good it is and how happy I am we met." Stephanie leaned across the table and kissed his lips.

Ali quickly pulled back, glancing on both sides of him and mumbled spoke quietly. "I'm sorry," he said, barely audible, "but we can get into trouble for something like that. You forget where we are."

Four men sitting at one of the tables nearby were staring at them. Stephanie lowered her head. "I'm sorry. I simply forgot," she said, looking down, and feeling embarrassed. "Look how they're staring at us."

Initially, Ali was ill at ease to reveal his past to Stephanie and every time she asked questions on the topic, he would promise, again and again, "I'll talk about it, some time." But when it came to the political and social situation in Iran, Ali was outspoken and inflexible. "The regime is leading the country to disaster," he had said. "Unemployment is higher than ever and the Ayatollahs control every sphere of our life. In recent years, Iran has become a loathed country, one of the three countries defined as the axis of evil." Stephanie was shocked by Ali's tremendous hatred for the regime. His words were very harsh.

"Ahmadinejad is a dangerous man," he went on. "He and his Revolutionary Guards. His attitude toward the West in general and the United States and Israel in particular will cost us dearly. Eventually, he will end up like Saddam Hussein. Unfortunately, Iran is on the brink of collapse, economically." Stephanie tried to interject a comment but he was lost in his own words and didn't notice.

"The last thing Iran needs is a nuclear program that sucks all the money from the sale of oil," Ali grew more passionate as he spoke. "Thanks to oil, we are one of the richest countries in the world, but many people here are desperately poor. You may not see them in the big cities, but you'll understand what I mean if you go to the countryside. Unemployment is up to thirty percent, and outside Teheran, they say it's over forty percent. No one tells us the exact rate but it's high."

Ali paused for a moment, shook his head in frustration and then went on bitterly. "The West doesn't know what's really going on because Iran doesn't encourage Westerners to visit. That's without even mentioning shutting up the Western media. Yesterday, an Italian journalist was arrested because she wrote an article saying the Ayatollah fell in love with the idea of an atomic bomb because it upsets Israel and the United States."

Stephanie had never seen such anger on Ali's face and it astonished her. But she couldn't think of anything to say to comfort him. And so he went on.

"And I'm not even talking about basic things like individual freedom or civil rights. Who really knows what's going on here in the prisons? What kind of humiliation and torture is there for prisoners? 'Privacy.' 'Rights.' Those words are labeled as vulgar and anyone who tries to act differently simply disappears and no one dares to ask what happened to him."

It was as if the men staring at Stephanie's expression of love for Ali had ripped something apart inside him. He could not stop his angry diatribe in a low voice.

"I know several Iranian families close to starvation. To survive, they sold their daughters to pimps or sheiks from the Gulf countries." Ali was unable to hide his indignation.

"Most leaders who are close to the regime are corrupt. They split money and invest in business opportunities in countries like Turkey, India, China and they even have investments in Canada. They are rich while most citizens can barely survive."

"What you are saying is terrible. It's out of control." Stephanie was searching for words. "And nothing can be done?"

Ali smiled, a brave, small smile. "Something can be done, but people are scared. The Ayatollahs regime, through the *habsigi* militia, their special force, threatens the people and they are afraid to utter a word."

Ali paused for a moment, his anger dissipated. He looked guilty. "I'm sorry," he said abruptly. "I got carried away. I shouldn't trouble you with all this."

"No, no. On the contrary. I want to hear it all. If it's part of your life, it matters to me."

Ali continued. "At one point, the country held presidential elections. Mir Hussein Mousawi, a reformer compared to the present regime, ran against Ahmadinejad. According to the official results, Ahmadinejad won over sixty percent of the votes, while Mousawi got thirty percent. Mousawi's camp claimed that the elections were rigged and his supporters took to the streets demanding new elections. They demonstrated carrying flowers and wearing green armbands. Ahmadinejad sent the Revolutionary Guard to beat them. Some were even killed.

Stephanie winced. "So there was never a recount?"

"The authorities agreed to hold a recount only after a few days of pressure," Ali explained, "when at least ten demonstrators were killed by the Revolutionary Guards. Anyway, the recount didn't change anything. More demonstrations, more young people killed or injured. Mousawi was detained, sentenced to house arrest and gradually everything calmed down. This is the Islamic Republic of Iran."

"If it's that bad," Stephanie questioned, "why do you stay here?"

"Believe me," Ali replied, "I've dreamed of leaving. My mother and my family depend on me. My situation is quite complex."

"You don't have to tell me if you don't feel at ease," Stephanie assured him.

"That's fine," he replied. "I feel comfortable with you. My father was drafted into the Iranian Army in the Great War against Iraq in the eighties and took part in the battle of the port town of Hormashar. He stepped on an Iranian mine and lost both legs. A few years later, both my brothers were killed by chemical weapons used by the Iraqis in the occupation of the Isle of Abdan. They were killed within a month of each other."

Stephanie lowered her head and murmured softly. "I'm sorry. I'm so sorry," she had to stop herself from reaching for his hand again, conscious of being watched. "I guess it was an awful trauma for you, your family, and your mother."

Ali didn't answer back. He remained seated with tears in his eyes. In that moment, neither cared what anyone might have thought of their behavior. Stephanie reached out a stroked his face. "I love Iran," he said, "but these days, I'm not proud to be Iranian. What can I do? I'm pretty scared to join the opposition, so like everyone else, I sit, complain and try to live for the day. I live in my little world, the academic ivory tower. Does it make me feel good? Absolutely not.

"Is there anything else you can do?" Stephanie asked.

"Nothing," he said, bitterly. "That's why it's so sad and frustrating. It's hard to believe how narrow-minded the people are, sitting in the Iranian parliament. Instead of bringing the country forward, they take us back to the

Middle Ages under the influence of religion and the Revolutionary Guard. You know that Iran is the only country in the world that executes children? It's confirmed." Ali shook his head. "Did you ever hear the name Atafa Rajabi Sahle?"

"No, I haven't." Stephanie replied.

Ali sighed and lifted his palms skyward, as if asking for help.

"Of course not," he continued. "I don't think that even in Iran many people know of him. Atafa Rajabi Sahle was sixteen years old when she was hanged in public in the town of Nequah. The authorities claimed she was 22, but I knew her very well, as she was my cousin. She had a difficult childhood. Her father was a drug addict. The militants of the *hibasij* militia belonging to the Revolutionary Guards arrested her several times, once for sitting in a café, once because she was with a guy. Stuff like that. Rather than trying to rehabilitate her, they arrested her, imprisoned her and brutally raped her. And most frightening of all, they tried to talk her into becoming a *shahid*, a saint who dies in the name of Islam. They wanted her to go to Lebanon and blow herself up, to kill one of the leaders of the Christian community there. When she refused, they hanged her. Can you believe such a thing happened here in the twenty first century?"

Stephanie was shocked, unable to speak for a few moments. "It's just awful," she finally said. "I had no idea of such things happening. On the contrary, I was pleasantly surprised by what I saw for the few weeks that I've been here. My mother told me she was fearful, and I didn't understand why. Now I do. But what I don't understand is how the world keeps silent. There are all sorts of organizations that could be helping."

Ali discouraged her statement with a wave of his hand.

"Amnesty writes and alerts, but as the saying goes, 'The dogs bark and Ahmadinejad's entourage keeps going.' Who here can rebuke Iran? Media, television and Internet are all under control of the Revolutionary Guards. People live in fear."

After dinner, while they were on their way to the car, Ali continued the extraordinary denunciation of the regime. "To me, it's pretty clear that President Ahmadinejad constantly defies Israel and United States on the nuclear subject in hopes of forcing them to attack Iran. Most people believe the President here is just an angry man, led by fury and rage. But he is very sophisticated. He knows that in case of such an attack, Iran will become the martyr, will unite different factions in the country and divert the real debate on economy and society to security; they will know how to turn the attack on Iran into a ritual to serve their economic and religious interest… and when that happens it's going to be a disaster for us and the entire region."

When they reached the car, Ali opened up the door and let Stephanie in. She watched him walk in front of the car to get to the driver's seat and felt butterflies in her stomach as she thought about how much she admired his passion and knowledge. When he got in the car, Stephanie leaned in to kiss him. Suddenly, there was a loud knocking on the car window.

They both stiffened when they saw four men in grey uniforms surrounding the car. Stephanie felt a wave of fear. "What do they want? Did we do something wrong?" she asked and quickly secured the scarf on her head.

Ali's voice was quiet and calm, in spite of his tense body. "They are officers of the modesty patrols. They will ask if we are married and what we are doing together. Don't worry," he assured.

Ali slowly rolled the car window down and began speaking to the men. The firm voice of the one talking to him didn't bode well, and Stephanie, not understanding anything, was frozen in her seat. Ali took a document from his pants pocket and gave it to one of the men.

"They ask that we get out of the car," he said, turning to Stephanie. "Come, we should get out immediately."

Stephanie remembered the letter her father had given her, in case she was in any trouble. She hurried to pull it out of her purse and handed it to Ali. "Give them this," she said. "It says that I'm a tourist. My uncle has signed it. Tell them he is a police officer."

Stephanie and Ali got out of the car, and, her voice trembling, addressed the head of the group in English. "I beg your pardon, sir. Sorry. I hope you understand English. I'm an American citizen. I came for a family visit to my uncle. His name is Amir Motaki. He is a deputy chief of the police in Teheran. Please read this." She pointed to the paper Ali had handed him.

The man who had barked at Ali, his face severe, stared at her with undisguised contempt. "American?" he growled at her. "We don't like America." Staring at the letter, he completed his inspection and gave it to a colleague. After few minutes that felt like an eternity, the squad leader handed her the letter and then returned to Ali his papers.

"Ma'am, you are in Teheran and you should respect our rules," he said harshly. "We don't approve such a vulgar behavior as yours and that of your friend. I hope Amir Motaki will explain to you the offense you have committed. If it wasn't for your uncle, we would arrest you both."

The first person Stephanie disclosed her unfolding romantic connection with Ali to was Zaher.

"I'm in trouble," she told her. "My attachment to Ali is

getting stronger and I know that soon, everything will be over."

"No one said that you have to leave so soon," Zaher reminded her.

"To extend my stay again is not a solution," Stephanie replied.

Zaher smiled. "I know quite a few women who would trade places with you. At least try to enjoy it while you can," Zaher advised.

Tahara entered the conversation. "What's the rush?" she asked. "What awaits you in the United States? You met a nice guy. You are happy with him…try to enjoy a bit."

"I know your parents would disapprove," Stephanie argued. "It doesn't look good."

"Calm down!" Tahara insisted. "It's true we live in Iran and some people think that what you are doing is immoral. But if we lived according to their views, we'd lose all grasp with reality. I'm sure father will understand. Mother may dislike it, but she won't say anything."

At the end of that same week, Ali suggested they take a trip together to Isfahan. "You must visit that town," he told her several times, "to be in Iran and not to visit Isfahan it's like you haven't been at all in Iran. Beyond that, it's my home town and it's also been declared a World Heritage Site by UNESCO because of its sites of historic interest." Stephanie tried to interject, but he continued speaking with excitement.

"Isfahan is approximately 350 kilometers south of Teheran," he went on. "It's an amazing town. My family lives there and they will be happy to meet my Hollywood princess. We can spend the night there. They will be glad to host us."

Somewhat surprisingly, her father didn't object when she told him about Ali's suggestion. "Let me think it over until tomorrow," he said, ignoring his wife's severe gaze. "I want to think about it calmly."

The next evening, he gave his answer. "You can go with him. It's fine with me," he said. "Just please take care of yourself. Don't forget for a moment that you are a member of my family and you are in Iran."

Zaher smiled broadly when Stephanie told her she had their father's permission to spend the night in Isfahan with Ali's family.

"If I know my father," she told Stephanie, "he investigated Ali and probably his entire family in Isfahan."

"I don't believe it" Stephanie said.

Zaher laugh. "About a year ago, I had an admirer; nothing serious, but someone who took a fancy to me and wouldn't leave me in peace. At the end, I agreed to go out with him. We met a couple of times, went to a restaurant, sat down in a café, and that was enough for father. One evening, the guy came to me in panic, saying that it would be better if we didn't meet again.

"At the time, I didn't understand what happened. Two months later, the Revolutionary Guard arrested the guy. Who knows why. Father didn't say a word about it and I chose not to ask him. Actually, I was a bit sorry for the guy. All in all, he was a good person."

Stephanie loved every moment together with Ali. He turned out to be a great guide, well informed about his hometown. With pride, he showed her around the city. But what really mattered for Stephanie was the visit to Ali's family home, in one of the southern suburbs of town. It was possible to see the river Hazinda-Rod that crossed the town. The house wasn't large but clean and well kept. Colorful carpets were scattered in all the rooms and various photos hung on the walls.

"This is my father. May his soul rest in peace," Ali said pointing to a photo of a mustached man, hanging in a frame in the center of the main room. "And these are my two brothers," he continued. "I told you about them. They were killed within a month of each other."

Ali's mother, Ahula, was a short woman, with gray hair and a shy smile. Vidad and Maharanjiz, Ali's sisters, lived at home, even though both were in their thirties; they had never married. None of them spoke English so Ali had to translate whatever was said. Despite the language barrier and the difference in age between them, Stephanie felt great love, even appreciation, from the three women.

"Mother says you look like a Hollywood star," Ali said as they went out for a breath of air after a hearty dinner. "She says you remind her of Rita Hayworth but you are more beautiful."

Stephanie smiled, embarrassed. "How does your mother knows Rita Hayworth," she smiled. "And besides, that's an exaggeration."

"She is not exaggerating at all. I think you have a breathtaking beauty," he looked deeply at Stephanie. "I cannot take my eyes away from you."

She reached out to caress his cheek. "You are so sweet," she said, feeling his rugged facial hairs underneath her fingertips. "For some time, I haven't felt this close to anyone."

"You know it's mutual," he said, putting his hand on hers, holding it against his face.

"Yes," she nodded, "and that's why I'm so sad. Apparently, one can't have everything in life."

Ali pulled her towards him, passionately. "If one wants, it's possible," he said, his face serious. "I know that it sounds a bit unreal; we've known each other such a short time, but I feel I have known you for years. I cannot stop thinking of you, dreaming of you. I never felt this way. I don't want it to end."

Stephanie didn't respond. In silence, she laid her head on his chest and closed her eyes.

"You have to go back to America?" he asked, holding the back of her head in his hand. "Is there any chance you can stay a bit longer?"

She shrugged. "You know it's not possible," she said quietly. "My life is there, my job. My mother lives there. It's not a *great* career and I don't have anyone waiting for me, but still."

"Please stay a little longer," he urged.

Stephanie sighed. "I have already lengthened my stay in Iran, Ali," she insisted. "I may be able to extend by one or two weeks, but eventually, we'll reach the same point and it's going to be more difficult. The more time we spend together, the deeper our connection grows. And then what? Then it's going to be much worse."

"So, marry me."

Stephanie pulled away abruptly. "What did you say?" she asked, looking up at his face. Ali's eyes were fixed on hers, as he took her two hands in his.

"You heard me," he said, speaking with confidence and certainty. "Marry me. I love you. Marry me."

She smiled at him, unable to speak.

"We'll have a family," he continued. "We'll be together. We won't have to hide any longer."

Stephanie gently clasped her hand over Ali's mouth. "Wait. Wait," she said, trying to regain her composure. "This is not a decision to be made hastily. We should think it over. It's not that easy. And I'm totally confused…I need to grasp what I just heard."

Stephanie told Zaher of Ali's marriage proposal and her dilemma. Zaher let out a cry of joy and she threw herself at Stephanie, hugging and kissing her. "*Mabruk, mabruk,*" she uttered between kisses. "Oh God, I'm so happy for you. It's amazing. Tell me when it happened, tell me everything."

"Lower your voice," Stephanie hushed Zaher. "I know it's great, but it's also very dangerous. I really don't know what I should do. Believe me, it's the last thing I thought would happen to me in Iran."

Zaher couldn't understand her. "What are you talking about? Stop tormenting yourself. You love him. He loves you. What else do you need?" she asked. "Ali is an amazing person; he's wise, liberal, a man of the world. Wait, I hope you are planning to live here."

Stephanie shrugged her shoulders, looking defeated. "He talked about it," she replied. "Anyway, he offered no other option and that's what bothers me. Despite my family here, I just don't see how I can start a new life here. I don't know Farsi, and the customs are so different."

"Does father know?" Zaher interrupted. "For him, it would be a dream come true if you decided to stay."

"Swear to me you won't say a word to anybody," Stephanie demanded, "not even a hint. You are the only one I told. Until I decide what to do, I prefer no one knows. Please, Zaher, not a word!"

The next day, she met with Ali, next to the university.

"I want to know if you thought of what we talked about," he said. "I'm so excited. I almost called my mother to tell her, but then I realized I'm rushing things. I suppose I should at least wait for your answer," he said sheepishly.

"I've been thinking about nothing but a life together," she said. "But I don't know what to do."

"Did you talk to your uncle?" Ali asked.

It took Stephanie a second to remember that Ali was still under the impression that Amir was her uncle. Could she really marry a man who she had not even be fully open and honest with?

"Not yet," she replied. "Only Zaher knows. Ali, I have a problem. I just don't know how to make this work."

Ali's eyes were shining with excitement. "It can happen," he insisted. "If we want, we can make this the most real thing in the world. It's up to us. Actually, it's up to you. I already decided, and I'm at peace with my decision, one hundred per cent. I want you with me."

Suddenly, Stephanie blurted out words that she had no idea were about to come out. "Come with me to the States."

Ali smiled and answered sarcastically. "Sure, tomorrow morning. We'll board the plane and fly to the land of unlimited opportunities," he scoffed.

"I mean it, Ali. Come with me," she insisted. "We'll do everything slowly. We'll live together for a while. If it works, we'll get married. If it fails, you can always come back to Iran. It would solve all my hesitations."

"Sorry, Stephanie. You know there is no chance I'm going to leave my mother and my sisters. I cannot do that to them. I take care of them. Mother will die if she hears I'm leaving her. Besides, I can't give up on my career. I won't get a year off. It took me a while to get where I'm—"

"Come on," Stephanie interrupted, annoyance creeping into her voice. "I have a mother, too. And what am I going to do here? I'm an American. I don't know the language and I have no profession here."

"We'll manage," he assured her. "I have connections. I'm sure your uncle, too, will help. And I have savings. Not a lot but I saved some money. We'll buy a beautiful house."

"I don't know, Ali," Stephanie insisted. "It's not an easy decision."

"You don't have much more time. You are supposed to go back to America soon unless you extend again," he pleaded.

"I can always come back to the United States and, after a month, return to Iran."

Ali's enthusiasm had disappeared.

"If you leave," he went on, "I believe you won't come back. His voice became soft. "It will be all over. From Los Angeles, Iran will look far away. I will lose you, Steph. I'm afraid I will lose you."

They walked in silence. It was the first time they'd had a disagreement. But their passion and their need for each was greater than ever. When, an hour later, they got to Ali's house, they rushed into each other's arms, kissing and undressing each other. This time, their lovemaking was exceptionally free.

Afterwards, Ali spoke with sadness. "When I think that in a couple of days it may come to an end, I go crazy," he confessed. "I'm sorry if I put pressure on you. Maybe you can extend your stay a little bit, so we can have some more time to think and be together."

The next day, Stephanie went to her father.

"I need to talk to you," she said. "I need to ask your advice on a particular subject."

Amir stared at her. "Something wrong? Are you okay?"

"I'm fine, really" she answered "I just want to discuss

with you a personal matter."

They met for lunch in a small restaurant nearby the police station. Amir was wearing his crisp, freshly pressed police uniform with his rank shining on the shoulders. All eyes turned to Stephanie as they made their way toward a small corner table.

A waiter approached quickly. "Yes, sir, what can I get you?" he stammered.

Her father turned to Stephanie. "What do you want to eat? Meat? Salad? All the food here is very tasty," he offered.

Stephanie shrugged. "I'm not really that hungry. Please order what you like."

He wound up ordering for them both and the waiter disappeared.

"Let's hear about the important subject," her father said. "Something happened?"

She smiled, embarrassed. "I don't know how to tell you. I'm afraid of your reaction," she said. "And I know how to make decisions. My being here proves that." Stephanie took a deep breath, unable to organize her thoughts.

"Stephanie, why are you going round and round?" her father said, warmly. "Tell me. What happened? Is it about Ali?"

She nodded. "Yes, yes," she spoke in a whisper. "He proposed to me. I know it sounds crazy. We haven't known each other a long time, but there is something really strong between us, that makes us want to be together all the time. Father, I'm in love."

A slight smile appeared on Amir's lips. "There is nothing like a woman's intuition. Dalram was right. Today, she suggested that you were going to talk to me about something of importance." He took a second to think, and his face grew serious. "But you hardly know each other. Why the hurry?"

She was embarrassed. "Maybe you don't know, but since we met, we've been spending a lot of time together. I feel so good with him. He is great, kind, intelligent. He loves me."

Amir asked the most difficult question. "Do you see yourself living in Iran?"

The waiter was back, carrying a large tray of plates and bowls of food. "I hope you'll enjoy. If you need anything else, I'm at your service," he said, and left the two in silence.

Stephanie looked around at the table, laden with food. She didn't recognize any of the dishes. Amir read her thoughts, pointing to a bowl full of thick liquid. "This is pistachio soup. We call it *sopa past*. It's delicious. I suggest you taste it."

She pointed to a small bowl and took a small taste. "This seems tastes interesting," she said. "What is it?"

"Stuffed quince. *Dolma-ya*. Start eating. Everything is delicious." He paused after he spoke. "You didn't answer my question: do you intend to live here in Teheran?"

Stephanie took one stuffed quince from the bowl in the center of the table. "That's what he wants, what he suggested," she replied. "If he would agree to come with me to the States, I wouldn't think twice. But I simply don't see myself living here."

Amir thought about her words for a while before responding. "Stay here with us as long as you wish," he said. "I mean, as long as it doesn't jeopardize your job. Then, go back to the States. Take your time. You know the proverb, 'Things are not what they seem to be.'

She exhaled, relieved. "Thank you, father. That's exactly what I'm going to do."

She extended again her stay with a short phone call to Kevin Shepard. He was glad to hear how happy she was. She knew he wouldn't make an issue of her being gone a little longer. He once again proved his friendship to her.

At dinner, Stephanie told the Motaki family that she had lengthened her holiday. The four women burst into shouts of joy. Little Lily got up in a hurry to hug Stephanie.

"My prayers were answered," Lily said, unable to hide her excitement. "You are my special sister."

Stephanie, moved by their reactions, hugged Lily and kissed her on the head. "You are the family I never had." Stephanie spoke, trying to find the right words. "You may have guessed this already, but Ali Hijazi proposed to me and—"

She could not finish the sentence, as the girls and Dalram shrieked in delight. Tahara and Zaher were quick to hug her. "Despite your short time together," Tahara whispered, "I knew. I knew that he was in love with you."

Dalram got up, and approached her with open arms and a wide smile. "Come, my daughter, come," her voice was booming with happiness. "I want to hug you. I'm really happy for you."

Tahara was bursting with excitement. "Now, tell us everything. Tell us how he proposed, where exactly it happened, what are you planning," Tahara spoke almost too quickly to understand.

Lily interrupted her. "When is the wedding?"

"I'm not sure how to answer. For the time being, nothing has been decided. There are many issues to think about and to be considered," Stephanie replied.

"But you said 'yes.'" Lily's disappointment was hard to witness.

Stephanie stroke the child's head. "I couldn't say yes. What I said to him is that I need some time. Of course, I want to be with him, but I haven't decided yet. Everything is going too fast in life." Stephanie paused.

"That's right," Tahara chimed in. "Everything is happening fast." Her tone quickly changed from agreeance to a sternness. "But it's much simpler than you make it. You are not a child. You trust him and you feel that he is the man with whom you can build a home and a family. Isn't that enough?"

Dalram came to Stephanie's aid. "Leave her alone," Dalram ordered. "From the outside, things always look easier and simpler… You forget that she has a life in the States. It's not that easy to give up everything."

"Exactly," Stephanie breathed a sigh of relief. "I think I'll do what father suggested. First, I'll go back to the States. I'll give myself a few weeks to size up what I really feel about all this." Dalram and the girls came to understand Stephanie's positon. Ali's reaction, however, was the opposite.

The following day, after she told him of her decision, Stephanie observed the strangest expression on his face. "I don't understand," he said, unable to hide his disappointment. "You said you love me."

Stephanie once again had to choose her words carefully. On one hand, she didn't want to hurt him, but on the other, it was important to clarify her point of view. "I would like you to understand, Ali," she spoke slowly to make sure her words landed. "It's not an easy decision for me. This is bigger than just a decision to marry you. This decision is going to radically change my life. You know for me to live in Teheran is not going to be that simple for me. And based on what I have seen and what you've told me about life here, I have doubts. Please, you must understand."

Although he appeared to keep his composure, Ali was upset. "If that's what you want. I'm sad, very sad. I thought there was something real between us," he barely managed to speak.

She held his hand tightly. "You know I love you," she stressed. "Believe me, if I didn't have any feelings for you, I would have gone back to the States long ago. I want to think. I've already made several mistakes, and I don't want to make another one."

Ali bowed his head, murmuring. "You are destroying my dream," he said, his voice shaking. "You'll leave here and go back to your life. I believe that you may think of me during the first few days, but after a couple of months, our time here will just be a nice experience, something to tell your friends."

"Come with me to the States," Stephanie begged.

He laughed briefly, almost bitterly. "You know I can't. I explained to you, my mother is here. I have to take care of her. Anyway, they won't let me go. You don't know the Revolutionary Guards. You don't know them. Just because my family gets government benefits due to my father's injuries and the death of my two brothers, just because I have tenure at the school, doesn't mean I can do whatever I want. It's Iran, Steph. Wake up."

"And that's what scares me," Stephanie replied. "That's what I'm talking about when I say I have to think twice about living here. I don't want to raise children in an environment where I have to worry about things like that."

"I understand," he countered. "But here, you have family." Ali paused for a few seconds, took a deep breath and continued. "Sometimes, I'm disgusted and scared to live here. We're losing our humanity and we accept things around us as a matter of fact. They have a network of informers everywhere. Why do you think that they asked me questions about you?"

Stephanie had a look of surprise. "When? I don't understand," she said. "Are you telling me that they interrogated you about me?"

"Before we went to Isfahan, they invited me for a conversation. I think that the people I met with were from the *Al-Quds*. They belong to the Revolutionary Guards but act independently."

"What did they ask? Why you haven't said anything until now?" she asked. "I can speak with my uncle."

Ali shrugged. "With all due respect for your uncle and his rank, I don't believe he can help when it concerns the *Al-Quds*. They don't respect anyone or anything. Ask your uncle. I'm sure he knows them better than me."

She was angry and revolted by the revelation. "What did they want from you?" she demanded.

Ali's voice had a note of resignation in it. "They asked about you. Actually, they seemed to know a lot already. They didn't need to ask me, but they did ask about our relationship," he told her. Stephanie was upset and could hardly keep her voice steady.

"It's none of their business what you and I do or feel," she spoke, almost yelling. "The whole thing is just unbelievable. Now, you see why I'm scared to commit? With all my love for you, and you know it, I don't think I want to live in such an atmosphere."

The next morning, Dalram asked Stephanie if she would invite Ali for dinner. "It's customary that the family meets the groom. I mean, the possible groom," she corrected herself.

As upset as she had felt since the proposal, she smiled at the idea of having everyone over for dinner. "I'll ask him," she replied. "He will be glad to meet you."

Ali came to their house for dinner, hopeful it would mean a change in Stephanie's opinion about the marriage. Amir was not in a good mood. He'd returned home earlier from work but he remained in his police uniform. Lily and

Dalram chose to greet Ali wearing clothes for a special occasion.

"Please sit down," Amir told Ali. "Make yourself at home. We are pleased to welcome you to our home. Considering that in the future you may be part of our family, we should know you a little better."

Dalram prepared a magnificent meal and the table was loaded with all the best food. She had made juicy *khoresh bar nazid* with quinces, pomegranate seeds, stuffed vine leaves and, of course, the royal rice, *jabar pulau*.

Stephanie sat next to Ali, thrilled and excited, even though she did not know what would result from the gathering. She looked around the table, appreciating being with family; family was something she had never known. She swallowed hard and tears rolled down her cheeks. She quickly wiped them away, not wanting to spoil the moment.

# *10*

Two days after the dinner, it was the beginning of the holy month of Ramadan. Stephanie was well aware of the importance of this Muslim annual holiday, and wanted to know more; Lily was more than willing to explain.

Over dinner, she stood in front of Stephanie with shining eyes. She obviously enjoyed her status as teacher. "The month of Ramadan is the ninth month of the Muslim calendar. Every Muslim pledges to fast from dawn until stars appear. It's forbidden to eat, drink and smoke."

Everyone smiled. Tahara teased her. "When you grow up, you will replace one of the Ayatollahs, I'm sure of it."

Zaher added, "You need to start preaching in the mosque."

Without paying any attention to her sisters, Lily stood, continuing to look serious. "Each day of the Ramadan, one gets up early to eat the *al-shaor*, which is the last meal before the fast. Then, just before dawn, the family comes together to eat the *al-iftar*, which is the meal ending the fast."

Stephanie tested Lily's knowledge. "Why do you celebrate this holiday?"

"Actually, the Ramadan fast represents one of the five pillars of Islam. The Quran says that this is the month when the Prophet Mohammed had his first revelation. We mark this event, *Lilat al Kadar*, towards the end of the Ramadan month, on an odd-numbered day."

Stephanie pulled Lily to her lap. "You know everything. You are a genius."

Lily slipped out of Stephanie's arms. "Wait, wait. There is also the feast of *Id-el-Fider*, which falls immediately after the Ramadan. On that day, the Muslim rejoices and thanks God for allowing him to fulfill the commandment of the fast. The holiday is a kind of reward God gives the believers for their devotion. It lasts three days and the tradition is to visit each other, give gifts and to visit family, neighbors and friends. Also, most take part in giving to charity for the needy and helping others."

"How lucky I am that I have such a bright sister who can explain to me everything. What would I do without you?" Zaher asked.

Later on, after the meal, Stephanie learned a different aspect of the Ramadan from Ali. "Actually, during the holiday, the regime always plans mass gatherings in the presence of the Ayatollahs. But I read that this year, the authorities are being very careful. They fear that these gatherings might become demonstrations against the regime, which happened in July after the elections. They're afraid that the Green movement, people affiliated with Hussein Mosawi, will inflame the crowds."

"Aren't the riots over now? All the time I've been here, it's been pretty quiet. I haven't heard much of anything."

"People are scared," Ali reminded her. "Don't forget that during the July riots more than a hundred people were killed. Hundreds of protesters were arrested and the majority of them have not been released. Following the riots, the security forces understood the importance of electronic communication. They purchased special equipment, allowing them to listen to phone calls and also intercept all the incoming and outgoing text messages. And that's beside their ability to monitor all e-mails. In the last decade, the issue of computer investigation has progressed quite a bit here."

Stephanie, disturbed to hear all this, didn't answer. As if he could read her thoughts, Ali said, "Yes, I know you're thinking that in such a country, you don't want to live. I know it's not the most appealing thing."

She put her hand comfortingly on his knee and changed the subject. "I suppose it's not easy to fast for a month. People must lose weight dramatically."

Ali caressed her arm. "People may fast all day long, but at night they have a really extravagant meal. You will not be here on *Id-el-Fider,* but on that night there is a real feast. I plan to travel to Qum and spend the holiday with my mother."

Stephanie leaned her head on his shoulder. "Maybe some other time."

"If there will be another time."

"Don't start. Every time you start, it breaks my heart. Let's try to enjoy the time left. I realize it's difficult but try to respect my decision."

Ali kissed her head. "I'm really sorry. I know I promised to give you time, but I cannot help myself. Sorry, Stephanie. Forget what I said."

* * *

On the second day of Ramadan, Ali returned for dinner at the Motakis. The atmosphere was much less formal than on his previous visit and the mood was cheery. Amir was home earlier than usual and greeted Ali with a warm hug.

"You are the son I never had," he told him, smiling

broadly.

The next day, Ali invited Stephanie for the end of fast dinner at the house of one of his relatives in Teheran. "It's a tradition," he told her. "Since I came to Teheran from Isfahan, I go to them for one dinner during the holiday. I told them about you and they made me swear to persuade you to come with me."

On that evening, Stephanie arrived at Ali's home, she found the door locked. All her attempts to locate him on his cell phone were unsuccessful. Just as she was about to return to the home of the Motakis, Ali arrived.

"I'm sorry," he said, breathing heavily, "I had a meeting with the university dean. It went on and on and I couldn't stop him. Sorry."

"I was worried. I called your phone several times."

He kissed her quickly on the lips. "I'll just change clothes into something more festive. We still have some time. I'm really sorry. The meeting wasn't planned. It was about new ideas for the academic year."

Ali behaved normally, but Stephanie sensed that things weren't right. She didn't know what is was exactly, but something deep down told her that something was wrong; Ali had changed.

Standing at the front door of Ali's relatives, she studied Ali. "Are you all right?" she asked.

He smiled at her and answered automatically, "Yes, sure. Why wouldn't I be?"

"I don't know. I have the feeling that something is wrong."

"I'm fine, Stephanie. Nothing happened. Come on, let's enjoy the dinner."

Dinner was pleasant. Ali's relatives, Hussein and Naima Hinaji, did their best to entertain the "young couple," as the hosts called Stephanie and Ali. The spacious house was situated in a northern, prestigious suburb of Teheran.

Naima, the mother, a skinny woman who dressed simply in jeans and a white shirt, bestowed lavish praise upon Stephanie. Her husband Hussein, who studied at a university in London and spoke excellent English, was polite and kept urging Stephanie to taste the dishes prepared by his wife.

Stephanie noticed that Ali had hardly touched his food. At first he complained of stomach pain. Then, he claimed not to be hungry. Although he participated in the ongoing conversation, Stephanie had a feeling that his mind was elsewhere.

"I'm not used to seeing you like this," she said as they walked to the car. "I know you, Ali. You're just not like yesterday. What's going on with you?"

"You are mistaken," he reassured her. "Nothing is wrong with me. I'm just a little sad because you are leaving soon. Nothing else. Really."

$$* \phantom{*} *$$
$$*$$

Her gut feelings proved to be correct when they were lying on the bed in Ali's apartment. She started to caress him gently. Usually, when they made love, a light touch was enough to arouse him but not this time.

She leaned over him and took his manhood in her hands, massaging him. This time, however, there was no response from him. She pulled back and lay down beside him, deciding to softly caress his chest. She had no doubts that whatever had been on his mind that changed him, was now affecting his sexual desire. She knew from experience that the best way to arouse him was first and foremost to create a warm and intimate atmosphere.

"I'm so happy we met," she said softly, holding his body close to hers. "The last thing I thought would happen to me here in Teheran was to fall in love."

"I didn't believe it could happen to me, either," Ali replied. "Sometimes it seems like a movie. Unreal. Know what I mean?"

Her hand moved slowly along his leg. "I feel I could stay like this for a week. I'm never satisfied. I'm addicted to you," she murmured. Stephanie gently began to stroke his penis. Slowly, it bulged between her fingers. Moments later, she raised herself on Ali's body and moved his penis inside her. "God, how good it is to feel you inside me," she whispered "I love you Ali…I love you."

As they were lying side by side, breathless and sweaty, she broke the silence by speaking. "You seem upset, Ali. I feel something is bothering you. What's going on?"

"I'm really worried about this situation. I don't know what will happen."

"I already said I'm going to think about it, back home," she reminded him.

"You know what? I'm coming with you to the States."

Stephanie froze. "What? What did you say?" she asked, exultant. "Are you serious, Ali? Say it again, please. I want to hear it one more time." Stephanie hugged him and covered his chest with tiny kisses. "I love you," she whispered happily, unable to hide her intense emotion. "You mean it? Ali, you mean what you said? You're coming with me?"

Ali started to laugh. "Yes, we are going to the States. My God, it sounds like some wild dream."

Stephanie paused. "And what about your mother? And you said the regime can prevent you from leaving. You said they can create difficulties."

"Everything is settled. My cousin Hussein arranged it all. He is a very important person in the regime. I told him of our problems and that you don't see yourself living in Iran."

Very concerned, she persisted. "And your mother and

sisters? You said they may be hurt."

"Hussein promised to take care of them. I trust him. He has already proved himself in the past. How do you think I got the job at the university? He is very connected to the Revolutionary Guards. Don't worry. Everything has been arranged."

She smiled and started to kiss Ali passionately. Suddenly, she stopped again. "It's amazing. I must tell my father and the family. I simply can't believe that it's happening. My God, we are going to do it, Ali."

Ali looked surprised. "Wait, wait, Stephanie. What did you say? You have to tell your *father*?"

Stephanie froze, thinking how to handle her gaffe. It was essential to keep secret that she was Amir Motaki's daughter. But now, she had slipped up. And how could she lie any more to Ali, who was willing to change his whole life to be with her? The confusion and pain was so great, she covered her face with both hands and started crying.

"What happened?" Ali asked with concern. "Stephi, calm down. What is it?

Stephanie closed her eyes and took a deep breath, trying to buy a few more moments. Telling the truth would endanger not only herself but also her father and his family. However, she knew that sooner or later she would have to tell Ali of her family connection with Amir Motaki.

Suddenly, she said, "I have to tell you something, but you must promise me that you will never talk about it with anyone. Please, promise me, Ali."

Ali took her hand. "Stephanie, you know that I would never do anything to hurt you."

"I want to tell you. I don't want it to stand between us. It's important to me to be honest with you. Promise me that you won't say anything to anyone. Please, promise."

"I promise. I swear to you on everything I hold most

dear in the world."

Stephanie hesitated and then started to talk. "Amir Motaki is not my uncle," she said and looked down, embarrassed by his piercing gaze.

"He's your father?"

She could only nod. Ali looked puzzled. He couldn't grasp what had just happened. Finally, he said, "Why did you hide it? You should be proud of his position."

Stephanie began to tell Ali the sequence of events, and even told him she had left to visit Iran despite her mother's strong opposition. She skipped the sensitive details about her mother the spy, the faked passport, and of course the conversations with the CIA agent who tried to prevent her from going to Iran.

"I'm not sorry I left the United States without my mother's consent. Thirty something years I grew up without a father. Then, I discover that he is alive and doesn't know of my existence. Isn't it an amazing story that I finally met my father and his wonderful family? Can anyone judge me for my actions?" she asked.

"I'm pretty shocked." Ali spoke slowly. "But, of course, I understand. It was your wish to maintain your privacy. I'm not judging you. It will be an honor to be Amir's son-in-law." He gave her a broad smile and took her in his arms.

As expected, the Motaki family was very happy to know that Ali intended to move to the States and be with Stephanie. Lily expressed her feelings better than anyone.

"It's sad, but also happy," she said and hugged Stephanie.

Zaher asked, "How come this change?"

"He said everything has been arranged. I have no idea how and haven't asked too much. If he's sure it's okay, I believe him."

Tahara asked, "Will you get married in the States?"

"Too early to talk of marriage. I think I'll first have an engagement party here in Teheran so that you and his family will be at the event."

"It's a wonderful idea," Dalram said with a broad smile. "I'm sure father will be pleased. It will make him happy. Anyway, I'm very happy for you. It will be some time before we deal with marriage with Zaher or Tahara."

Zaher was enthusiastic. "Maybe we can have another party for our friends, too."

"Don't forget that I'm supposed to leave soon," Stephanie reminded her.

"Please stay a few more days."

"It's really impossible. They did me a favor at work and I had to beg them. Even though they like me, I don't want to risk losing my job."

Stephanie was greatly surprised when her father received the news about Ali going with her to the States. He seemed quite reserved. "It sounds good," he said. "I'm happy for you that things are working out the way you want." His enthusiasm was dampened.

"Amir, the kids are thinking of giving a small party before she leaves for the States," Dalram informed him. "We need to organize quickly since Stephanie is going back in a few days."

Stephanie noticed her father and his wife exchanging glances. At first, she didn't pay any attention, but a few hours later, just after midnight, when she woke up and went to the kitchen, she saw her father and Dalram standing in the dining room, whispering.

"Is something wrong?" she asked.

They exchanged a quick look and Dalram, smiling, answered, "No, not at all. We were talking about the engagement. We don't have much time, so we thought the party should be the day before you leave. I hope that's fine with you."

"I suggest you ask Ali to give me a call," her father said. "We'll have a meeting and it's important you are there, too. I want to coordinate everything. The sooner, the better."

Again, Stephanie's instinct told her something was wrong. She had been right about Ali and she worried what it might be this time with her father. She opened the fridge, took out a pitcher of lemonade and asked, "Do you want some?"

"No, thanks," said her father. "I'm really tired. It's been a hard day. I'm going to bed. Goodnight."

Dalram was left standing beside Stephanie. A long moment went by. Then, she said, whispering, "Your father is worried."

"Worried?" asked Stephanie. "About what?"

Dalram shrugged and spoke gently. "He is a little bit concerned about Ali."

Stephanie stared, astonished. "What is he concerned about? I don't understand. If it's about the party expenses, don't worry. I don't want you to pay for it."

"No, it's not that," Dalram answered. "He is concerned about Ali. He doesn't understand how he can leave everything here and go with you to the States."

"Very simple. He loves me. He was afraid that if he didn't come with me, we'd never be together. He doesn't want to lose me."

Dalram didn't answer. Her black eyes gazed upon Stephanie and she was smiling sadly. "It's not that simple. It's not so easy to decide all of a sudden to get up and leave Iran. If they allowed anyone to leave, every day, hundreds, maybe thousands would do it."

"Ali told me he has connections. He said he has arranged it with a close family relation. It's the same man who arranged for him to get the job at the school."

"Your father knows that not everyone tells everyone everything."

That night, Stephanie couldn't fall asleep. Dalram's words echoed in her mind but she didn't know how to perceive them.

She got up earlier than usual and rushed to the kitchen. As usual, Dalram was already sitting at the table. "Good morning. You got up early today. Sit down. I'll make you tea."

"Good morning, Dalram," she answered. "I'll get it myself. I couldn't sleep much last night. I was thinking of what you told me." She poured a cup of tea and sat down next to Dalram. "I want to know why father is concerned."

Stephanie had barely finished the sentence when her father came into the dining room, wearing his neatly pressed and spotless uniform.

"Good morning," he said and sat down on his chair at the head of the table. "Why did you get up so early?"

"You seemed worried last night," Stephanie said. "I would like to know why."

"I'm worried," he answered with a serious look. "Because when you started the relationship, I did some checking on Ali in the police records at my disposal. I found out that he is a man with no criminal past, a school teacher. He lost two brothers in the war against Iraq. What worries me is this change. How come he is suddenly able to drop everything and leave for America?"

"He loves me and cares for me. He realized that if I'll go back to the States, he will lose me. It's as simple as that. Why is this hard to understand?

Amir waited until his wife put his breakfast on the table. "Maybe. Maybe it's not so simple," he said without looking up. "I want to check on him somewhere else."

Stephanie reacted quickly. "Dad, what do you have to

check?"

"I would prefer that you don't hurry. I suggest you go back to the States, analyze your feelings for Ali. If you miss him, invite him to come over. Why this haste? I cannot say much more. I just have suspicions."

"What are you talking about?" she asked in a shaky voice, "What suspicions?"

"Amir," insisted Dalram, "you must explain to her what you fear. You cannot suggest something and then say everything is fine."

Amir Motaki looked straight at his daughter. "Trust my instincts, please. Everything looks legitimate and logical, but I'm concerned. You don't know how things are here. Some people are not honest. They take advantage of someone else's weaknesses."

"Are you suggesting that Ali is using me to run away from here?"

"Maybe yes and maybe no. I believe Ali loves you and his intentions toward you are real and sincere. But remember you are also potentially providing him a way to leave Iran."

Stephanie remained seated, speechless.

Amir got up and said, "I will check during the day. Meanwhile, don't say a word to Ali. Believe me, I will be very happy to find out that I am wrong about this."

In the morning, Stephanie joined Ali at the big rally held on campus to celebrate Ramadan. Ali noticed Stephanie's gloomy mood. While among thousands of students packed into a public square, Ali told her that the main event was a speech by Ayatollah Ali Khameini, the country's powerful Shiite leader.

"This is the man who decides and controls more than

anyone else," he explained. "The Shiites believe he is the successor of the Prophet Mohammed. Even President Ahmadinejad knows that if he doesn't follow Ayatollah Khameini's will, he'll find himself ousted from the political stage. The antagonism of the president towards the United States and Israel is a result of his desire to please Khameini."

Stephanie listened to Ali but her thoughts were far away. The fear her father had raised hung over her. She had a hard time maintaining a relaxed appearance.

"Are you okay, Stephi?" Ali asked, barely resisting the urge to pull her towards him. "Something wrong?"

She shook her head and smiled. "I'm fine. Really. It's just the pressure I'm feeling about leaving soon."

"*We* are leaving," Ali quickly corrected. "Don't forget. We are leaving together."

"Yes," she murmured softly.

A burst of applause from tens of thousands of young people interrupted their conversation. A bespectacled old man with a gray beard, wearing a gray suit topped with a black cape, appeared on the big stage a few hundred feet from them. He looked around at the crowd of students standing in front of him and a slight smile appeared at the corners of his mouth.

Stephanie didn't understand one word of the speech. Still, she could tell he enjoyed huge support from the students, who interrupted him several times with roars of approval. Ali, from time to time, leaned toward her, trying to translate some of the words.

Stephanie became bored after fifteen minutes. Ali was aware of it and asked, "I think we have had enough, right? Let's leave. I believe you experienced enough local politics for one day."

Stephanie looked at him with gratitude. This was one of the reasons she loved him so much: his ability to understand what she was going through without her even needing to speak.

They made their way with difficulty through the thousands of young men and women. Soon, they were sitting at one of the small restaurants near the campus that specialized in home cooked dishes. Following Ali's advice, they ordered two portions of a dish called *sabazi*.

"Trust me, you'll enjoy it," he told her, smiling, "My mother is an expert in preparing *sabazi*. It's a dish of tender beef with sour green herbs cooked with black, dry Persian lemons."

In fact, she was hungry and the meat was tender and juicy, but she felt enveloped in an emotional anguish that prevented her from enjoying it very much.

"Do you know Persian restaurants in Los Angeles?"

Stephanie shrugged. "Personally, I don't know any, but I'm sure there are Persian restaurants. Los Angeles has a large community of Iranians."

Ali smiled. "I will search the Internet for Iranian recipes. If I miss Iran, we will cook dishes like the ones at home."

"I can't eat anything else," she said softly. "I'm really full."

Ali looked at Stephanie's plate, still filled. "You didn't eat anything. What's going on, Stephi? You said you were hungry."

Stephanie looked down. "I was hungry. It's fine."

"Do you want something else?"

"No, I don't want anything."

Ali wasn't ready to give up. "You worry. What's happening to you, my love? Tell me what happened. I will understand everything."

Stephanie reached across the table and took Ali's hand, ignoring a group of men sitting next to them. "Do you love me, Ali?" she asked.

"You know I do," he answered quickly. "You know you are the most important thing in my life. I mean it and you know that. Do not doubt it for a moment."

"If you really love me and truly care about me, I want to ask you something and I want you to calmly consider it."

"Anything you say. You know I'll do anything to make you happy."

Stephanie took a deep breath and her fingers lightly touched his. She weighed her words and at last said, "I would like to return to the States alone."

"What?" Ali said, trying to hide his surprise. "What are you saying? I thought that—"

She interrupted him, her voice now steady. "I think it's better for me to take some time to be on my own, to find out what I want. I hope you understand. It's not easy for me to say that, but I'm convinced is the right thing to do."

Ali withdrew his hand. "I don't understand," he said in anger. "What is all this? I thought we had an understanding. I agreed to come with you to the States. I'm shocked. What made you change your mind?"

"Nothing. I just feel the right thing for me is to take time out. I don't want to make a mistake."

"What mistake? You said you love me, that I'm the best thing that happened to you for a long time." Ali was getting more upset by the moment. "Do you understand the situation all this is going to put me in? I informed the university that I'm leaving. It's absurd. I really don't understand."

"I suggest we continue this conversation outside," she said as she noticed people staring at them. "Please, Ali. We're making a scene in front of everyone." She got up quickly and left the restaurant and he followed her outside.

"I don't deserve this," he said angrily. "It's not fair. I believed you loved me. I believed there was something special between us. That's what you also said."

They walked rapidly, side by side, on the narrow street. Stephanie found it hard to see Ali so upset. She was sorry to have raised the issue. "You know I love you," she said. "You know I believe there is something special between us. All I'm saying is that I want a break. That's all. I don't want to do anything in a hurry. Please, Ali, I beg you, try to understand."

"No, I really don't understand you!" he shouted. "I don't understand and I can't understand. What happened to make all your plans change? You were the happiest person in the world when I told you that I was willing to leave everything behind and move with you to the States. What happened? What is it that affected you so much to radically change all your plans?"

"Nothing happened, Ali. Really."

He stood next to her. "You know what? I don't believe you! It must be your father who talked you into this."

"Why my father?"

Ali answered with bitterness. "I don't know. Maybe he thinks I'm not worthy of his daughter. He is a senior police officer and I'm just a history teacher. The truth, Steph. What did he say to convince you?"

Stephanie was not going to share with him the events of the previous night, so she said softly, "I'm sorry you feel that way. You know I love you."

"After all this, I really don't know what your feelings for me are. If you really loved me, you wouldn't change your plans."

# *11*

Stephanie did not recognize the number that appeared on the display of the cell phone given to her by her father, a few days earlier. "Yes," she blurted out, worried. "Who's this?"

Her father's voice was heard. "I'm on my way home. I'll be there in fifteen minutes to pick you up. We must talk. Wait for me up the street, by the grocery store."

"Why don't you want to come up to the house? What happened?"

"We'll talk in a few minutes. Wait for me outside," he said in a calm voice.

She left the house, filled with concern. Waiting for her father, the minutes passed slowly, tense with expectation. Was her decision to go back to the States by herself correct? What did her father discover about Ali?

She noticed his car and waved at him. He arrived alone, without his chauffeur and without the bodyguard, stopped the car by the side of the road and Stephanie hopped in. Amir's facial expression gave way to the turmoil he was going through.

"We have a huge problem. We're in real trouble," he said quickly.

Stephanie stared at her father. He glanced at the rear view mirror and plunged the car forward, entering into the flow of the traffic. "It seems they know exactly who you are. They know everything."

"Who is 'they,' Dad? What happened?" She was hardly able to conceal the trembling in her voice.

Amir steered the car nervously, changing from one lane to another at great speed. "They know exactly who you are. They know everything about you. They even know things that I didn't."

Her father's words shocked her. The CIA agent's explicit threat about the professional abilities of the Iranian secret service now echoed in her ears.

"They know about me and the passport?" she asked softly.

"Stephanie, is that true?" he asked nervously. "What were you thinking, damn it? Where did you get the nerve to actually do this stupid act?"

"Dad, I wanted to see you so much. I couldn't tell you. I knew it was problematic and didn't want to worry you. I didn't want you to get upset."

"If I had known, I would have done everything to stop you from coming here. I wouldn't have met you. This is very serious."

Stephanie couldn't hold back the tears. "I'm sorry," she mumbled. "I wanted to meet you so very much. Mom didn't want me to go. I wasn't about to give up. It was the only way for me."

Amir was breathing deeply. "They know who you are. I believe you have been under their surveillance since arriving here. And as I feared, they watched you with Ali."

Amir passed a van at high speed, attempting to avoid any possibility of being followed. His eyes fixed intently on the road as he ignored the curses hurled his way as he passed the van.

She froze in her seat. "How do you know all this?" she asked in a feeble voice.

"I have a good friend working for the Iranian intelligence. Your mother might have mentioned his name: Mahmoud. I asked him to check on Ali. I met him only a half hour ago. He saw Ali's file and there he found data concerning you."

Stephanie stared at her father, cheeks wet from tears. "This doesn't really make sense."

Amir turned the car into a small street and parked next to a building. "Listen to me. The game is over. This is a serious and dangerous matter. We have no time and every minute counts. The most crucial thing now is to get you out of here as soon as possible. We have an advantage, since they don't know how much we know. I have a plan. You must continue to play out the affair. First thing, I'm organizing the plane tickets for you and Ali. Later I'll check the option of passing Zahra's passport to you. We're checking to see if any of our people can help you pass through border control."

"What?" she cried out.

"I don't know what your plans are but you need to tell Ali that you want him with you in America. You will go together and purchase two plane tickets for next week. Act normal. It's important that you don't tell any of this to Ali. At the same time, we will buy another plane ticket through a different travel agent, under a different name, for the earliest flight possible. I know a travel agency that can do that. This is the only possible way to get you out of here. We have to try to calm things down, continue as usual and make them feel that they've trapped you, and then disappear."

Trembling took over Stephanie's body. She had so many questions to ask but she understood it was better to stay quiet. Her father reached out his arm to caress her head. "It will be okay," he said tenderly. "Do you understand what you must do?"

She nodded. "You said they spotted me with Ali."

"Exactly. Don't get this wrong. He's a good man. But the minute they tracked him, they got him to cooperate. I know how they operate. They promised to look after his family. They promised him a salary. He was supposed to watch you and report back to them."

Stephanie had trouble believing that. "You think he is in on this? What do they want from me? What good can I do them now? It doesn't make sense."

"As I explained to you, you're in a position that can help them immensely. The Immigration Department, the issuing of passports and entry visas. They're successful at infiltrating their agents into the States, but with you, it will be even easier."

"To get people in illegally? Iranian agents that will damage America? I wouldn't cooperate if my life was on the line. They can't make me do things against my will."

"My dear daughter, you're naïve. They would find a way to make you, just as they did with Ali."

Stephanie shrank in her seat while thoughts were racing in her head. She found her father's words very hard to digest and felt the ground was shaking under her feet. "I thought I could fool everyone," she mumbled, unable to control her tears. "I only hope I didn't get you in trouble... all of you."

"It will be fine, Stephanie," said Amir in a calm voice. "I've been in this situation before and I promise you, we'll overcome this too. What's important now is to get you out of Iran as quickly as possible. I hope that we are indeed one step ahead of them and that they don't arrest you."

"Arrest me for what? They don't—"

Amir shot a glance at her, now showing annoyance. "They have all the reasons in the world and we both know it. Don't forget you got in with a fake passport. That definitely could be enough for them. I honestly don't understand how you got the nerve to forge an ID, a passport… you… you can't even conceive what mess you got yourself into."

Stephanie was standing frozen on the corner, the same spot her father had picked her up, as she watched his car quickly drive off back into traffic. Her father's words made a strong impression on Stephanie. "They know everything about you," his voice echoed in her ears. She suddenly felt insecure, and began to thoroughly examine every person that passed her by, and gazed suspiciously at every car that drove by slowly. Her father had decided the best plan of action would be to send her home, and for her to act normal. He knew she would be safe, at least until she made it to the airport, as long as she acted as if nothing had happened.

She wandered around the neighborhood aimlessly, pondering what to do next. How was she supposed to go on as if she was fine, knowing that now her secrets had all been revealed, and that danger was possibly lurking around any corner? She decided she had to trust her father.

Finally, she went to the playground near the Motaki house and sat on one of the benches. The light wind was pleasant. She closed her eyes, allowing the thoughts to roll in her head.

It was hard to accept that the Iranian intelligence service was using Ali in order to recruit her. How could she not have suspected anything? How could she have been so naïve allowing Ali to manipulate her? What would Ali's fate be after she escaped? What would happen to her father and his family?

She felt extremely lonely and an intense longing for her mother rose up in her. Ever since she had left home, she navigated her way in total independence. But she always knew that her mother would be there for her. Indeed, after Tom had died, her mother was her greatest means of support.

The thought of her mother finding out that she was actually in Iran and not travelling in India made her shudder. She never wanted to hurt her or to disappoint her. "I'm sorry, Mom. I've been so stupid," she whispered to herself.

Stephanie was angry with herself, her stubbornness. She realized that as the years passed, this characteristic has become more and more dominant in her nature. The definitive "no" that she got both from her mother and the people at the CIA regarding the trip to Iran had, in fact, increased her motivation to do just that.

The incredible ease with which she was able to issue a new passport for herself had given her confidence. The thought that this entire affair was going to be revealed horrified her. She was also ashamed at the thought that she would have to face Kevin, her boss and trusting friend.

She realized that she might pay heavily for her actions. She was aware of the fact that forging a passport was a severe federal offense. Now, she also grasped the fact that she would not be the only one to pay a price. Kevin, too, would have to provide explanations and might even be dismissed in disgrace.

"Come over," she told Ali over the phone, trying as hard as she could to sound cheerful. "I'm sitting in the garden waiting for you. I've something to tell you that'll make you happy."

Ali arrived quite quickly. Stephanie followed him with her eyes from where she was seated as he walked briskly along the asphalt path. The closer he got, the more her feelings of discomfort intensified. The thought that from this point on, she would have to deceive him with every word that she uttered caused her grief. The fact that he agreed to cooperate with the Iranian regime did not make it any easier on her. Her feelings for him were real and sincere; she couldn't change them so quickly. She put a faint smile on her lips while he leaned to kiss her.

"Why didn't you wait for me at home? What's so urgent?" he asked, taking the seat beside her.

Stephanie tried to keep her cool. "Soon, you'll hear it all. But you've got to promise me that you'll do everything I ask of you."

He smiled at her. "What's the matter, Stephi? You know I always do what you ask." She reached out and touched him lightly on his knee, the way she used to every time they sat side by side.

"I've been thinking a lot these past days," she said with a severe expression. "I've been thinking about my life. I've been thinking of us. I thought about what I'm going to do after I leave." She sighed heavily, all the while her hand stroking his knee. "I've come to the conclusion that what I want is to be with you. I think our love deserves a chance. The idea of living together in America appeals to me more than ever."

Ali pulled her toward him. "I'm so happy to hear this. You have no idea how important your words are to me. I—"

"But our families can't know of this," Stephanie cut him short, "so what we have to do next is quite simple. On the outside, we act like 'business as usual.' As far as they know, I'll be going back to the States supposedly on my own and you are staying here, until we decide otherwise. In reality, first thing in the morning, we go to a travel agency and purchase two plane tickets to the States. No one has to know you're coming with me."

The wide smile and glow in Ali's eyes showed his happiness. He pulled her head close to his and kissed her warmly. "Wonderful, wonderful," he repeatedly mumbled. "You have no idea how happy I am." He leaned in to kiss her but Stephanie put up her hand to stop him.

"Wait, Ali. I want you to promise not to tell anyone about this plan of ours, not your friends, not your family. No one. It must be kept secret. Just me and you. No one else should be involved. I have no doubt this matter will hurt my father, in case he discovers what I did behind his back. I have no intention of doing anything that will insult or anger him. Once we're in the States, you call anyone you wish. I'm asking you to promise me, Ali."

Ali had trouble calming down. "Promise. Of course, I promise."

"Wait, one more thing," she said. "I don't think it will be right for us to go together to the travel agency. We should place two separate orders. Only after I buy my ticket, you will go and order yours on the same flight. In a couple of days, there is a Lufthansa flight to Stuttgart in Germany that continues to Los Angeles."

"Okay. And perhaps we should also arrive separately at the airport," said Ali.

"Obviously," said Stephanie, "we'll meet on the plane. You'll get there early and get on the flight before me. My Dad and his family will probably want to accompany me and

I wouldn't want you to run in to each other, not even by chance."

"Don't worry," he said, smiling. "It will be fine. I understand exactly what you're saying. It will be fine. We'll meet on the plane."

Stephanie felt a little relieved. It seemed that he had bought into her plan without asking too many questions, just as her father predicted.

"It's done, then," she said, bringing herself closer to him.

"Done," he smiled. "You can't imagine how happy you've made me. Do you want me to take you home?"

"No need. It's so close, I'll walk. I'll call you tomorrow morning."

The pages of a small notebook became the main communication channel between her father and her. Amir decided to take extra measures of caution. He was positive that the *Al-Quds* militia was not only tailing Stephanie wherever she went, but that his own house was illegally wired with sophisticated eavesdropping devices. A day earlier, waiting until all the women were out of the house, Amir made a few inspections inside the house and in the electrical closet attached to the exterior wall of the house. He found no device but saw some marks on the wiring that had not been there before, and it aroused his suspicion.

"From now on," he wrote in the notebook, "we are not saying anything about our affair out loud but writing it down instead. You are not to tell anything to any of the girls. Dalram knows everything. I trust her one hundred percent. In any case, you continue as if nothing happened. Keep your cool."

Keeping her secret was not easy for Stephanie. She found it hard not to share her feelings with her sisters, and even more, to lie to them. As her father instructed her, she made sure to tell the girls her return date to the States and even showed them the plane ticket.

"Five days from now," said Lily sadly, holding the ticket. "And when will you be coming back again?"

Stephanie caressed Lily's head. "Soon," she said, forcing herself to smile. "And maybe you'll come and visit me. Would you want to visit me in the States?"

"I'll come to your wedding to Ali," said Lily with a broad smile. "We'll all come for that wonderful day."

"If only," mumbled Stephanie to herself and pulled Lily between her arms. "I will miss you so, little one."

By her father's strict orders, Stephanie made sure to spend time with Ali, just as she used to up until now. It was not easy on her, emotionally or practically. "We have to let them feel all is normal," her father wrote in the notebook. "I know this isn't easy for you but there's no choice. They must not suspect that anything is happening."

As Ali had agreed to with Stephanie, they arrived separately at the travel agency and purchased plane tickets to the United States with a stopover in Germany.

"I still can't believe we're doing this," Ali said.

Stephanie listened to Ali's words but was constantly tense. Her attention shifted to a young man in blue jeans and a black tee-shirt, walking parallel to them, on the sidewalk across the street. She was certain she had seen him during her stay in Teheran but could not remember where.

"What do you feel like doing?" asked Ali. "You should take advantage of each day left to see more of Teheran. Or maybe you prefer to go to my place?"

"I want to buy something for the family," Stephanie stated. "I think each one of them deserves a small gift from me after all they did for me. Do you feel like coming to Teheran Mall with me?"

Ali was disappointed that Stephanie did not want to go to his house. Since they met, hardly a day passed without them having sex.

"Don't worry," she told him smiling, "We will have plenty of time together. You know, I'm just not in the mood. This situation with my Dad is stressing me out. I'm not used to lying."

A few days prior to her leaving, Stephanie decided to break her own rule about not giving in to Ali. He had collected her that day around noon with his car."Hi, my love," he welcomed her happily. "How are you today?"

Stephanie kissed him lightly over his lips. "I'm fine. What do you feel like doing?"

"Do you want to get something to eat? Yesterday, someone told me of a great restaurant at the market."

"Let's go to your place. It's been a while since we've been together and I miss feeling you."

Ali reached his hand out and stroked her leg. "That's a better plan than I could have thought of," he said, hardly concealing his excitement. "You can't imagine how much I miss you."

"Me too."

They made love passionately and stayed lying on the bed, exhausted. While Ali's urge for Stephanie was very physical, Stephanie's passion for Ali was driven by her wondering, worrying about their future.

Stephanie gave herself to Ali completely, as if she was sure this might be the last feeling of ecstasy forever between her and him. But still she was not able to climax. The thinking and the fear had their effect. She did not want what could potentially be their last time together to seem like he had not satisfied her, so she created passionate groaning and spasms to convince him. She thought afterward, *I am lying to him, even with my body.*

Ali brought Stephanie back to the Motaki home. He leaned and kissed her gently on the lips. She knew this would be the last time she would see him.

"Wait," she mumbled. "I want one more kiss."

"Gladly. You know I love your lips."

Stephanie wrapped her arms around his neck and pressed against him in a kiss. "Bye, Ali," she said smiling.

"What's that look?" he asked.

"What look?"

"The one you just gave me, after the kiss."

Stephanie was startled. "What are you talking about?" she asked, restrained, "What look are you talking about, Ali?" She tried to smile to dismiss his concern.

"I swear, you had this odd look," he said. "It wasn't your normal way of looking at me. I don't know."

She maintained a calm voice. "Did anyone ever tell you, you're an odd man, Ali?" She continued a forced smile. "I guess I tired you out so much today that you're completely losing your mind."

Without a doubt, the hardest moments for Stephanie were those she spent with the three Motaki sisters. That night, Lily forced them to play Monopoly. She managed the game with an iron fist and criticized anyone who was taking too much time. Despite her extreme tiredness, Stephanie did not want to part from her stepsisters and go to sleep. Her frequent yawning made Tahara and Zaher smile.

"Someone here is very tired," said Zaher, giggling.

Tahara smiled. "Yes. Poor thing. I guess one has to make the most of the days left."

"Cut it out," she said, embarrassed. "You shameless women."

Tahara bent over Stephanie, wrapping her arms around her neck. "You know we're happy for you. I wish I had the chance to get tired like this once in a while."

When they were through playing, they sat down to watch TV. Lily went quickly through the channels, trying to choose a worthy program to watch. She paused over a channel that showed the American president, Barack Obama. "This is your president and he doesn't like us," she said quickly, her eyes fixed on the television screen. The picture turned to thousands of women and men walking the streets, roaring in anger.

"This is the demonstration that took place today in Teheran," was Lily's hurried explanation. "That's why Dad will probably be late today. The Americans don't like Iran and want to destroy it, and people here say they are not afraid of the Big Satan. But you don't hate us, right?"

Before Stephanie was able to answer, the door opened and her father walked in. "Good evening to you all," he said.

Lily happily hurried to him. "Daddy, Daddy, you came earlier than expected."

"And how was our guest's day?" her father asked, trying to act as if it was business as usual. "You'll never guess what surprise I arranged for you tomorrow, Stephanie. Do you remember me telling you that I have to travel to Mashhad? Well, tomorrow, it's happening." Stephanie knew he meant that tomorrow she would be leaving to go home to the States.

"Why do you have to drag her such a huge distance before her flight? We don't have much time with her. Please, don't take her." Lily pouted.

Amir sat at the head of the table, as the discussion moved into the kitchen. "I don't know when Stephanie will visit Iran again. She's here now and that's why she should experience as much of the country as possible. I will go to my meeting and she will be able to tour the city. I already planned with one of my policemen to give her a tour. We leave tomorrow at 4:30 am. I have to be there precisely by eight."

Stephanie got up immediately after the family had finished their supper. "If you don't mind, I'll go to bed. Especially if I have to get up at four tomorrow." She embraced the three girls and Dalram.

"Good night," said Dalram. "I wish you a good trip."

"Thank you, thank you," Stephanie mumbled excitedly, finding it hard to decide whether she referred to the trip to Mashhad or her planned flight back home.

# 12

Stephanie entered the terminal of Teheran International Airport. Despite the early hour, there were hundreds of people, children, women and men. The choice to get on the first plane departing Teheran that day wasn't accidental. Amir told her that the work shifts changed at that time and therefore, their alertness was lower.

Stephanie looked timidly at the passport. Although the picture was hers and also the birth year matched, the name on the passport was Rachel Baadani. She flipped through the document marveling at the skillful forgery.

She put her ticket on the Lufthansa counter, trying to keep cool. The young woman, with blue eyes and an aquiline nose, smiled at her from across the counter.

Stephanie looked around. At first glance, there was nothing unusual. Right behind her in the short line was standing an older couple, a tall man in dark glasses and a skinny woman with curly hair. Their eyes were fixed on the attendant. In the distance, two young men in jeans looked a little lost in the huge hall. A group of some twelve women dressed in black from head to toe stood behind the men.

There was no sign of security people, except for two soldiers positioned at the far end of the terminal.

Just as she used to do in her childhood whenever there was a danger, Stephanie decided that if she counted to ten and nothing happened, everything would be fine. She started to count and when she reached ten, she sighed, relieved.

It was then that the woman at the counter picked up the phone at her side.

Stephanie stared at her, trying to read her expression. The young woman on the other side of the counter kept a straight face.

"Something wrong?" asked Stephanie with a forced smile.

"All is fine. All is fine, ma'am."

Stephanie felt fear cover her entire body. She thought that she would give anything to go back in time and agree to her mother's request not to go to Iran. She saw in her mind her mother learning of her arrest, while Sharon watched the news on TV. She tried hard to remove the image from her mind.

There was no reply on the other side of the line, so finally the woman, irritated, put down the phone and told Stephanie, "I'm sorry. You will have to wait."

Trying to speak in a natural tone, she asked, "What's happening? Anything wrong?"

"It's okay, Mrs. Baadani, just a standard procedure. I will now ask you to move to the side and let the nice people standing behind you move ahead. I promise I will attend to you shortly."

Stephanie stood where she was. "I think I deserve to know what happened," she said firmly. "Why do I have to wait? My flight is about to leave soon."

"I'm sorry, ma'am. You are delaying the line," answered the woman. "I asked you to wait a few minutes. I'll be right back with you."

She tried to remain optimistic. *In the worst case*, she tried to convince herself, *if they arrest me, I'll be released in one or two days.* She had no doubt that the United States would do anything and everything to free one of their citizens, particularly an employee of the Department of Immigration.

However, as soon as she landed in the States, she'd have to hire a good lawyer because of the forged passport she had issued to herself while working in the Department of Immigration. This was a serious offense. She had no idea how she would be punished except for, of course, the loss of her job.

The phone rang. The woman at the counter quickly picked it up. Although Stephanie didn't understand what she was saying, she knew that the conversation concerned her.

Two men in dark suits came out from one of the small offices at the back. She could feel her pulse pounding at her temples, her head spinning and she felt a stabbing sensation in her stomach. She stared at the two men as they quickly walked the distance between them. They stood on either side of her. Stephanie noticed the tiny earphones they wore.

One of the men picked up her passport from the counter and began to examine it. Some seconds went by until he raised his eyes and looked at her.

Stephanie froze.

"Come with us," she heard his voice.

"I don't understand," she murmured, unable to overcome the shakiness in her voice. "Is something wrong? Someone please explain to me what's going on here."

"Ms. Baadani, some details are not clear. I think it would be better to clarify the issue privately. Please come with us." He reached for her bag, grabbed it and said, "Let me help you."

"That's fine. I can manage," Stephanie answered, but

the man held the bag. Stephanie didn't try to resist. She felt completely helpless.

She looked around the terminal. Except for a group of women and men standing in front of the Lufthansa counter waiting for their turn, none of the hundreds of women and men in the terminal noticed what was going on. Stephanie was led into a small side room, not far from the terminal.

"Wait here," said one of the men.

"May I have an explanation as to what's going on?" she asked in an aggressive tone.

One of the men smiled at her. "Soon, we'll explain everything. Be patient. It may be a misunderstanding but it must have an explanation. Wait here. I will not be long."

"What misunderstanding are you talking about?" She didn't get any response. The security men left the room and shut the door.

She ran her hand over an inside window and assumed that it was a one-way mirror. She sat down heavily on one of the chairs, feeling exhausted. The fear of the unknown intensified. Time passed slowly and each minute seemed like an eternity.

About half an hour later, she couldn't bear any longer the inactivity. She got up and gripped the door handle firmly with both hands, trying to open it. The door was locked.

"Hello," she called out. "Hello. Can anyone answer me?"

The door opened and the security man who had spoken before appeared. "Yes, ma'am, we are here. We didn't forget you. Patience."

"I'm afraid I'll miss my flight."

The security man smiled at her. "We are aware of it. Don't worry. We will book you on the next flight. There is a small problem."

"What problem?" she asked. "I want to know why you

are detaining me."

The security man didn't answer. He left and closed the door.

Over ten minutes later, the two security men came in together with a tall and broad man with a black beard. The look on his face was serious and intense.

"What's your name, please?" he asked without even introducing himself.

"Rachel Baadani," she answered, trying to keep her voice steady. "I would like to know what's going on here. Why are you detaining me?"

The man who was sitting across her stared at her. "I see that name on the passport. I'll ask again, who are you really?"

Stephanie pretended to be surprised. "I don't understand. What are you talking about?" Her mouth was dry. She decided to use her father's name. "I'm Rachel Baadani and my uncle is deputy chief of a police station in Teheran. I'm sure you know him."

The bearded man bent down and a slight smile appeared at the corners of his mouth. "You know exactly why you are here," he hissed through his lips. "You are not Rachel Baadani. We received information that you entered Iran under a false identity. Your passport is forged. I'm asking again: What's your name?"

A cold sweat came over Stephanie's body. She realized now that the worst scenario was coming true. "I belong to the Motaki family," she said weakly. "You must know my uncle, Amir Motaki."

"We know all about your relationship with Amir Motaki," the interrogator said. "Unfortunately for you, Amir Motaki cannot help you any longer. Who are you? How did you enter the Islamic Republic of Iran? Who sent you here?"

"I don't understand what you are talking about. I came

to visit the Motaki family. I'm American, a tourist and—" Stephanie couldn't complete the sentence.

"You are lying!" roared the interrogator, now sitting across from her at the table. "I think you don't understand the gravity of your actions. You entered the Republic under false identity of a Regine Damir. And you are now trying to leave Iran under another forged passport in the name of Rachel Baadani. I'm asking you a very simple question: What's your real name?"

Stephanie realized that her father was right. The authorities definitely knew all along her true identity. "I want to see the British ambassador," she said in a firm voice that surprised even herself. "I'm an American citizen. I know that we don't have an embassy here. So, I demand to see the British ambassador or his representative, to be present here."

Asking for the British ambassador in Teheran as well as to mention her father's name were two of the suggestions her father had proposed in case she was detained at the airport.

"God bless you, child," her father had told her. "Let's hope everything will end up well and you won't..."

"What?" she had asked.

"I don't want to even think what might happen," Amir had said. "If they question you, don't admit anything. Try to keep cool as much as you can. If you admit anything, all is lost. If you don't, there is a chance they will decide that your arrest doesn't justify all the political issues it may lead to."

The interrogator hit the table hard with his fists. Stephanie gasped and swallowed. She opened her mouth to say something but couldn't speak. The man looked at her threateningly. "Answer me. What's your real name? Who are you?"

"I don't know what you want from me," she murmured

quietly with downcast eyes. "I want to see the ambassador. I want to see Amir Motaki. I have the right—"

"You are in Iran! You really don't understand that you have no rights. You have no rights whatsoever. I'm the only one who has rights."

The black eyes of the interrogator were fixed on her face and Stephanie noticed his jaw moving angrily. "I have all the time in the world, but you, your time is running out. If you had answered my questions, you would be on the plane now."

Stephanie tried to stop shaking with fear. She willed herself to be a little calmer. "I want to see the British ambassador," she murmured in tears. "I'm an American citizen and I have rights."

The interrogator looked at her cruelly, calmly collected the papers he had brought in and got up from his seat. He said in a calm voice, "As I already told you, I have all the time in the world. If you want to stay in Iran, it's fine with me."

Stephanie couldn't utter a word, and the interrogator left the room quickly.

Less than a minute later, he returned to the room.

"Come with me," he ordered her.

"Where?" she asked "Where are you taking me?"

As she was leaving the room, she was relieved to see her father far away, down the corridor. She wasn't sure if he had seen her. She tried to call him but her throat was constricted. Amir was now accompanied by two muscular men in suits. They disappeared into a room. The momentary sense of relief she had felt at the sight of her father was gone.

It was nine thirty in the morning when Stephanie,

escorted by three security agents, entered the Gaamar prison, a grey, two-story building whose entrance was a small door. Although the Gaamar prison was in the city center, just behind the hospital of the same name, most of the residents were unaware of its existence.

The prison was run by Iranian intelligence, the Al-Quds division, and known to organizations for human rights as one of the most brutal detention facilities in Iran. Political suspects who were going through the first stages of investigation were detained there.

The fact that all the employees, including the administration, had to sign an unconditional confidentiality document prior to working there, had contributed to its secrecy. In the past, there had been two cases of employees who spoke of the existence of Gaamar. Both were executed without a trial.

The complex included a small yard, four investigation rooms, eight solitary confinement cells and eight small detention cells. Its nickname, given by the agents of the Iranian secret service, was "café for the deaf."

Stephanie walked down the narrow corridor, her eyes scanning the white walls closing in on her from both sides. A young man, wearing jeans and a green tee-shirt, led her into a small room whose door bore the number six. At the center of the room, there was a small table and two wooden chairs.

"Wait here," ordered the man. Stephanie sat down heavily on one of the chairs, inspecting the small room. The tiny beam of light coming from a fixture above gave the place a scary appearance. And then, she felt two hands gripping her from behind and holding her tightly to the chair. A strong smell of onions rose to her nose. Handcuffs were secured to her hands and a black cloth put over her eyes and tied at the back of her head. Stephanie let out a loud scream of protest.

"What are you doing?" she demanded. "What is going on?"

A strong punch landed on her face and knocked her down onto the floor. She was in shock. Her head was spinning. A strong smell of onions rose again to her nose.

"If you don't want to worsen your situation, I suggest you keep quiet," she heard a man's deep voice above her say. "It's time you stop playing games with us. Otherwise, you'll spend quite a few years here."

Someone picked her up and put her on the chair. She could feel the blood from her nose run down into her mouth. She could taste the cold iron flavor on her tongue. The fear paralyzed her. Fingers forced their way into her hair and pulled back her head. She made a choked scream.

"Better you do what you are told," she heard the man who smelled of onions say. "You can choose to cooperate. If not, you will not recognize yourself the next time you stand in front of a mirror."

"I don't know what it is you want from me," Stephanie murmured softly. "I really don't know. I just came to visit—"

The hand holding her hair tightened and pulled her head back. "Who sent you?" she heard the man ask. From the smell of onions, she realized that the examiner's face was very close to hers. "Who sent you, the Great Satan or the Small One?"

The deep voice sounded familiar. It sounded like the voice of the taxi driver who had picked her up upon her arrival to Teheran and drove her to meet her father at the police station.

"Who sent you?" roared again the voice of this new interrogator.

"Nobody sent me," she whispered. "I swear that no one

sent me. I came for a visit. I have family here. Motaki family. They can confirm it."

Then, the hand holding her hair shoved her head forward and it heavily smacked the table. Stephanie cried out in pain. The cold water that was splashed on her face revived her. With great effort, she lifted her head, fearing any movement. She could feel the interrogator's breath.

"I see you have decided to continue playing with us. You don't leave me much choice."

Suddenly, she heard a female voice speaking in English. "It's a shame that a woman as beautiful as you will be prey to a band of men in this jail. But at night, when the lights are off, they will do things to you. One by one. They are animals."

The female voice was soft and melodious. Stephanie wanted to say something but was unable to mutter even one word. "If you are counting on your father for help, you can forget about it. At the moment, he cannot even help himself."

Stephanie took a deep breath, trying to overcome the tears. "No. Please. I really don't know what you want from me."

The female voice continued, with contempt. "We know exactly who you are. We know your real name is not the one on the passport. We know your relationship with Amir Motaki. All we want from you is your confirmation. That's all. I don't understand your resistant attitude."

Stephanie did not reply.

The woman continued. "I'll tell you the truth. We have no intention to hold you. You are meaningless to us. The last thing Iran is interested in these days is to get into further direct confrontation with United States. We have a lot more serious matters to deal with than you. Therefore, your confession is just a normal procedure."

"I want to see the British ambassador," Stephanie mumbled. "I want to see the ambassador."

Silence fell around her for a seemingly long time. "I see you choose not to cooperate." The female voice was soft but hostile. "I thought I could help you, but I see you are not interested in that."

Again, there was silence. And then, hands roughly grabbed her, and tore off her blouse. She cried out. One rough hand grabbed at her breasts, while she desperately squirmed. The sound of laughter of several men resounded.

"You are going to enjoy today, bitch," she heard a man's voice nearby. "The three of us are going to check to see if you are a virgin."

She flashed back to painful memories when she was rapcd by Tom, her husband. "What do you want from me?" she asked pleading, "Please…I didn't do anything."

The rough hand greedily grabbed her breast. "It's good for you? It's been a long time since I saw such a beautiful body. You like it, bitch?" He grumbled as he brutally tore apart the dirty prison pants. As he began to penetrate her, she screamed and then lost consciousness.

When she awoke, she was sitting on a chair, the naked upper part of her body covered with a big military blanket. Pain tore through her body. Blood ran between her legs. They showed no mercy on her. One by one, they had entered her, tearing into her. The fact that Stephanie had thrown up more than once didn't prevent them from continuing; in fact, they encouraged each other. They went on and on even after she fainted.

"Those are our methods of investigation," said the familiar female voice, "in particular when it concerns spies for the Great Satan. We don't always use electric shock on the feet or the nipples, and only rarely do we extract teeth without anesthesia. Yet, I have warned you."

Stephanie heard the female voice above her. She was trembling, unable to control it. "You know that here in the Republic, a woman who has been raped will never go to Heaven. You are at fault. You caused all this. Is it not a shame?"

The room fell silent and Stephanie moved her head to track the location of the woman now talking to her, moving about the room. "Let's forget everything. I repeat my question: Who sent you to Iran? Do you work for the Americans or the Israelis?"

Stephanie rushed to answer. "I have nothing to do with Israel. I came on a trip. I wanted to visit my family, the Motaki family. I swear to you that's the truth."

"Okay. Let's say you are telling the truth. What's your real name, not the one on the passport you had."

"Stephanie," she finally said softly, trying to hold back the tears that threatened to come again. "My name is Stephanie Simmons. That's my real name."

The female voice sounded amused. "You see, that wasn't so bad, after all. Now tell me, how did you enter Iran with a passport using the name of Regine Damir? How did you get that passport? And why did you try to leave with a passport in the name of Rachel Baadani? And who provided you with the forged passports?"

Stephanie dried her tears and couldn't decide what to do. "I got the passport of Regine from my work," she finally said softly.

"You are lying!" the female voice roared. "Again, you are not cooperating. Who are you trying to protect? I repeat that we know everything. Do you want to deal with those men again? Where did you get the passport with the name of

Regine Damir?"

"I issued it at my job," Stephanie said, her voice a little louder than before. "Nobody knew about it. I took advantage of the fact that requests for passports go through me."

"Where do you work?"

"At the Department of Immigration in Los Angeles."

"Why did you need the passport?"

Stephanie weighed her possible answer. She had already said much more than she had planned. "I bet with a friend who works there that I could not only issue myself a passport, but I could also succeed in using it to get out of the United States."

"How did you succeed in issuing yourself a passport?"

"I have told you. I'm a secretary in the Department of Immigration. Requests to issue or renew passports go through me. I sent a request for a new passport for Regina and used my picture. I'm very thirsty. Can I have some water?"

"First, answer me. Why did you need a forged passport? Why couldn't you enter under your real name?"

Stephanie realized that mentioning her mother might lead to death for either or both of them, eventually. She could hardly speak. "It was my bet with one of the women in the department. I wanted to prove to her that the Immigration Department needed to tighten its security. Can I have something to drink? Please."

"What's the name of your friend?"

"I would like to go to the bathroom. I would like to wash myself," she pleaded. "Please. Something to drink. My body hurts all over."

The female voice answered quickly. "First, answer my question. If you will cooperate, you'll get what you want. What's the name of your friend?"

"Mary Chiatro," Stephanie answered quickly. "She works in the legal department as a senior secretary. Now, can I have something to drink please?"

After another silence, the door opened and Stephanie could hear as the woman took a pitcher and poured something into a glass.

"Here, drink," she heard the female voice nearby. The glass was moved close to her mouth and she rushed to sip the cold water. A pleasant feeling filled her body as the cold water ran down her throat.

"Do you want more?"

"Yes, please," Stephanie whispered. "Thank you."

Stephanie drank quickly the cold water. "We don't have the whole day," said the female voice. "You want to get on the plane, right? Let's go back to your job. I repeat my question: where exactly do you work in the Department of Immigration?"

"I work in the Department of Immigration for Kevin Shepard, but…"

"But what, Miss Simmons?"

"Soon, I'm supposed to work at the Los Angeles City Hall," she finally said, trying to keep her voice steady. "They transferred me to the personnel department of the Los Angeles City Hall. I was supposed to start working there immediately after the holiday. I thought that I would have more of a chance for advancement. At the Department of Immigration, I was just a secretary."

Stephanie was shoved into a cell and, exhausted, she fell asleep quickly.

# 13

In the middle of the night, a hand shook Stephanie. "Get up, bitch. Get up." She vaguely heard the voice above her. The hand grabbed her arm and pulled her up aggressively. Stephanie didn't react and her body fell heavily on the floor of the cell. "They want you in the interrogation room."

She could barely stand on her feet and she couldn't keep her balance so she collapsed onto the floor. Now the hand gripped on her arm.

"Get up cunt!" She felt herself being dragged into another room where she heard a shout above her. "I told you to get up. Don't you understand? There is no time." She had been kicked and beaten, unable to protect herself. "Move, you rotten bitch… do you need a special invitation? Get in."

With great effort, Stephanie crawled into the dark cell. Behind her she heard the iron door being slammed shut. She was left lying on the concrete floor, the coldness seeping through her body. Despite the intense pain, the silence along with the cold brought her some kind of relief. As she got used to the darkness, she tried to get up but failed. Leaning against the wall, she tried to free her hands and feet until the physical effort wore her out. At last she gave up, the tears streaming down her face.

The intensive interrogations went on for hours. At this point, Stephanie could no longer remember what she had said. She felt no more pain nor humiliation, only anger and fear.

The soft female voice once again asked her all the same questions. Stephanie lost track of time. When she started to pass out, a rough male hand slapped her face. "Who are you? Who sent you to Iran? What's your relation with the Motaki family? Where did you visit during your stay in Iran? With whom did you meet while in Iran? What's your relation with Ali Hijazi?"

Stephanie repeated her life story, doing her best to clarify. It turned out that the examiner wasn't satisfied by her answers. She didn't rest. "Don't forget we know everything," she said. "We followed you from the time you entered the country. All we want now is for you to reconstruct the facts in your own words."

"I have already told you everything," Stephanie murmured helplessly, "What else do you want from me? I told you everything…really".

"Who sent you? Who issued the passport? Who asked you to come to Iran? Did you meet C.I.A. agents before coming?"

"I swear to you that nobody sent me. It was my idea. I wanted to visit the Motaki family. You know that he is my father. It was my own idea…I issued myself the passport."

"You lie!" the examiner's voice roared. "You lie shamelessly! Do you think you can fool me?"

Stephanie burst into tears. "I am not lying. It's the truth. I swear to you. It's the whole truth."

"Tell me the truth," roared the examiner. "You don't

leave me much choice but to bring back the men…"

The threat achieved its purpose. Stephanie was horrified at the thought. "I swear it's not a lie…" she pleaded. "Nobody sent me. I bet with a friend at work that I could issue myself a passport. I decided to visit Iran after I succeeded. Nobody sent me. I wanted to see my father." Stephanie again and again repeated the same information.

"You lie!" the female voice roared. "Do you think you can fool me?"

Stephanie burst into tears. "I'm not lying. It's the truth. I swear to you. It's the whole truth."

"You leave me no choice," the female examiner sighed. Suddenly, several pairs of hands grabbed her and put her on her feet. The blanket covering her upper body dropped, leaving her completely exposed.

"No, wait," she begged. "I'm really telling the truth."

"Time to eat your own mess," said the examiner.

Hands reached for her pants and she fell back in horror, feeling the chill of the wall on her back. She could clearly hear the man breathing.

"Please," she murmured.

"Please…enough…enough…please…" Her pants were removed roughly, despite her objections. She remained standing, stiffened with fear, weeping bitterly. Stephanie, stuck to the wall, felt completely humiliated and utterly helpless. Her breath was heavy and she cried painfully. And then suddenly, several pairs of hands seized her and pulled her quickly to the table. A hand gripped her neck and bent the upper part of her body towards the table. Her breasts were firmly pressed against the table.

"Don't move, bitch," a voice ordered her. The hand pulled her hair with force and pressed her head to the table. She was standing on her feet, her bare bottom sticking out, her upper body sprawled on the table. She felt the touch of one of the men's body rubbing her, and soon an intense pain pierced her from behind.

"America…America," she heard the man on her back bragging to himself in ecstasy, while penetrating her with up and down movements. A minute or two later he withdrew from her, pulled up his pants, and left the room.

She tried to free herself and began to lift her upper body from the table. The hand of the other man in the room gripped her neck and banged her head on the table. Pain shot through her head and her forehead was covered with blood. She burst into a strangled cry.

"Stop…leave me…I will talk…please…I am ready to talk…"

"Don't like it?" she heard a voice above her. "We thought you like this position, rotten bitch." Stephanie felt an object pierce her bottom. The pain was sharp. She screamed and her whole body began to shake. Her legs barely sustained her and a strong dizziness enveloped her. In utter bewilderment, she wept bitterly.

"Enough," she murmured, "Please…enough…I can't anymore…I'll talk… I beg you…" The last man who had entered her left the room, and the female examiner removed the bag from over her face, revealing the room to contain only her and someone in a white coat. Stephanie looked straight in the examiner's cold eyes and begged for her life.

"Please can I have my clothes…please, I am in pain…and I am very cold".

"It's up to you," the female examiner replied "But I'll see what I can do. Meanwhile, I want you to answer several questions…but this time it's better if you tell the truth."

Stephanie shrank in her seat. "I told you everything," she whispered, "I swear that's the truth."

The woman's soft hand touched her shoulder and Stephanie jerked. "You have nothing to fear from me. I'm not going to hurt you. Trust me, I want your own good. Do you think I'm proud of what those men did to you? It's hard to see you like this, but I think you don't understand the gravity of your situation. Who are you trying to protect? Is it worth all the misery you are going through?"

Despite the shock, Stephanie was well aware of "the carrot and the stick" method that the examiners were using on her – one hand cuddles and soothes, while the other one hurts and offends. Because the female examiner's approach was in total contrast to the violent and harsh treatment of the male examiners, Stephanie greeted the female examiner's attempts to connect with her with great caution. She had no doubt that this pretense was part of the approach of the investigation – solely intended to soften her.

Obviously, Stephanie opted for the relationship with the female examiner. For her, the female examiner was the lesser of two evils, a deceptive ray of light in the dark, literally and metaphorically. She had no doubt that if she had been entirely at the mercy of the male examiners, her situation would be much worse.

Beyond the severe pain, she felt humiliation and helplessness. Her fate didn't rest with her and no one in the world could save her. Stephanie's mind flashed back to the moment she saw her father in the airport, accompanied by policemen. She remembered thinking *here comes the hero to save the poor girl, and fly me back home to America.* Now, as she lied completely brutalized on the table, reality began to sink in.

"Come on, let's finish this business quickly, and then I promise you a good meal and a shower." Stephanie didn't respond.

"Pay attention," the woman ordered. "On the table is a paper with the details of all you have told me. I need you to sign it. Very simple. After that, you'll get a good meal and we will let you sleep, and then go home."

Stephanie was in pain, humiliated, tired and hungry. "OK," she whispered, "Whatever you say."

Several seconds later, the handcuffs were removed from her hands and feet. The examiner's voice sounded behind her. "For your own good, sign the statement. I'm sure you know by now that I am not playing games with you."

Stephanie sat down heavily on the chair and let her body relax. A sense of relief enveloped her and she was pleased by the silence around her. She now had the opportunity to review the small room, whose walls were white. She looked at the paper lying on the table. Stephanie slowly raised her hand and held the paper. She didn't need more than a second to find out that the document was written in Farsi.

"Excuse me," she exclaimed, too afraid to look at the examiner. "Excuse me. Miss…hello…would you come here please?"

The examiner's voice sounded through the door. "I can hear you… what's the problem?"

Stephanie spoke weakly. "I don't understand what's written here. How can I sign this if I don't understand it?"

Through the door came again the examiner's voice. The woman's tone had changed. Now, she was angry. "I explained to you, it's a summary of all that we have discussed. You don't need to understand it. Sign and that's it."

Confused, Stephanie mulled over the situation. "I want to sign a document in English," she said softly. "I don't understand what this says."

The woman was pitiless. "There is no one to translate the document. We will have someone do that tomorrow. If you won't sign now, you can forget sleeping. We can go on till morning, if that's what you want…"

Stephanie lowered her head, considering what to answer. "I want to sign a document in English, please," she whispered. "Please, I don't know what I am signing…" Before she could even finish her sentence, she heard the door burst open and in an instant, felt a fist hit her head. The force of the blow slammed her head on the table in front of her. The pain was intense and bursts of light flashed before her eyes. She lost consciousness.

When Stephanie woke up, she found herself blindfolded and handcuffed again, and completely naked. She could hear voices in the room with her. Suddenly, she began coughing, and the talking ceased. A hand seized her hair.

"Did you miss me?" a male voice rumbled. "I hope that you understand…this time, nothing will help you. You can beg till tomorrow." The rough hand of the examiner greedily cupped her breast and his breathing became heavy. "We are going to party once again…you, me and my two friends…I heard that you like this very much. Your boyfriend, Ali Hijazi, told us a lot about you…let's see if he was right…"

Stephanie sat helpless in her place. The examiner's threatening voice made her shiver all over. "I am sorry," she murmured in a whisper, trying to overcome the choking in her throat. "I am sorry…I will sign the document…I will record whatever you tell me… I promise. I want to sign, really…please. Please, I just want to see and understand what I am signing."

She heard the voice of the female examiner on the other side of the table. "I explained that at this time there is no one to translate the document. Sign now, and tomorrow morning I promise you'll get the translation of the document. All you need to do is to sign the document. What is written here is exactly what you told me."

"I want a translation," she whispered. "Please, I will

sign. I just want to know…please." Stephanie was trying to stall for as long as she could. Somewhere in her mind, she held the belief that her mom would come to save her, if only she could hold out just a little longer.

A punch that hit her again in the face shook her whole body. The pain quickly spread to her head, and a trickle of blood started flowing from her lower lip. Her head was spinning and she would have fell from her chair and collapsed on the floor if two arms hadn't been holding her.

The examiner's voice rose to her ears. "You still don't understand that your foolishness and stubbornness are causing you problems? If you had signed, you would have spared yourself the misery you are going through and you could also have slept several hours."

Stephanie's whole body was aching, her lower lip had swollen and blood covered her face. Even if she had wanted, she could not speak. She was overcome by exhaustion. She felt the room grow dark once again, and she passed out.

When she woke up from the blackout, she found herself lying on the floor of the interrogation room. And just as before, she heard the singing voice of the examiner. "You can't say I didn't warn you. Now you must decide what's next. You can sign now or I can have the guys come back to have more fun with you until morning. Make up your mind."

At this point, she didn't care about anything. Stephanie had lost her will. She could no longer bare the pain, least of all, the humiliation. The decision was to do as they were asking. Whatever the consequences will be. She realized there was no point to resist, and that the examiners will continue to torture her as they pleased. All she wanted for now was to close her eyes and to be freed of the handcuffs on her legs and hands. She wanted to rest her body, and most importantly, rest her soul.

"I'll sign," she whispered. "I'll sign."

"Good. Sign now. Tomorrow, you will record a video clip and finish with this matter." Stephanie became slightly optimistic by her decision to do whatever they ask. She was even somehow relieved. She reassured herself that she had made the most appropriate decision, considering the pressure exerted on her. And so it was, her hands and legs were released from the heavy chains, and the blindfold was removed once again.

"It seems you got some sense knocked into you," she heard the female voice. "Sign and let's finish with this issue. You are not the only one who wants to sleep. I need a few hours of good sleep, too. Come, let's finish this and you will sleep a bit… eat… think what you would like us to prepare for you…"

Stephanie sat down heavily, letting her eyes adjust to the light in the interrogation room. She reached for the pen and without thinking, she scribbled her signature at the bottom of the document and put down the pen. The woman who interrogated her took the document and quickly left.

It was finally over. Stephanie felt a wave of relief sweep over her body. She closed her eyes, took a deep breath, and wanting to believe that everything had come to an end, let her head collapse. Within seconds, she fell asleep.

A push woke Stephanie up from her sleep.

"Get up," a woman's voice was ordering her. "Get up…this is not nap time. Get up immediately!"

Stephanie looked up and stared at the tall, young woman standing next to her. The desk in front of her was empty and there was no sign of the document. She held tightly to the blanket covering her naked body. With difficulty, she lifted her head, as she felt a hand slipping a cover on her eyes and fastening it at the back of her neck.

"Get up", ordered the voice. "I am telling you to get up!"

She barely managed to get up, feeling a sense of relief as she remembered that her legs had been freed. She dragged her feet as she was pushed through the corridor. A male hand held her.

"Careful, there is a step," he said. Stephanie allowed the man to lead her as she cautiously went down the steps. "Come on, come on," she heard the voice of the escort. She increased her pace. "Stop here," she heard his voice behind her, "Stay put." She stood where she was, and felt hands quickly remove the cover from her eyes. "Get in," said the man tapping her back. She barely opened her eyes, and saw a green door. "Come on," said her escort "Move, open the door."

Stephanie opened the green door with a hesitant hand and slowly walked into the room which was just slightly larger than the interrogation room. A small table and two chairs stood at the center of the room and in a corner, against the wall, sat a raised bed. Across the room, near the front door, stood a long cabinet. In another corner, she noticed a small mirror above a sink.

Stephanie fell down heavily on one of the chairs. The door opened and a woman of about fifty entered, carrying a bundle of clothes under her arm. The woman was wearing a floral dress over dark pants and a big green scarf around her head. She stood in front of Stephanie.

"It's for you," said the woman in broken English with a heavy Persian accent. Her voice was a stark contrast to the soft and melodious voice of the examiner. "Now, you get dressed… fast… now you get dressed."

The woman laid the clothes (a brown shirt and pants) on the table between them. In a hurry, Stephanie removed the blanket covering her body, ignoring the woman's severe stare. Quickly, she took the shirt and put it on. Then, as fast as she could she put on the pants, which were several sizes too big for her. She stood silently in front of the woman.

"Wait here," the woman snapped at her, as she walked around the table, opened the door and left. Stephanie, aching, humiliated, and tired, sat in the room she didn't recognize. Fear enveloped her as she felt her body long to sleep. She had been able to develop a method to escape the great humiliation and frustration: close her eyes and fall asleep, and wake up thinking of another imaginary reality, where all is well. She rested her head on the table, and immediately fell asleep again.

When she woke up, she was sitting across from a tall, bespectacled, bearded man, wearing a white jacket. "There is a sink. I suggest you wash your face," he spoke in perfect English. "Looks like you could use some medical treatment."

Stephanie got to her feet, crossed the small room and stood by the sink. She got the chance to examine her face in the small mirror above the sink. At first glance, it was hard to recognize herself, and she barely stopped the scream that began to rise in her throat. She was horrified at the sight. Her face was deformed due to the swelling and dried blood was smeared all over it.

She turned on the faucet and was amazed by the running water, a luxury she had taken for granted until she had been without it for so long. She gently started to wash but felt intense pain each time she splashed the water on her face. It took her several attempts to completely remove the layer of dry blood that covered her face and hair.

She opened her shirt and began hastily to wash her body. The pain she felt each time she splashed water on her body, reminded her of all the torture she had to endure. She could barely lift her arms without wincing.

"Are you OK?" she heard the voice of the man in the white coat. She turned her head, and saw him standing next to her, a tube of ointment in his hand. "Come, I want to rub this on the open wounds… or maybe you prefer to do it yourself."

Without a word, she took the tube from his hand and tried to read what was written on it. She gave up as she realized it was in Farsi. She walked to the mirror, quickly opened the tube, and began to rub her face with the white cream. The contact of the cream caused her to moan in pain.

"It hurts?" asked the man. The soft tone of his voice made her feel safe. She nodded.

"What cream is it?" she asked. He approached her with another tube. She looked at him, curious.

"Aloe Vera. It's a good disinfectant and will make you feel better. Come here, please. Let me see you."

"Are you really a doctor?" Stephanie asked, allowing the man to rub her aching body with a greenish ointment. The man nodded and smiled as he rubbed the cream on her wrists, covering the deep wounds from the handcuffs.

"You lost lots of fluids and your iron level is low. I will give you something to strengthen you. I hope it helps."

# 14

Stephanie woke up to the noise of the opening of the iron door in the small cell where she was sleeping. She felt much better after the rest, with the help of the doctor.

"Get up," called a male voice. Stephanie was growing tired of this routine. With an effort, she rose to a sitting position, her eyes on the tall man with a black beard standing in the doorway. "Get up, follow me," he raised his voice and at the same time put his hand on the gun secured at the belt of his jeans.

Stephanie got up from the cold mattress and moved heavily towards the door, surprised to realize that, despite the strong pain, her legs were stable. She didn't know for how long they let her sleep, but it was enough to fill her with renewed energy.

No doubt that also the meal she had, after the doctor's treatment, helped her to gain strength. She was not at all surprised when she realized that the examiner's promises that a special meal will be prepared for her soon after signing the document, had no real basis. Instead of that festive meal she had imagined, she was given a tin bowl with a brownish-black brew of some potatoes and beans. Stephanie looked in disgust at the brew. The smell from the bowl put her off and she made do with the four slices of stale bread lying next to the bowl. As unappetizing as the food appeared, the hunger overcame her, and she quickly swallowed the bread slices.

"Still, I suggest you eat," the man in the white coat had told her. The compassionate look in his eyes gave Stephanie some comfort. "If you want to survive you must put something in your stomach," he said quietly. "I can assure you that you won't die from it. It may look disgusting, but if you ignore the smell, eventually it's edible." The voice of the man with the black beard stirred her from her thoughts. "Come," he said aloud, and stepped aside to let her through the door. "Come on," he hissed at her as she walked by with her head bowed. "Come on! Here."

Stephanie walked slowly along the narrow, stretching hallway, feeling the pain cutting her lower body. No one else was in the hallway and she could hear the footsteps of the man with the black beard walking behind her. Her attempts to estimate the time of day were unsuccessful. The lights that were on all over caused her to lose track of time, and therefore, she had no idea of the hour or even if it was day or night.

She was surprised that for the first time, they let her leave the cell without being blindfolded, and with her hands and feet no longer cuffed – something that gave her hope. Even her medical treatment – although negligible – seemed a good sign.

But then, she started to think of the document she had signed without having any idea what was written on it. She remembered her father's words from earlier, warning her not to sign anything, not to confess to anything. The thought that it may have contained false information in order to incriminate her, made her shudder. What if she indeed had signed a statement that she was sent to Iran under a forged passport to spy, whether on behalf of the CIA or the Israeli Mossad?

The idea of spending years in prison, maybe her whole life, horrified her. She could not erase the terrifying scenario from her mind.

"Stop immediately!" called her escort from behind. She froze on the spot. The tall man with the black beard bypassed her quickly, and knocked on the door. The door opened and a short, bald man of about sixty showed up at the doorway. Stephanie noticed that the dark suit he was wearing was several sizes too big.

Her escort pushed her into the room. "Get in," he ordered. It was another interrogation room. She remained standing, her head bowed and her hands crossed over her chest, dreading what would come next. "Sit down, Stephanie," the man in the suit ordered her. A smile flashed briefly across his face. "I have a few questions for you, and I expect you will answer straightforward. This way, we'll avoid any inconveniences for both of us. I hope you understand what I mean."

Stephanie nodded obediently.

"What's your name?"

"Stephanie Simmons."

"What's your father's name?"

"Amir Motaki."

The man paused and then stared long and hard at Stephanie. "Where is your mother living?"

Stephanie rushed to respond. "San Francisco."

"What is her job?"

"My mother works in a jewelry store."

"How old are you?"

"I'm thirty-three," she answered.

"Where were you born?"

"In New York."

"How did you enter Iran?"

Stephanie paused. "Under a forged passport with the name of Regine Damir."

"Are you here on a private visit or on duty?"

"On a private visit," she said in a choked voice. "I know that I was not supposed to come as I did. I'm sorry. I know I made a mistake." Her throat was dry and she could barely speak. She coughed slightly. "I'm sorry," she whispered. "Can I have some water?"

Unfazed, the man turned and left the room, leaving Stephanie was left sitting on the chair. The fact that she wasn't blindfolded allowed her to review the room, which she noticed had no windows but only an iron door. Her eyes paused on the table next to her. *Was this the table where they abused me?* Her mind started to panic.

The reappearance of the man in the suit interrupted her thoughts. He walked to the table and placed the glass of water on the table. She reached out for it and drank a long sip, then stared at the man who was now standing over her. His cool tone filled her with great concern. He sat down next to her, gazing upon her with his black eyes. A moment later, he pulled out a thin brown file from one of the table drawers. He browsed through the document inside.

"Very interesting," he murmured. "I'm glad to see that you have cooperated with us," he said smiling. "It saves all of us from pleasantries. Eventually the truth comes out, in one way or another, right?" Stephanie remained seated in silence, her eyes fixed on the examiner's face. As the examiner lifted his eyes from the documents, she looked away. He pulled out one document and put it on the table between them.

"Is this your confession?" he asked. "Do you recognize your signature?"

"I signed the document, not knowing what's in it," she

said with downcast eyes. "This document is written in Farsi and I don't understand the language…I asked the examiner to get a translation."

"I don't understand what you are talking about," he said smiling, quickly drawing closer to her, the document in his hand. "This document is in English, the one you signed. How can you say you didn't understand what you signed? Are you trying to make fun of me?"

Her eyes darted quickly over the English writing. "I've never seen this document," she hissed between her lips. "I never signed a document in English." She managed to read only the first two lines: "I, Stephanie Simmons, am signing on my own free will, this confession, and I confirm that it is right…" She felt her blood start to boil. "I never signed this. I never even saw this," she said desperately. "I begged to get a translation… she explained to me that there was no one to translate it. She promised I would get a translation in the morning. I swear to you I have never seen this."

The man stared at her. "Slowly, slowly…you are too excited. You may not remember, but you will notice, there are two signatures, one on the Farsi document and one on the translation. How do you explain that?" he asked. "I am sure you were confused. You probably forgot." The sentences on the document bounced in front of her eyes one by one. She was shocked as she read the following words:

"I entered the Islamic Republic of Iran on a forged passport under the name of Regine Damir. The passport had been issued for me in the United States by the CIA, the Central Intelligence Agency of the United States. The purpose of my visit was to hire two academics whose families are connected to the construction of nuclear energy plants."

Angered, Stephanie pushed aside the document. "I didn't sign this document. I would never sign such a document. Everything here is a lie! The only thing that's true is that I entered Iran with a passport that had someone else's name." She spoke with a desperate sort of certainty, with hopes to minimize her wrongdoing.

"That's not what we were told," said the man, quietly. "We have a signed statement that confirms you have offered people the chance to work for the CIA."

"It's a lie!" she stammered.

The man opened the file and pulled out several documents and pictures. "Do you recognize the people in the pictures? Look at this one here. You look like a couple in love."

"It's Ali, my boyfriend," she answered.

"That's what we thought… and this is Ali Hijazi's statement. 'I declare that Stephanie Simmons suggested that I give her information to one of my cousins, who works at the Institute for Nuclear Energy in Isfahan, and in return, she will help me, through her connections with U.S. Immigration, to get me American citizenship.'"

"It's impossible…it's not true…" Stephanie whispered unable to hold back her tears. "Ali and I were supposed to get married. I don't believe he would say anything like that… Ali is not a liar. This can't be happening."

Calmly, the man collected the document from the table and returned it to the file he was holding. Then, he pulled out another document and placed it on the table. "And here we have a signed statement by Tahara and Zaher Motaki. You know who they are, right?"

"Yes," she answered quickly.

"We know that you stayed with them you entire visit."

Stephanie sat frozen. She nodded. The man slowly returned everything to the file.

"As you realize, even without your confession, we have enough people who will testify that you tried to recruit them to betray our country.

"I don't believe it," Stephanie snapped. "I don't understand how any of this can be true."

"Let me help you understand," he grinned. "Here is the statement Tahara wrote." He held it out in front of her. Stephanie didn't move. "Ok, then I will read it to you. 'I didn't know that she had chosen to enter Iran with a fake passport and if I knew, without any doubt I would have rushed immediately to inform the authorities…it's a very serious offense.' Is this a false statement, too?" he snickered.

Stephanie remained seated, her head bowed. She realized that the optimistic scenario she had made up of a quick release, was fading fast. Suddenly she became dizzy, and everything blacked out. She fell on the floor. Someone poured water on her face.

"Wake up," she heard the voice of the man. "I have some more to share with you from Ali's statement." He began to read. "'Stephanie bragged about the good life she has in the United States, and she criticized sharply the regime of the Islamic Republic. She is the one who asked to join me on the visit to my family in Isfahan. Later, she tried to convince me to take her for more trips. She told me that she went on a trip to Qum with her father, Colonel Motaki, and because of his connections, she was able to go to areas that were normally restricted for tourists. She told me she took a lot of interesting pictures.'"

He looked at Stephanie. "Are you OK?" The man seemed to be taunting her. "You are very pale. Do you want water?" He quickly opened the door. "Salim!" she heard his roaring voice. "Please bring a pitcher of water. Quick."

A couple of minutes later the pitcher of water was on the table.

"Here. Drink," said the man. "You are very excited by what your boyfriend says of you. I can imagine it's not pleasant to hear. Shall I continue?" Without waiting he continued to read.

"'She told me that she had come on a mission for the CIA and suggested that I cooperate. In exchange for the information I give, she said I will get a monthly payment that will be transferred to me by a German computer company as a consultant salary, in addition to my American citizenship.'"

"I cannot believe Ali signed a statement like that," Stephanie responded bitterly.

"Here." He flashed her the document. "You can see it. Here is his signature. If you still have doubts, we can watch his video statement. Or if you insist, I can bring him in."

"Bring him. Yes. Please. I need to see him and hear this directly from him."

"As you wish," he sighed. "Do you also want Amir Motaki or maybe Tahara to come in? Whatever you want." The man put the file on his lap. "Actually, I was going to offer you something that could get you released. But I see that you are stubborn and there is no use in going on." He got up, the file under his arm, and continued in a firm voice, "I suppose you would rather stay here. Perhaps you like your male visitors. It makes me wonder what you are more of: stupid, silly, or stubborn." He turned to leave.

"Wait," she called out. He stopped. Stephanie sat there, mulling over her options. After a few more seconds she asked, "Please. Don't bring them back. Just tell me what I need to do to be out of here."

The man approached the table. He laid down the file and sat on the chair. Stephanie raised her head and their eyes met. "Listen to me," he began. "There is a lot of tension not only between Iran and the United States, but also between Iran and most of the European countries. You know, the nuclear program, the sanctions."

Stephanie moved uncomfortably in her seat, trying to guess where his words were leading.

"If you say that I told you this, I'll deny it. But I believe that you have no connection with the CIA and you had no intention to spy for the Americans on your visit to Iran. I'm the only one who believes and knows exactly why you are here." She let out a small, hopeful sigh. He continued.

"I tell you these things personally. I know exactly how you signed your statement, and I know how they edited the video cassette where you are seen signing the document. But that doesn't mean that we will not use your confession. Your arrest 'fell' at the right time. I mean that in this situation you are a very welcomed asset for us- a bargaining chip. No misunderstandings; we will definitely play the card that is Stephanie Simmons." The man took a deep breath. "You see, we have multiple confessions, and an incriminating video. This is more than enough for us. As far as we are concerned, you are a spy. You shall be put on trial without a lawyer, and without being allowed to say one word. According to Iranian law, the best you can hope for is life in prison. The worst: the death penalty by hanging."

Stephanie felt her throat turn dry and sore.

"I want you to listen carefully. In three days, we are to execute by hanging seven people who have confessed to spying for the Great Satan, United States, and the Small Satan, Israel. The execution is according to the president ruling. The hanging ceremony will be held in Teheran, in the main square, Ayatollah Ruhollah Khomeini. If you do not cooperate, you will be the eighth."

"What do you want from me?" she whispered. The man took his chair and pulled it near hers.

"Good question…" He paused, and then immediately continued. "If you will cooperate, I can promise you that within two, three weeks at the most, you will board a plane and leave Iran. Moreover, I promise you that if you cooperate, from now until your flight back, you will stay in a hotel and get an accommodation unlike the one you've experienced: a hot shower, good food, and sleep in a real, comfortable bed…"

"What exactly do you want from me?" she asked desperately.

"All we want is to expedite the proceedings. We would like you to appear in a video. We will give you a list that you will read. You will specify the names of several CIA agents who are spies working in our area, including that same 'Blondie,' whom you met in Santa Monica. You will also specify how exactly they have recruited you."

Stephanie felt a bolt of electricity run through her. "Blondie? How do you know about him?" She was shocked by how much information they had on her. She tried to change the subject. "Please believe me. The CIA never recruited me. Never!"

The man lost his patience. He stood up and collected quickly the file on the table. "I really tried to help you, but if this is the choice you are going to make, you will have to deal with the consequences."

Stephanie remained seated, motionless unable to answer.

"Think" she heard his voice, "Think carefully of what I have suggested to you. It all depends on you. From what I heard, those men will be happy to have another go at you." Stephanie stared at him, silently, knowing that any decision she made at this point would be a bad one for her.

"Stephanie… you are really silly." The man walked away, leaving her behind.

When she opened her eyes, she found herself standing

naked, her face some feet from the brick wall. Her hands were chained from the ceiling and her feet were handcuffed to the floor.

She couldn't remember how she got to her present condition. The last thing she could remember was the man's sentence "Stephanie… you are really silly." She could see the look of disappointment on his face as he left the room, slamming the door behind him. She did recall feeling a pair of hands hold her arms and then cover her face with a bag smelling of oil, and then everything went black.

Now, helpless, Stephanie closed her eyes as little by little, an intense pain swept her back, wrapping her body. Each minute felt like an eternity. Her desperate attempts to find a position allowing some rest to her aching back failed. The fear that her captors had forgotten her increased as the minutes passed without being able to assess them. She couldn't bear any longer the growing pain. She began to think about the deal she had been offered.

"Help," she screamed with her remaining strength, unable to withstand the intense pain that swept her, wave after wave. "Please…help… Anyone? Help!"

The pain took over her body, and the overwhelming smell of the oil bag outweighed her remaining ounce of energy as she passed out again.

She reawakened as cold water washed her whole body. Seconds later, she came back to her senses. The bag and chains had been removed, and she could finally breathe again. She found herself lying on a mattress, wearing a brown shirt and pants. She slowly opened her eyes and was somewhat relieved when she saw the man in the white coat, the jail doctor, watching her. He held in one hand a glass of water and two pills in the other one. "You have lost a lot of fluid. Here, swallow these. It will ease the pain."

The door opened and there stood the bald man in the

black suit, the same one who had tried to persuade Stephanie to admit to being a spy. The two men exchanged a few words in Farsi.

"Come on, take the pills," said the doctor.

With effort, Stephanie got up, took the glass of water and swallowed the pills. She suspected they were not painkillers, but she understood it was pointless to worry about it.

"Come," said the doctor, and he pulled her to her feet. "Try to clean yourself up a little bit. Here, you have a mirror, a comb and some makeup. We want you to look as good as possible, so we don't worry anyone in your family."

She dragged herself to the small sink. She gasped when she saw her reflection in the mirror. She couldn't believe how mangled her face looked. Black and red blood stains were still smeared over her face, her eyes were red, and her lower lip was swollen. She reached for the comb lying on the rim of the sink and began combing her hair. It took a while before she could easily run it through.

"Come on, it's not a beauty parlor here," she suddenly heard the voice of the bald man say. "You have to hurry."

"Right away," she whispered and turned on the water tap. "I want to fix myself a bit more, please."

Stephanie washed her face. For a moment, she considered using the makeup but changed her mind, fearing that it might contain chemicals that could affect her judgment. She took one last glance in the mirror. She couldn't remember the last time she saw her reflection. Finally, she turned towards the man in the suit. His black eyes were fixed on her.

"You are a beautiful woman," he said, and opened the room's door.

Stephanie found herself once again walking along the narrow hallway. She walked slowly, her eyes scanning the walls closing in and the locked doors. This time, too, there was no one around.

"Stop," she heard the man's voice behind her. He rushed past her and opened one of the doors. "Come here," he blurted out. Just then she noticed he was holding a brown folder. They entered the room.

"Sit down," he ordered, and gestured at one of the chairs. "Come on, we don't have all day," he yelled. Stephanie sat down heavily, watching the tall man seated in front of her. Quickly, he pulled out a document from the brown folder.

"Here is something we have prepared which reflects your confession," he said quietly. "I want you to review it now."

Stephanie took the paper. She quietly read the document out loud and was filled with dread. "My name is Stephanie Simmons, a resident of Los Angeles and an American citizen. I am in good health and getting fair treatment. I am here on my own free will and my own initiative to clarify a few things…"

Stephanie took a deep breath and kept reading the document. "I confess to entering Iran under a forged passport using the name Regine Damir, on a CIA mission." She took another deep breath and read on. "I was sent to Iran to recruit local academics and create an intelligence network. During my stay in Teheran, I was in contact with several people and I tried to persuade them to cooperate with me. Among those I managed to convince were a school teacher, Ali Hijazi, and a high ranking police officer, Amir Motaki."

She choked. She felt anger and rage boiling up inside of her upon reading the last sentence concerning her boyfriend and father. Despite the pains and confusion, she realized that it was a clear-cut implication of the people she loves, and she knew they would pay with their lives.

"It's not true," she said between her gripping teeth. "I cannot say that. I cannot do that to my father."

The bald man quickly pulled the document from her hand. His black eyes were furious. "I thought you learned your lesson," he growled. "I see you need a few more hours to realize you have no other choice." Stephanie watched the man get up from his chair and nervously shove the paper into the brown folder. "If that's what you want, it's what you'll get. If you think you can play with me, then you are mistaken, very badly mistaken."

"I am willing to say anything about the truth," she pleaded, "but please not this. I cannot do this to my father… Please." The man didn't even turn his head. He walked quickly to the door and opened it. "Wait, wait…a minute please," she begged. The man stopped, one hand on the door knob. He turned his head towards her. Stephanie couldn't carry on any longer, unable to bear anymore of the humiliation or the pain. She bowed her head and murmured softly. "Ok, ok. I'll do it. I'll say whatever you want." Then she burst into a bitter cry.

# 15

Curled up in pain, Stephanie lay on the new, clean, comfortable mattress. She had just finished her bowl of soup that had been her reward for her cooperation. Stephanie would have never imagined herself being able to betray the people she loved, the family that took her in with no questions asked, even knowing the danger of the circumstances. However, the pain and the humiliation exhausted her to the point of giving in.

She recalled she had never paid much attention to that conversation with Kevin Shepard, when he had told her in confidence of the investigation the FBI was conducting in the passports division, on suspicion that one of the employees had illegally issued working permits and passports to a group of Islamic extremists.

She was furious at herself. She thought, *how could I forge a passport, knowing of the ongoing investigation? How could I think I knew better than my mother and the "Blondie" from the CIA?*

She realized that her father would be hurt as well as his family. She had no doubt that the incident would endanger her mother's life. *What a fool I am,* she thought angrily. *God, how could I be like that? Why? What exactly did I want to prove that*

*I am…smart? Stubborn? Or just audacious? It's me, Stephanie Simmons, the same one who had never thought to copy an exam in school, and here I find myself lying to my mother, underestimating a federal agent, and forging a passport, all while taking the risk to get involved with the American authorities. What kind of vicious bug got into me?!*

*I remember how happy I was when I first got married. So young and hopeful. Then Tom died, and my lover Yasser left me, and life became dull. But I got into a pretty relaxed track with work, friends, and despite the disappointment of being unable to make it into Hollywood, by all accounts my life was peaceful then.* The idea that this was all her fault became too much to bare.

Stephanie began to find relief searching for someone else to blame. It was the only way she could cope with her guilt. First she blamed her mother, who hadn't had the nerves to tell her about her past. Then, Kevin Shepard, who had suggested she work at the Department of Immigration, Professor Yasser Ashraf, who hadn't warned her, and even her father, who hadn't made sure she'd leave Iran on time. Stephanie wasn't satisfied to only blame her family, and decided that also the taxi driver who drove her to the airport, in Los Angeles, was guilty. If the driver had been late for the flight due to traffic jams, or if he would have been involved in a traffic accident, she might have been spared all she was undergoing now. She didn't even spare the pilot, who had taken off to Germany on time. Her all-consuming thoughts were interrupted by the opening of the cell door.

"Get up," she heard a man's voice above her. She looked up and saw a security man with a black beard who she had never seen before. He stood on top of her with his legs apart, staring at her torn shirt from which part of her breast was visible. Stephanie hurried to pull it up and cover herself.

"Get up," he ordered her again. He said a few sentences

in Farsi, which she didn't understand, and then he grabbed her arm. Stephanie stood on her feet. Despite the pain all over her body, she was glad to find out that she had regained some strength as a result of the hours of sleep and the meal she was given.

"Where are you taking me?" Stephanie asked, "Where?"

Stephanie began walking down the narrow, whitewashed corridor. The memory of the previous events rose to her mind and a sense of rage started to shake her. She couldn't accept the fact that she had agreed to her captors will and worst of all, incriminated her father.

From an invisible opening at the end of the corridor, three men suddenly appeared in front of her. Two of them were wearing jeans and black shirts, and guns stuck out from their trousers. The third man, the tallest of the group, in black pants, white shirt and a black vest, walked briskly at the head.

As they approached her, Stephanie felt an acute pain in her stomach. She again felt a sense of helplessness and her throat choked up. The two men in jeans held her, facing the corridor wall. They handcuffed her and covered her eyes with a large head scarf. She panicked. The hands holding her pulled her, and one of the men said in English, "Come on, hurry…you are coming with us."

Her legs struggled to carry her body. Had it not been for the strong arms holding her tightly, she would have collapsed on the floor. Now, as she was being dragged down the narrow hallway, she was shaking with the fear of going through more torture and humiliation. She couldn't bear the thought of having been so naïve as to believe her captors would release her within a few days.

"This way," ordered one of the men holding her. "Careful, there is a step." A few seconds later, she heard the squeak of a door. "It's okay," the same man said, "we are outside the building. Soon, it will be over."

Stephanie's heartbeat intensified. She was going to be executed. Stephanie stiffened and her legs didn't respond. "Sit down," ordered one of the men. Stephanie let her body slump. The slamming of the door and the roar of the engine signified that she was now in a car. She felt herself shaking. Where are they taking me?

Someone released her from the handcuffs and removed the blindfold from her eyes. She was in the back seat of a car, between the two men in jeans and black shirts. The blue-eyed man, sitting in the front seat next to the driver, turned around to address her. He smiled at her.

"I hope you are all right."

She didn't answer. After days of not seeing daylight, the streets of Teheran seemed to her the most charming on Earth.

"Stephanie," the man in front said, "Relax. You are in good hands now. My mission is to get you out of here and back home to America."

Stephanie stared at him, barely able to comprehend what she had just heard. She couldn't find any words to speak due to her shock, but hearing the word "home" was all it took to get her heart beating rapidly. At that moment, after many days, she smiled.

"My name is Mahmoud Srkaawi. I know your mother and father have mentioned my name before." Stephanie's hands began to shake with happiness. She, indeed, remembered his name. Her mother had mentioned it when she told Stephanie the story of how he helped her to leave Iran when Khomeini raised to power. She also remembered her mother and father saying that Mahmoud Srkaawi still had a high ranking position in one of the elite units of the Iranian central intelligence.

She nodded. At first, she couldn't believe what she was

hearing. She feared it was another scheme by the examiners, but this time she didn't mind if it was true or not...this time it was worthwhile to think positively, even if it was just a lie she was being told. "If this is really who you are, then yes, yes I heard a lot about you," she answered smiling. "Thank you, thank you. Thanks. You have no idea the hell I went through…"

"I'm sorry I couldn't come earlier," Mahmoud apologized.

"What's happening with my father? How is my family?"

"They are all fine," the man assured her. Stephanie wasn't willing to settle for a general answer.

"But I saw they arrested my father at the airport. Is he ok?" she asked.

"Yes. They arrested him after they arrested you. He was questioned and he confirmed that you are his daughter, but he denied he knew you had entered Iran with a forged passport. They released him within a few hours. Anyway, they suspended him from his job for now. I hope it all works out for the better. Let's hope... Inshallah."

The car drove into a side alley and stopped next to a three-story building. The two men sitting on both her sides rushed to jump out. One of them reached out for her. "Come on, Stephanie, we must hurry. Every moment is critical." Mahmoud was insistent. Stephanie grabbed the outstretched hand of a security man and quickly got out of the car. Mahmoud was at her side. "Come, a pleasant surprise is waiting for you," he said.

When they got to the second floor, Mahmoud stopped in front of one of the doors. He knocked four quick times on the door, and waited. The door opened and Amir was there. Stephanie rushed to him, threw her arms around his neck and hugged him.

"Father," she whispered excitedly, unable to stop the

tears, "I'm so glad to see you. I was afraid I would never see you again."

"I'm glad to see you, too. We were so worried. Did they hurt you? What did they do to you, my daughter?"

Stephanie shrugged. "I'm fine," she murmured, not wanting to talk about what had happened to her in jail. She was offered bottled water and a cheese sandwich. Stephanie noticed that her father wasn't wearing the police uniform he liked so much. The man who was so careful of his appearance was unshaven. And the confidence and self-esteem were gone, replaced by a look of anquish and exhaustion.

"How are Dalram and the girls? I was afraid that something would happen to them because of me. You have no idea how worried I was about you all."

"Everybody is fine, Stephanie," he said, overcome by emotion. "We'll be fine. It's essential that you leave Iran as soon as possible. Right now."

"Wait, I don't understand. I'm not free? They promised me—"

A look of hate showed on her father's face. "Do you still believe in their promises?" he snapped at her. "Without Mahmoud, who was willing to risk his life, you wouldn't be alive."

"I don't understand."

Amir's voice roared. "If not for Mahmoud, who heard this morning of the intent to hang you in Teheran's main square, you wouldn't be here right now. They said they had a confession that you are a spy and would execute you by hanging. Without a trial or anything." Stephanie was stunned.

"It was a direct order from the president," added Mahmoud. "He was furious after earlier this week a special unit of Marines, who were still in Iraq unofficially, killed a cell of Iranian intelligence agents. It turned out that one of the members of the cell was a relative of the president. In revenge, he ordered to hang you and seven other spies in a few hours."

Stephanie sat, slumped, her heart beating wildly and breathing heavily. It was explained that without her knowledge, she was part of a secret Iranian plan called "twenty-fifty." According to the plan, as her father told her, the Iranians had the intent until 2020 to recruit for intelligence purposes, fifty American citizens of Iranian origin with sensitive positions in the American government and economy.

"I'm just a clerk in the Department of Immigration," Stephanie responded.

Mahmoud smiled. "But you deal with entry permits and the issuing of passports. And to this we must add, of course, the unusual relationship with your boss, Mr. Shepard."

Stephanie was dumbfounded. "Shepard? How do they know about Shepard?"

"They know everything about you, Stephanie," Mahmoud explained. "They are professionals, extremely thorough. At the request of your father, I read your personal file. You even have a code name, 'Queen of the West 028.' They also knew of your relationship with Professor Yasser Ashraf, who was one of them. But at the last moment, he changed his mind and firmly refused to recruit you. He really loved you and paid for it with his life."

"Yasser? He was one of them? They killed him?" Stephanie was shaking now.

"Yes. Yasser had a very senior position in the organization, the *Basij*, maybe the most senior on the American West coast."

"I can't believe it…Yasser Ashraf, that plump and bespectacled professor of mine…was an Iranian spy? What's happen to his baby and the rest of the family?"

Mahmoud was aware of the intimate relationship between her and the Professor. He noticed her eyes restlessly running from side to side. He added, "Stephanie, Yasser Ashraf, was married with a woman who lives in Teheran, they have no children. During his time in America as a professor, he succeeded in tasks of first priority on behalf of the Iranian Intelligence, but this one time he chose not to complete his mission. He didn't agree to recruit you, and for that he paid with his life."

"I cannot believe it. I thought that what I went through till now, was more than enough…" She mulled this information over while looking with downcast eyes at her father who stood somber aside.

"We have to hurry," her father urged her. "If they catch you, they'll torture you to death. They have the Army and the Revolutionary Guards looking for you. Mahmoud arranged for you an escape route."

Mahmoud announced, "We will take advantage of the Shiite pilgrimage to the holy sites in Iraq. My friend, Radek, will take you by train to the town of Karmanshah. From there, you'll proceed to Iraq, to Karbala and then to an American Army base." Mahmoud opened the door. A man entered the room, carrying a bag. He looked to Stephanie like a Shiite cleric.

"Meet your husband," said Mahmoud. "His name is Radek. You'll do everything he tells you. Do not say a word. He knows exactly what to do." Stephanie looked at him skeptically. Radek was about fifty years old, of medium height, slender and a black beard adorned his lean face. This was the man she was going to trust with her life? As if reading her thoughts, Mahmoud continued, "You can trust him one hundred per cent. For many years, this man was the number one intelligence man in Iran. Don't be misled by his external appearance. He can kill with his bare hands."

Mahmoud took the bag from Radek's hand and gave it to Stephanie. "It's a *chador*. I want you to remove any clothing that might reveal your identity. You can leave only the underwear."

Stephanie didn't say a word but only nodded, looking back to her father, who nodded back his approval of the plan. "We were able to get for you an identity card on the name of Fatwa Haamiz," Mahmoud emphasized. "Remember the name: Fatwa Haamiz. Radek is listed as your husband. His identity card says he is married to you."

Stephanie took the bag from Mahmoud and headed to a bathroom. She closed the door behind and began to remove her ragged clothes, a reminder of her stay in jail. She shuddered from the memories and then drove them from her mind. When she returned and stood in front of the three men, she was wearing a chador and faded sneakers at her feet.

"Make sure only your eyes are visible," her father told her. "It's important that not even one hair emerges. You must be focused. You cannot make any mistake. Even a small one might cost your life."

Stephanie moved to her father and hugged him. "I'm sorry I caused all this," she murmured softly. "Father, I put you at risk. I couldn't hold on, because of their torture methods." Her choked voice trailed off.

Amir embraced her and kissed her head. "I know their torture methods from my own experience. Anyone would have admitted crimes he didn't commit much earlier than you. You were very strong. Your family loves you."

Stephanie laid her head on her father's chest. "And what will happen to you, father? What they will do to you?"

"*Inshallah*, it will be okay. I hope our future will be better."

"But how they will react when they know I escaped? What they will do to you all?"

"Stephanie, it would be insane for them to deal with me. As you know, I was arrested soon after you and your mother escaped…even then everyone believed I had no chance to stay alive. At first, the investigators didn't believe you were on the plane that crashed, then they said that I am part of the same British mole…after a month of tough investigations, to say the least, suddenly they released me, and more than that they sent me back to work in the police. And they have a reason, Stephanie. I hold intelligence material very sensitive and confidential related to the Iranian strategy. The material I was exposed to is like a "ticking bomb." If such information reaches the media it will compromise them with their allies: Russia, China, and North Korea… they are scared. They know that if something happens to me, someone will take care to disclose the "doomsday weapon" that will implicate them in such a way they will never recover, and the Islamic Republic will collapse like a banana republic"

Stephanie was stunned. "Wow, Dad. That explains a lot of things. Maybe the time has come to take action and save the millions of Iranians from the jaws holding them every day. Father, with such a move you can give hope and a bright future to most of the moderate people."

"No. It's not the right time for war…I will choose the timing," Amir replied vehemently. Amir Motaki tried to convey calm and confidence to his daughter so she could go on her way safely, free of concern for them, and added: "This information has been revealed to very few people. The Ayatollahs, in the name of Allah, will sell their mother for those religious interests. Anyway, I don't want to pursue the subject. At the moment, your exposure to this matter is just pointless. Your failure to escape Iran will cause a major catastrophe to our family, the whole family. Stephanie, you must be careful and alerted, there is no room for mistakes. You have learned how cruel they can be. I don't want to even think what may happen if…"

"I will be fine, father. Don't worry," Stephanie assured him. "After all, I am your daughter, and now your's and Mother's genes are giving me strength, I am stronger than ever. No way will I be caught or go back to prison."

He took her hand and looked at her. He felt the pain and suffering she had gone through in jail, and bowed his head. "Damn them and their world," Amir snapped. His voice was calm, but he was obviously very angry. "They are not human beings… they are beasts… animals."

Mahmoud interrupted their moment together. "We have no time. Every second counts. Stephanie, you won't say a word. Your husband Radek will talk to you only in Farsi, and you will nod. You will act as a submissive Muslim woman. Make sure to keep your head always down, and don't look straight ahead. You will not do anything by yourself, unless Radek tells you."

A nervous voice came through the radio hidden in the pocket of Mahmoud. Stephanie felt like something was happening, and she was right.

"You have to go now, Stephanie," her father said, softly. "We may meet again in the future. Who knows what will happen." Her father hugged her tightly.

Mahmoud looked tense. "The guys in the car say there is a growing movement of military personnel. They are probably looking for you."

"Dad, I love you. I'm glad I came. I'm glad we got to meet, even if it's only this once."

Amir shed a tear, held her firmly with both hands, kissed her forehead, looked right into her eyes, and said in a strangled voice, "My treasure, go in peace and may God be with you." Something about the way he had spoken, so deliberately, so focused, made every hair on Stephanie's body stand up, and this feeling grew in the pit of her stomach. She felt as if he was trying to tell her something bigger

Suddenly, a barrage of fire sounded outside the building. Everyone in the room fell silent, exchanging glances. A voice in Farsi gushed from the radio. Mahmoud said something in the speaker and hid it back in the pocket of his pants. His expression didn't hide the tension he was feeling.

"We need to move as quickly as possible," he said. "Fighters of the Basij of the Revolutionary Guard are in the area. Stephanie and Radek, go first and soon after, we will leave. We must not be found here. Go, Radek. Now."

In fluent English and a calm voice Radek told her, "Come, don't panic. Remember: Whatever happens, in any event, you don't stop. A car is waiting for us close to the rear exit door... don't worry, it will be OK. Come." Mahmoud Srkaawilranian approached the man with the black beard. "I trust you Radek... do exactly what I ordered you and everything will be all right... do you remember all?"

Radek nodded. "We will be all right. I'll take care of her."

"The most important thing is not to stand out. Try to mix with other people. I count on you, brother. I trust you with a precious treasure. I will never forget what you are doing. Come on, go... get out from the back, through the emergency stairway."

Again a barrage of fire. Stephanie suppressed a cry of fear and tightened her grip on Radek's hand. Seconds later, she found herself hurrying down the emergency stairs in the back of the building, holding Radek's hand tightly.

"Don't stop," he said. "We are on the ground floor. We're almost there." They burst through a door and quickly got into a car waiting for them. Stephanie looked back, trying to locate the source of firing. To her surprise, the alley was empty, except for an elderly man in a white galabya sitting at the entrance of one of the buildings.

She heard Radek's voice: "On the floor, face down. Quick."

Stephanie slid silently to the bottom of the car, curling into a tight ball in the space behind the driver's seat. The car tore down the alley and into traffic.

Stephanie sat terrified on the speeding train, staring out of the window and repeating to herself the name on her new identity card, Fatwa Haamiza. From time to time, with her hand, she checked that the head scarf, which almost covered her entire face, was in place. Radek, who was sitting next to her, had placed a pillow under the chador, which gave the impression of advanced pregnancy.

The hustle in the train coach was great. A multitude of men, women, and children filled the narrow place. A heavyset woman sat in front of her, clad in a black *chador*, regularly scolding her four children, who spoke loudly and had trouble staying still. The heavy woman turned to a man in a black suit, sitting across from her, next to Radek. The man got up and in a squeaky voice scolded the children, while waving both hands. The children went quiet for a few moments, but soon enough, they went back to their mischief and their noises again filled the heavily crowded coach.

Five young men added to the clamor. They stood in the corridor and didn't stop chattering loudly, trying to overcome the train noise. From time to time, they burst out laughing, drawing the attention of all. Stephanie couldn't ignore the stares of some of these young men.

A tall man with green eyes, standing near, was particularly staring, and she caught him multiple times looking over at her. The fact that she was with a man, and all the signs indicated she was a married woman with child, didn't prevent the young man from staring at her lustily.

Stephanie met his eyes only once but she could have sworn he had a little smile at the corner of his mouth. Faithful to her given instructions, she focused on the landscape outside. Her thoughts were on the uneasy situation she was in. She had no doubt that if caught, the Iranian authorities would not hesitate for a moment to execute her.

In her mind, she saw herself being brought to Teheran's main square, her hands and feet handcuffed, a bag over her head. She imagined the huge roar from the crowd filling the square. She could see the scaffold and the noose swaying at the top. She shivered at the thought that, while she sat on the train, seven people accused of spying would be led to the gallows.

Then, Stephanie thought of her father and his friend Mahmoud. What happened to them after she had left the hideout apartment on the outskirts of Teheran? Were they able to flee without being harmed? The thought that her father might have been killed in a gunfight that broke out around the hideout building, while she managed to escape with Radek, made her ill. Even if her father was able to escape the place, what would happen to him next? And what about Dalram and the three girls? What kind of a life could they expect?

Tears flowed from Stephanie's eyes at the thought that the Motaki family would have to renounce the secure and comfortable life they could only afford till now because of her father's rank as deputy chief of the city police. *Will they have to give up the large and spacious house? And what will happen to Taher's studies? And what will become of little Lilly? And will Zaher stay on at the hospital in her senior job? Will they all be considered traitors? And was there really some secret information held by her father that could really help them? Or did he just tell a story to reassure me?*

Then, suddenly, the train came to a screeching halt, and there was commotion among the passengers. Three of the young men standing in the passageway fell at the sudden stop. Cries of "Allah Akbar" erupted from all corners of the coach. Radek read her thoughts. He glanced at her, shook his head slightly and gently laid his hand on her arm. Stephanie understood he was asking her to remain seated at her place, and exercise restraint.

The young man with green eyes, who during the journey had stolen many glances at Stephanie, walked to the window. He pulled it up and with the encouragement of his friends, leaned out. He looked right and left, withdrew his head and began talking to his friends. Even though she couldn't understand a word of what he was saying, she knew he was telling those present what he had seen. The group of young people got very excited at his words. She looked at Radek and was surprised to see he had his eyes closed.

Radek opened his eyes, leaned very close to her and whispered in her ear, "Stay calm. Don't talk. Even if they talk to you. Police and soldiers are searching the train." Stephanie's heart was beating wildly. She remained seated, petrified, her eyes searching the eyes of the people on the coach, desperate for some sign of reassurance that it would be ok. Loud shouts arose from the outside. By instinct, everyone in the compartment looked out the window.

Outside, Stephanie could see two chador-clad women marching side by side. Four policemen marched behind them carrying assault rifles. As the two women and the policemen walked away from the train, a booming voice came from inside. When Stephanie looked toward the compartment door, she saw security force men pushing their way through the passengers, waving guns in their hands.

One of the security men approached the man with the screechy voice in the black suit next to Radek. The man hurried to pull out some documents from the pocket of his pants. His hand slightly trembled as he handed them to the security.

Despite not understanding the conversation, Stephanie could gather from the man's gestures that he was introducing the security man to his family (his wife and four sons.) The security man examined the documents carefully, then returned them to their owner.

The security man turned to Radek, and in spite of the unbearable heat under the *chador*, Stephanie was bathed with cold sweat.

# 16

Stephanie was huddled in her seat, trying her best to breathe regularly. In spite of the emotional state she was in, she managed to keep a straight face. She didn't dare to lift her head and meet anyone's eyes, but that didn't prevent her from observing what was happening by using her peripherals.

Slowly, Radek reached under his black cloak and pulled out several documents that he handed to the security man who was standing pompously over him. Stephanie shut her eyes, her blood pounding through her temples. She squeezed her legs together, hoping no one would notice them tremble.

Long seconds elapsed (that to Stephanie seemed like an eternity) until she heard the voice of the security man. Soon after, she heard Radek's voice. Stephanie remained sitting, her head bowed and her eyes shut, trying, without success, to understand the conversation between the two men.

She felt a light touch on her left arm and was quick to open her eyes, but she didn't raise her head. She saw Radek rising from his seat. He said a few sentences in Farsi, and then Radek slowly followed after the security man. His hand gesture was enough for her to understand that she must stay seated. The heavy woman opposite Stephanie told her something in Farsi, looking sympathetic. Stephanie, not understanding but reading the woman's expression, quickly nodded.

For a split second, Stephanie had the idea to get up, leave the train, and try to blend into the crowd that was outside. She quickly realized it was a silly idea. It was evident that with only the identity card she had, she wouldn't go far, especially being unable to speak the language, and having no idea where she was in the country. Now, she wished she had surrendered to Lily's pleas to learn more Farsi.

Once more, her mind was flooded with horrific scenarios. First, she saw the prison cell and the interrogator who smelled of onions. Then, she visualized being led, hands and feet handcuffed, to the city square, on her way to be executed. Her father's face appeared in front of her, and soon after, her mother.

She looked outside and gasped when she saw Radek encircled by four security men. From his gestures, she understood he was trying to explain something to the group of armed men surrounding him. The security men moved off, taking Radek with them. Stephanie watched in shock as they left the train station.

The train began to move, gradually increasing its speed. Stunned and frightened, Stephanie didn't move, unable to grasp what was happening.

Where did they take Radek? Why did the security men choose not to arrest her? Who could she turn to now? Stephanie looked around the compartment, to see the reaction to the incident. As expected, the eyes of most of the passengers were fixed on her. The young man with green eyes, standing in the corridor, openly stared.

Stephanie considered the rest of the journey. She realized that she would not be able to get through without

Radek, and even if she was lucky enough to not be arrested during the ride, her chances of crossing the border into Iraq on her own were nonexistent. She decided she would get off at the next stop, hoping to get on a train traveling in the opposite direction, to return to Teheran. Perhaps, she could find help from her father, assuming her father was not in jail, or worse: dead.

The young man with green eyes made his way toward her. He sat down next to her and Stephanie felt his leg rubbing hers. She was quick to distance herself away from him by shifting towards the window. For a moment she considered getting up and sitting somewhere else, but decided it was better to stay and deal with the new situation rather than draw more attention to herself. She looked out at the window, keeping her back to the young man.

Her mind continued to race and plot. She reconsidered going to Teheran. If they were searching all over for her, she had a better chance of staying under the radar in the countryside. Stephanie felt a catch in the throat and tried to fight off the tears. They were slowly falling down her cheeks, so with her hand under the veil she hurried to wipe them off.

And then, almost like a seeing a mirage, she sat in disbelief as she saw Radek entering the compartment. Slowly, he made his way through the crowd toward her. The green-eyed youth next to her jumped up from his seat, as if he had been bitten by a snake. Radek took the seat beside her. She barely managed to suffocate a scream of joy that was rattling inside of her.

In spite of the noise of the train and the terror she had just been through, Stephanie fell asleep. She woke up as a hand slightly touched her shoulder. When she opened her eyes, she saw Radek standing over her and gesturing with a nod of his head to follow him. She had no idea how long she had slept nor where she was. Stephanie stood up and followed Radek past the group of youngsters standing in the aisle of the coach, their heads bowed. Even if she hadn't seen anything, she could feel the green eyes of the young man watching her. She walked quickly past two children sitting on the floor of the train near by the door, ignoring their cries.

Once off the train, she continued to walk slowly behind Radek. They exited the station, and were met by the noise and commotion of a town. Everything looked strange and threatening. As she slightly lifted her head, she noticed Radek a few steps ahead, waiting for her. Exhausted, she increased her pace and approached him.

"Are you okay?" he whispered.

"Yes, yes, just a bit hot. Where are we anyway?"

"In Kermanshah," Radek whispered in her ear. "We are not far from the border. But they've increased security at the border crossing. They know that during the holy pilgrimages, many try to leave the country illegally, mainly through the Kasser-Shirin crossing. Very dangerous."

Stephanie's face sank. Radek tried to cheer her up. "Don't worry. We have another plan. Here in Kermanshah, we have Kurdish friends, opponents of the Ayatollahs regime. At night, they will take us across the border by foot. We will get to Badara, a small village in Iraq not far from the Iranian border. There, a car will be waiting for us, and if all goes well, *Inshallah*, tomorrow morning we'll be in Baghdad."

"Why are we waiting? Isn't it dangerous to be out here in the daylight?"

"It is dangerous, but there is no choice," Radek spoke lowly, scanning the surroundings. "Our friends know we are coming. They're probably making sure Iranian security is not following us. They are very careful. They are certainly watching us right now. Don't worry."

Sure enough, a few minutes later, a blue van stopped close to them, raising a cloud of dust. Scared, Stephanie stepped back. A man with a mane of black hair stuck his head out of the window.

"Get into the car," Radek said urgently. Stephanie hesitated, eyeing the driver. "Quickly," he urged as he slid open the side door. Stephanie plunged into the back seat. Immediately, Radek joined her. The car jerked from side to side as it took off and Stephanie reached out to firmly hold the back of the seat in front of her. The driver turned back and Stephanie noticed a large scar on his face that made him look threatening. She could not understand the conversation between him and Radek.

"What's going on?" she asked.

The man with the scar smiled at her. "Everything fine," he answered in broken English. "It will be okay. You don't worry."

Stephanie wasn't assured. "What's going on?" she asked again, looking at Radek.

"Large forces of police and the Army are in the area. We did well not to cross the border by train. According to him, since early morning, more than a thousand people have been arrested, mostly smugglers and some drug dealers. There is a feeling of great tension all around."

Stephanie's eyes darted between the man with the scar and Radek. "So how long will it take to cross to Iraq?" she asked.

In his usual calm voice, Radek stated, "We are now going to a hideout where we'll wait until night. Then, we'll travel by car to Badra, and from there, we'll continue on foot. Like I said before, if all goes well, we'll get to Baghdad at first light."

The man with the scar added, "Everything under control. Don't worry. We have done this route dozens of times. Really, you can relax." The car left off the main road and turned onto a dirt path, leaving behind a trail of dust that penetrated the car. Stephanie quickly closed the window next to her and began to cough. Eventually, the car drove into a small courtyard alongside a two-story building. Two big men holding guns greeted them with waves of their hands.

"Welcome to our small house," said the man with the scar. "I hope you'll enjoy our poor hospitality." Stephanie opened the car door and stepped outside. She inhaled fresh air into her lungs. Two young men quickly covered the car with a brown canvas. They all went in.

Stephanie found herself in a long, dark room, lit only by one small lamp. A young woman in jeans greeted her.

"Welcome," she said in English, "My name is Jamila."

The driver spoke. "You take time to rest a little. If you would like to, we have a shower."

"Thanks," murmured Stephanie, "I could use it."

"We are honored to have you here. Jamila will be help you, if need you being anything," he added. His broken English was almost endearing.

Radek ended a phone conversation and said, with a smile, "You have warm regards from your father. He sends his love."

"Is he okay? What happened? And Mahmoud? They managed to get away from the house in Teheran?" Stephanie couldn't get her words out fast enough.

"I spoke also with Mahmoud. He too sends his regards. They managed to get away from the hideout. It turned out that the presence of the Army in the area was not at all connected to you. It was a search for a corrupt banker. They were able to leave the place without being detected. You can relax."

Jamila took her hand. "You probably want to take off

the *chador*. You must be terribly hot under that thing." Stephanie followed the young woman to a room, removed the chador and the pillow meant to make her look pregnant, and lied down on a small bed, falling asleep almost immediately.

Stephanie felt a gentle touch on her hair. She slowly opened her eyes.

"I'm sorry to wake you up, but there is no choice," said Jamila. "You have to go. They are waiting for you in the other room."

"What's the time?" she asked in sleepy voice. "I lost track of time. Did I sleep a lot?"

"It's now ten at night. You have slept since three in the afternoon. You must have been very tired."

"I needed that rest," said Stephanie stretching her arms. "I hardly slept for almost a week. Plus, the delicious meal you prepared for me. I always fall asleep after a heavy meal. What did you give me?"

"It's a traditional Kurdish dish. We call it *jiujia bedan jian*. It's made with chicken and eggplant. You are not the only one who enjoyed it. The men too eat it with great pleasure. My mother taught me how to make it."

The voice of the man with the scar came from the next room.

Jamila answered. "They want us to hurry up," she said, "They set a meeting at the border at 2 AM and they don't want to be late. Come, let me fix the pillow."

They left the house and got into the van. She sat next to Radek.

"Okay, here we go," said the man with the scar. "It's approximately an hour and half journey until we get to the meeting point."

Stephanie felt the warm breeze coming from the car window. They traveled with no lights and were surrounded by total darkness. She curled up in her seat, her thoughts going back to the conversation when her father and Mahmoud told her that she had been under surveillance by the Iranian security services for many years.

She now looked at her previous life under a different light. She shivered, thinking about working at the Department of Immigration. Had an invisible hand also accelerated her position at the job?

Stephanie no longer knew what to think and what to believe. Could it be that Kevin Shepard was part of all this? Could it be that he was ordered to develop their relationship? And who was behind all this? The American or the Iranian intelligence services? And what happened to Ali? Was he also a victim of the espionage? Or was he part of it since the beginning and she had fallen, easy prey, into his arms? Since Yasser was an agent, how did he really feel about her?

Now, she had disturbing questions about her mother. Was it really true that her mother, despite all the precautions she had taken and despite being under close surveillance by American intelligence, hadn't known how closely she and Stephanie were monitored by the Iranians? She felt a stab in her stomach at the thought that her mother's life was in danger, and she might pay a heavy price – maybe even with her life – because of Stephanie's reckless action. Stephanie's experience of the cruelty of the Iranian security services made her very concerned about her mother's future.

And of course, there was Yasser, her lover, the man to whom she had given her spirit and soul. In spite of the harsh words of her father and Mahmoud, it was hard to accept the fact that their relationship was, at least initially, a huge pretext.

She had mixed feelings, knowing that Yasser paid with his life for not following his superior's instructions by refusing to pursue her recruitment. She thought this fact must have meant that he really had loved her.

And Tom's death in a car accident? She wondered. Was it possible that the Iranian security services were responsible for that accident? Could it be that Tom was still alive? The idea that the CIA must have been aware of the ordeal she had gone through in her marriage, including the rapes she had experienced, horrified her.

Stephanie was the daughter of a spy mother and a father who was an Iranian police officer. To think of it that way amazed her. It was now clear that all her life, without knowing it, had been essentially a big illusion. She realized now that she had been manipulated like a puppet throughout much of her life. In every direction her thoughts were going, she ran into big question marks. She couldn't decide what in her life was real and what had been shaped by all the intelligence services.

Could someone have steered her even without being present in each stage of her life? What about all her friends and acquaintances? Were they, too, a part of the show she had starred in? Was it possible that Vicky, her closest friend, was part of it? And what about Mona Hussein, the young woman she had met while working at the Department of Immigration?

Stephanie recalled what her father and Mahmoud called "plan twenty-fifty," and that Iranian intelligence had a file on her labeled "Queen of the West 028." What's the purpose of the plan? How would it impact the United States? How come that the American intelligence services, considered among the best and most efficient in the world, failed over the years to uncover that plan? The whole situation was completely surreal. The last thing she could have ever imagined was getting into the bizarre situation that she was in now. It was the closest she had ever been to a Hollywood action movie. Now, her life in Los Angeles seemed far away, belonging to someone else.

*Good God*, she thought to herself, *how did I get into this? Will I ever be back to the quiet and peaceful life of my past?* Her thoughts were interrupted by Radek's words.

"We are approaching the border," he said.

"Everything all right?"

"I hope so. We'll know in a few moments. In any case, if something happens, it doesn't matter what, you must get out fast from the area. You will not look back. Just run away."

"What do you mean? Where am I supposed to run?" she asked, unable to hide the fear in her voice.

"I am hoping that everything will proceed well, but if something happens, and I don't rule out the chance of running into the Iranian army – you run away fast from the place. You don't look back."

Radek then pulled out a black bag and handed it to Stephanie.

"Your father and Mahmoud asked me to give this to you. It contains several important items that may help you in the coming days, and you are to keep it as close to you as possible at all times."

Stephanie held the bag tightly, and asked about its contents, but Radek had no time to answer. A barrage of gunfire ripped through the silence of the night and bullets hit the moving car. The car swerved from side to side. Stephanie screamed and ducked down. She heard Radek shout, "Hold on tight!" Then the car overturned.

Stephanie opened her eyes to the silence around her. To her surprise, except for a strong pain in her right arm, she wasn't hurt. Heavy dust filled the car and she had trouble breathing. With difficulty she managed to straighten up a bit and settle, trying to see what was going on around her. She quickly opened the upper part of the chador and pulled out the pillow, still tied to her belly. Then with the pillow to protect her hand from the heat, she pushed the heavy metal above her. She noticed a pair of frozen eyes fixed on her. Despite her efforts, she was unable to identify who it was in the darkness. She leaned forward with great effort.

"Stephanie." She suddenly heard Radek's voice.

"Yes," she answered quickly, relieved to hear his voice. She could barely make out his pained and bloody face. Another barrage of gunfire sounded closer. Stephanie froze in fear.

"Radek," she whispered, "Radek, do you hear me?"

"Try to get out," he choked. "Quick. Run to the mountains on the left. Fast, Stephanie, and don't forget the bag. Take care of it."

"What about you?" she said with a trembling voice. "Let me help you out."

Radek's voice was determined. "What did I tell you? I told you to run. Get out now before the car explodes. Now! Do you hear?"

"What will happen to you?" she cried out.

"Now!" his voice boomed, making Stephanie jump. "And God be with you," he added quietly. Stephanie didn't hear the last of Radek's words, because she immediately began to use all of her efforts to crawl out through the shattered glass windshield. She landed on the ground with a thud. Quickly, she got up and began to search into the darkness. The fear didn't paralyze her but it gave her a strength she never thought she could possess. She took one last look back at the mangled car, then turned to what she hoped was the mountains, slowly increasing her pace, until at last, she began to run.

# 17

Stephanie managed to walk some forty meters away from the overturned car, when she suddenly heard a loud explosion behind her. An intense heat wave that instantly enveloped her propelled her forward. She barely managed not to fall, but dropped the black bag. She stopped quickly and bent down to recover it.

When she turned her head toward where the explosion came from, she saw a big mushroom of fire rising from the overturned car. Stephanie froze, standing motionless and completely horrified, until a barrage of fire struck the silence of the night. She fell to the ground, clutching tightly the black bag. The bullets whizzed above her, forcing her to stay down in the dirt.

Her attempts to track down the source of the fire were unsuccessful. Total darkness surrounded her and the dust in the air obstructed her vision. While on the ground, she tried to remain calm and instinctively she reached for the bag and opened it. She began to feel around inside, hoping that there was something in there that could possibly save her in this situation. Her hand stopped when she felt a cold metal. She pulled out the object, and could see it was the barrel of a gun. She pulled it out, placed it on the ground beside her, and stuck her hand back in. She discovered a Blackberry and a GPS. With another reach into the bag, Stephanie pulled out a fist-full of American dollars. And finally, almost too small to notice, she felt a small plastic device in the bottom corner of the bag, and pulled it out to reveal a flash drive. She examined it closely, wondering what its significance could be.

The sky was lit up by several flares. She quickly scanned the lighted area and found out she was on a hillside. She frantically gathered everything and placed them safely in the bag, double-checking to make sure she had not left anything behind. With a new sense of direction from the light of the flares, Stephanie got up and started to run up the hill holding the black bag in one hand and the gun in the other. More shots were fired, and Stephanie could feel the whizzing bullets flying nearby. This time she did not stop. Racing to the top of the hill, Stephanie could see some buildings at a distance of a few hundred feet that looked to be abandoned.

Stephanie carefully moved in the dark down the hill and ran as fast as she could towards the buildings. The longer she ran, the more she could feel her heart pounding in her chest. With every passing second, she could see the shadows of the dark buildings becoming clearer. She was encouraged by the thought that if she could get to the buildings, she could find a safe place to hide and lay low.

Suddenly, Stephanie lost her balance and fell down, landing in a pit. It was a powerful blow. Stunned and aching, she remained lying there, until she heard a squeal of car brakes and voices. A light beam passed over the top of the pit. Stephanie huddled as much as she could into the bottom of the pit, trying to avoid the light. Her ankle throbbed with such pain, she barely managed to stop the scream of pain surging from her throat. She wondered if it was broken as she reached down to touch it and felt the swelling. The pain overcame her, and she passed out. When she awoke, she found herself still lying in the dark pit, trying to follow what was going on above it. Except for a distant barking dog, all was quiet.

She removed quickly the large quantity of weeds from her body and took a deep breath of fresh air. She lied there for a short while, making sure the silence was lasting, and then got up very carefully. With much effort, she managed to get out of the pit. She ignored the sharp pain in her leg, and limped the short distance between her and the row of abandoned buildings.

The place was in ruins. Here and there, she noticed discarded syringes, empty food cans, and also piles of brush and wood for fires. She sat down heavily on a wide stone, opened the black bag, and pulled out the cell phone. She turned it on but wondered how and whom to call. The second the phone was on, it began to vibrate. She wondered whether it was wise to answer it. Finally, she pressed the green button and put the phone up to her ear. Several seconds later, a voice came through.

"Stephanie? Are you okay?"

Stephanie didn't recognize the speaker's voice, and although the question was asked in English, she wondered whether to answer.

"Who is this?" she asked hesitantly.

"My name is Aoni. I work for Mahmoud. I'm not far from you. Listen, the danger is not over yet. The soldiers are still looking for you. You must not under any circumstances, leave the place where you are."

In a panic, Stephanie looked around the abandoned building, for any sign indicating Aoni's whereabouts. "How do you know where I am?" she asked.

"Keep your phone on. Stay where you are. Don't be

scared. I was sent by your father and Mahmoud. I'll rescue you." She was overwhelmed with a sense of relief by the words coming from the phone, and found herself relaxing a bit.

"Okay," she whispered. "Thank you."

The line went dead. She hung up and put the phone back in the black bag beside her. She noticed she was covered with a considerable amount of dirt. She didn't even try to remove it. She bent over and touched her leg in order to feel the swelling. A sharp pain pierced her body when she touched her ankle.

The sky was growing lighter. She had no more energy. Instead of worrying whether the soldiers or Aoni found her first, she said a silent prayer and drifted off to sleep.

She awoke to the sound of a vehicle in the distance. Her heart jumped into her throat, and her entire body tensed up. Then, the Blackberry began to vibrate again. She quickly dug it back out and placed it to her ear.

"Yes," she whispered, while peeking out over at the car coming in her direction.

"It's Aoni. I'm in the car in front of you. Do you see me?" She watched the headlights flashing.

"Yes," replied Stephanie, suddenly hopeful.

"Come, get in." She heard the voice of the man. She quickly collected the black bag and left the building. The car stopped to a screeching halt next to her.

Stephanie hurried to open the door and sat next to the driver. Only then, she noticed the green eyes staring at her.

"Hi, I'm Aoni. I'm sure you remember me," he spoke, almost smiling, "From the train."

Stephanie couldn't help but remember the pair of green eyes that kept glaring at her openly throughout the train ride. Now, on closer scrutiny, he looked much older than she recalled. The car took off.

"I would never flirt with a married woman, certainly not in public," Aoni said with an embarrassed smile. Stephanie chose to ignore the comment. She was baffled at how calm he seemed.

"How did you find me?"

The young man pulled out a Blackberry. "This device is amazing," he said with a broad smile. "Several months ago, we installed a fantastic navigation software in our phones that allows us to find the location of any device belonging to the organization. This is how I knew all along where you were."

"Should we call Mahmoud?" she asked. "Is he updated on what happened tonight? I mean about Radek and…" Her voice faded as she remembered the explosion.

"For some reason, it's impossible to get his location. I have been trying for hours to call him, but he doesn't answer. I don't get it."

Stephanie recalled his terrified eyes, begging her to run. "He didn't make it." Stephanie's voice was full of guilt.

"You don't know Radek." The green-eyed man replied. "I'm sure he is fine."

Stephanie shot him a look of disbelief. She felt uncomfortable. This young man didn't inspire confidence, the way he seemed so care-free and nonchalant.

"Where are we going?" she asked, unable to hide her concern. "What do we do from here?"

"First, we get away from this area as fast as possible. I think it would be wrong to try again to cross the border here. Too dangerous. The best thing is to get to Hormashah. There, we have a hideout apartment. We'll wait a couple of days until things calm down. On the way, I'll try to reach Mahmoud."

As he drove, Stephanie felt restless. "Hormashah?" she asked. "How far from here?"

The guy with green eyes pointed to the GPS in front of him. "We are heading south. It's one hundred and fifty kilometers from here. Maybe a bit more."

Stephanie kept silent, realizing she had no choice at this point but to trust him. He almost read her thoughts.

"You really don't have to worry." He broke the silence. "You can trust me. Really. I was born in Hormashah, so I am familiar with that area and I know people there that can help us." The sincerity in his voice softened her distrust of him.

"How old are you?" she asked. "When I saw you on the train with all the other young people, I was sure you were a student."

"They were students at the University of Teheran, going home on holiday. They thought I was a student, too. I'm really twenty-nine, but those who don't know me think I'm twenty at the most."

"How did you get to do what you are doing?"

"Thanks to Mahmoud. I owe him my life. I was part of a smuggling gang. He got me out. I would do anything for him." He sounded very passionate about it. Then he continued. "I grew up in Hormashah. It's a port town so there always is something to take or move. Sometimes, we would also handle people, as in your case." Aoni glanced at Stephanie and then continued.

"I'm Arab, like many of Hormashah residents. We don't really love the Shiites and in truth, not the Sunnis either. They have always screwed us. My story with Mahmoud begins after I was arrested on illegal trade. At first I played along, and because of the tortures I admitted to the crimes I was charged. I was supposed to get many years in jail, but who knows if I would have gotten out at all. He recognized my potential. We hit it off well and he decided to recruit me. I became his source. Since then, I'm with him, and most of the time I am working for him."

Stephanie was tense. She recalled the events of the night, the burning car, the whistling bullets nearby, the blood-stained face of the man with the scar, the pit, the flashing beams searching for her. To her surprise, now the events she went through left her almost completely indifferent. She didn't feel sorrow, compassion, fear or pain. Something deep down had been shut off that allowed her to look at things from afar, calmly, as if they were not her business. She felt numb.

"Do you have something to drink?" she asked. "I'm very thirsty."

"There is a small water container in the back," he answered quickly.

Stephanie reached into the back of the car. She struggled but managed to get the container. "My God, I didn't realize how thirsty I was," she said after the first sip.

Aoni smiled. "I guess last night was pretty rough. When I saw you crawling out of the car, I couldn't believe my eyes. I didn't expect someone to get out of that alive."

"You saw that?" She looked at him. "How could you see? Where were you?"

"I was in the abandoned buildings. I have night vision binoculars we stole from a Russian base. Trust Mahmoud. He is an architect, a genius, nobody like him. He assigned me to be your shadow.

They finally reached the end of the dirt road and got on the main road. Aoni came to a screeching halt. "We have to adjust," he said.

"What?"

"It would be suicide to travel openly on the main road. At the same time I want to leave this area as soon as possible."

"What do you suggest?"

"I think it would be better if you move to the trunk." He almost sounded apologetic. "It's a place where we store equipment and weapons."

Stephanie turned her head back, examining the small trunk. "I don't believe I can fit in there," she said doubtfully.

"With the special permits I have, it won't be a problem for me to go through the roadblocks, but it will be hard to explain why you are with me, especially if they managed to circulate your picture to units all over the country."

Stephanie nodded and moved to the back. After a couple of forced tugs, she pulled the back seat down to reveal a very small trunk.

"I will never be able to get in there," she complained. "Not a chance."

"It's our one and only option," Aoni replied. "After all you've been through, I'm sure you can manage to sit inside a trunk for a little while."

"What am I going to do with my bag?" she asked. "It contains personal stuff."

Aoni replied quickly. "Leave it. I can say it's mine. Just take the cell phone."

Stephanie slowly crawled into the narrow space. It took her a while to settle down into it. "I will choke in here," she mumbled, struggling to make herself comfortable.

"Don't worry." Aoni attempted to soothe her. "I promise I will get you out as soon as possible. We just need to get away from this area." Aoni reached behind him and with great effort, pushed the seat back up to conceal the trunk, trying his best not to hurt Stephanie. Everything went black for Stephanie.

"Are you okay?" he asked.

"Yes," a dim voice spoke from the trunk.

After some hours, Stephanie felt the car stop. She heard the door slam open, and suddenly the trunk opened to reveal

Aoni looking down at her. Stephanie was on the verge of fainting. Aoni reached his hand in and pulled her out, but she couldn't stand on her feet. She collapsed on the ground and layed on her back in total exhaustion.

"I am done," she whispered, her eyes closed. "I can't feel my hands or my feet. I'm exhausted. I'm dehydrated."

It turned out that the decision to hide in the trunk was right. Throughout the journey, Aoni had to stop at over five roadblocks. He went by three of them quickly, after showing a card confirming he was a member of the Iranian intelligence services. At two of the checkpoints, the soldiers were very suspicious. They were not impressed by the card he showed them and demanded to search the trunk.

"How did you convince them not to?" Stephanie asked.

Aoni pointed to the black sling bag. "I began to rummage into the bag, as if I was looking for the keys, and I showed them a bunch of your dollars. Once I saw the look in the soldier's eyes, I knew I had the upper hand."

"How much did he take?"

"Less than what it should have cost," Aoni replied quickly.

Stephanie smiled. "Where are we now?" she asked.

"Near Harmashah," he said. "We will cut through the fields. I suspect there is a checkpoint at the entrance to the city. It looks like they got all the soldiers out of their units to look for you. I have never seen so many soldiers on the ground. Why do they want you?"

"You don't know who I am?"

Aoni shrugged. "I don't ask questions. I told you, Mahmoud tells me what to do and I do it. The only thing he said is that if something happens to you it's on me. As far as he is concerned I will be cut out… and the last thing on earth I wish for myself is to get in trouble with Mahmoud Srkaawi."

"Did you manage to get in touch with him? Does he know what's happening?"

Aoni shook his head. "No, I didn't. I tried to reach him from several places. I'm pretty worried. I even called him at home, but his wife doesn't know where he is."

The car entered a narrow street. Along both sides stood two- and three-story buildings. At the entrance of one of them, Stephanie noticed two women in grey *chadors* standing and chatting. On another corner of the street, a group of children played ball. A young man riding a motorcycle passed nearby. A sense of relief at the sight of the town enveloped Stephanie, and she settled back on her seat. The thought that in a few minutes she would be able to remove the *chador* and shower and maybe even sleep a bit gave her new energy.

Aoni drove, skillfully maneuvering between the cars parked at the edge of the narrow street. Then, as he executed a sharp turn into one of the streets, he brought the car to a screeching halt.

"What happened?" asked Stephanie.

Aoni pointed down the street. "There is a checkpoint. Do you see it? We have to get out of here fast." He tried to make a U-turn and suddenly they heard gunshots.

"Get down!" he shouted at Stephanie.

Several bullets hit the car. Stephanie cowered, holding her head in her hands.

"Bastards," she heard Aoni growl. "What did you do that they are so anxious to catch you? Are you a spy or what?"

"It's a long story," she replied.

More bullets hit the car and it started to rock from side to side. Stephanie felt a sharp pain in her left leg and cried out.

"What happened?" Aoni shouted above her.

She looked down at her leg. "I think I've been hit."

"Hit? Where? Hold on, Stephanie." He tried to hide his panic. "I will shake off the bastards. Don't move." Stephanie touched her leg and when she looked at her hand, it was covered with blood. "Hold on tight, Stephanie… These bastards don't know who they're dealing with." Aoni briefly lost control of the car, but soon after, raced forward.

"We are going to park," Aoni replied cheering. "Here come the motherfuckers." Aoni swerved into a parking garage, whipped the car between two others and then turned off the ignition. He quickly jumped to lay on top of Stephanie. "Do not move. Allah help us."

A parade of vehicles zoomed by the parking garage. After a few minutes,

Aoni got back up, started the car and began to drive again, slowly, cautiously, with occasional glances at Stephanie and her wound.

# 18

Only when she reached the entrance to the safe house, on the first floor of an apartment building on a small street, did Stephanie notice the blood stain covering Aoni's shirt. He stood with his back turned to her, dealing with the lock. She reached out and touched his back.

"My God," she muttered in concern. "I see you got some, too. You're covered with blood."

"Yes," he answered, "I got hit with some glass right at the entrance to the parking lot."

"Does it hurt?"

"Not too bad. I got a bullet in my stomach once, six years ago. I was in the wrong place at the wrong time. I was hospitalized for a while, out of active duty for two and a half months. This is nothing compared to that. How's your leg?"

"It hurts," she said. "But a little less than it did."

The apartment was filled with a sour stench and it was hard to breathe.

"I think we should air this place out a little," she said and landed on a large sofa, covered with a green cloth. "Looks like no one has lived here for a while."

Aoni rushed to the window and opened it. "I haven't been here for more than six months."

"Whose apartment is it?" she asked.

"Mine. I mean, my family's," he corrected himself. "I lived here until two years ago, when I was transferred to Teheran. My younger brother Hosni moved in here after I left. I haven't heard from him in two months."

"So, is he in the family business, like you?"

Aoni shrugged. "Let's just say he's in import-export… that's the best way to put it."

"So… he's a businessman?" Stephanie asked.

Aoni burst into laughter. "I guess that's how he sees it. But the truth is, he's into smuggling. Here, in this city, if you can't find a regular job, you find yourself involved in smuggling one way or another. There's always a guy who knows a guy. I know that two months ago, last time we spoke, he was messing around with fake Viagra. He found this source in Basra who sold him hundreds of thousands of pills. You have no idea how popular that stuff is around here. Wait, you know what? I just remembered I have a first aid kit I once stole from an army base." He hurried out of the room.

Only now, spread out on the sofa with her eyes shut, did Stephanie realize how tired and aching she was. She knew very well that if it wasn't for Aoni's resourcefulness and courage, the security forces would have arrested her. "The parking lot trick" as Aoni called it, proved itself above and beyond. Once they left the parking garage, they abandoned the car in a narrow alley and walked the rest of the way.

Aoni came back into the room carrying a rectangular, white tin box. He put the box on the table and kneeled next to her. "Let's see your leg," he said.

"Don't you think we should treat you first? Your back is covered with blood."

"I'm fine," said Aoni, taking a pack of gauze pads and a tiny bottle out of the box. Aoni took the tiny bottle, opened it, and poured some of the liquid on the gauze he held. Then, very carefully, he began to clean the blood from Stephanie's leg. Despite his gentle touch, she started to feel pain.

"It hurts," she muttered, struggling to hold in a cry of pain. "When you touch it, it hurts…"

Aoni chose to ignore her. He looked at her leg closely. "I see the bullet caused an abrasion here," he said knowingly. "It created a deep cut, but the bullet didn't penetrate the leg… that's very lucky… I've seen it happen before. You're lucky."

"How do you know all these things?" she asked in astonishment.

Aoni shrugged again and a little smile appeared in the corner of his mouth.

"It's my specialty. I know a little bit of everything," he said smiling, finishing up bandaging her leg with remarkable skill.

"You wrapped that bandage as if you've done it a hundred times before."

Aoni smiled at her. "I've bandaged wounds more than I can count. The truth is, I did an advanced first aid course as part of my work. I'm no expert, but it helps me understand these things a little. Anyway, I can assure you that it won't kill you, so you can be calm."

"Thanks," muttered Stephanie. "Now let's see what happened to you."

Aoni started to take off his bloody shirt. Stephanie got up, looking at Aoni's sculpted body with admiration. She reached out to help him take off his shirt and then told him to turn around. His whole back was covered in blood. She began to treat his wounds when a phone rang.

He quickly reached into his pocket and took out his phone. As Stephanie cleaned Aoni's back with the antiseptic, her attempts to learn something from this phone call came to nothing. But she could her the tension in his voice. Aoni hung up.

"Just bandage it already," he demanded abruptly, revealing how upset he was. "I have to go meet someone."

"Who was that on the phone?" she asked, struggling to understand the change in his manner. "Did something happen?"

"The situation is not good," he answered quickly. "The whole of Iran is looking for us. I must go see someone. Come, put the bandage on fast."

Stephanie took the bandage and started to wrap it around Aoni's waist. "You have to see a doctor… I think the bullet is still in there. The wound doesn't look good."

"We don't have time" he said impatiently. "The man I just spoke to says they can't find Mahmoud." Aoni took the bandage from Stephanie's hands and with one quick movement, tore the end of it in two and tied it off. "Anyway, you stay here in the house and don't open the door for anyone. You can shower, rest, and gather your strength. I hope to return as soon as possible."

Before he left the house, Aoni went to the black bag and took out the bundle of dollar bills. "I'm taking some money. I hope you don't mind." He took out a few bills from the stack. "By the way, I saw a flash drive in the bag. Do you know what's on it?"

Stephanie shook her head.

"You better check. It must have some special value. There's a computer in the bedroom. It's a little slow but it works."

After much effort, Stephanie managed to figure out how to work the laptop, which was very outdated. Opening the flash drive required a password. She remembered how someone from the immigration department, a hacker, showed her how to solve this sort of problem.

"The basic assumption is that the password is a combination of birthdays, names of family members, and streets that the user knows," the expert had told her.

Stephanie began to write down all the possible combinations she could think of: her birthday and her mother's name, her father's and her sister's. Again and again she changed the letters and numbers, but all her attempts came to nothing. Stephanie took a short break, drank from the chlorinated water and returned to the computer. She sat down, staring at the dirty screen, when suddenly she remembered that special moment, the last thing her father told her as they said goodbye, the last time she had seen her father. His eyes communicated something else. It wasn't only concern. There was a message there. He had held her and looked into her eyes and said those words that made every ounce of her body feel the weight of some sort of importance. *What was is he said?* She tried to remember. She closed her eyes and concentrated, until finally, she heard her father's voice: "My treasure, go in peace and may God be with you."

She studied the screen. Could it be that simple?

"My treasure." She typed out, and hit enter.

"Access denied." The error message blinked at her again.

"Go in peace." She wrote hastily.

"Access denied."

She slammed her fists on the desk in frustration. By now, she had lost count of how many passwords she had entered. She dropped her face in her hands, and rubbed her eyes. She thought of her father, and the look of importance he had in his eyes when he had said those last words to her. Her head popped up. Could it be?

"God be with you." She typed speedily. She pressed enter.

"Access granted" the computer chimed. Stephanie jumped out of her chair and screamed with excitement. She had figured it out. She really did have her parents' genes. Now, pulling up the flash drive file, she had no idea what to expect. *This better be good*, she thought to herself.

On the flash drive, she could see two folders. One folder included a list of about two thousand names of men and women. Next to the names were addresses, identification numbers, phone numbers, bank account numbers and e-mail addresses. The second folder included a list of about one hundred names of commercial companies. Next to each of the names was the company's address and what appeared to be names of shareholders. This list, too, had details of bank accounts.

At first, the lists seemed arbitrary and meaningless. Stephanie couldn't understand why her father gave her the flash drive. She skimmed through it again, trying to find a familiar name, but she did not recognize even one. She pulled out the flash drive, deliberating what to do with it. Then, like a bolt of lightning, she suddenly remembered what Mahmoud said about the "twenty fifty plan."

"They will conquer Europe in 2050 without shooting one bullet. Think about the demographic. The average European household is 1.3. The Muslim population has grown to 5.8. They will simply walk in through the front doors of European universities and business companies.

They will take over financial hubs, become the doctors, the lawyers, the judges. The Ayatollahs have thought far and wide… they embedded smooth systems for the day of the Islamic revolution," Mahmoud had said.

Rattled by this thought, she quickly re-inserted the flash drive. Now, she carefully read through the list of names. Two pieces of information jumped out. The first was where these people lived. All of them, without exception, lived in the larger cities in the U.S.: New York, Washington, Los Angeles, Chicago, Boston, and San Francisco.

The second discovery was their place of employment. The list included the Senate, House of Representatives, the military, Secret Service, the Navy, the Federal Aviation Administration, Wall Street, IRS and a number of major newspaper editors.

Stephanie began to wonder if this was a list of the sleepers in America. *Could this be the key to the Iranian's plan to take over America, that same way* Mahmoud had explained that they had already begin to take over Europe? Stephanie grew excited by the very thought of holding in her hands one of the top kept secrets of the Iranian government. She then remembered what her father said: "Inshallah it will be alright. I have the power because I hold top secret information, information they don't want me to release, information that could complicate their relationship with allied countries such as Russia and China. A complication like that would devastate the entire economic well-being of Iran."

Now Stephanie understood a few things. The first was the reason why they never harmed her father. He knew how to keep this information as a "doomsday weapon" as he put it. The other is how much power she now held in her hands. But she was startled to realize that maybe this was why the Iranian Security Services were trying so hard to catch her.

Stephanie pulled out the flash drive and tried to decide what to do with it. In the end, she chose not to put it back in the black bag but rather, tuck it in the pocket of her chador. She entered the bathroom, took off her clothes, and eased herself into the yellowish tub and turned on the water. She closed her eyes, succumbing to the feel of the trickling water, ignoring the rust which adorned the tub walls. She started to soap her breasts, then her waists and thighs. A pleasant shudder ran through her spine and she sighed quietly.

Suddenly, she felt someone watching her and instantly opened her eyes. She looked to the doorway and jumped to see two men standing there. One was tall with black, thick hair, and the other was shorter with a large knit cap that covered almost all of his face. Stephanie let out a startled yelp and covered herself immediately. The young men took a step back, but their eyes were fixed on her naked body. A wide smile appeared on the face of the black-haired man and he whispered something in his friend's ear.

Stephanie turned and faced away from them. "Get out! Get out of here!" she screamed. "Go away!"

The black-haired man grinned from ear to ear, his eyes passionately reviewing her body. "You…who?" he asked in broken English.

Stephanie tried to reach the *chador* on the floor. With a quick movement, the shorter one kicked the *chador* out of her reach. Stephanie was taken aback.

"I'm a friend of Aoni" she stammered.

The door was slammed and Aoni's voice echoed in the apartment. "Stephanie? Where are you?"

The two men rushed out of the bathroom.

"I'm in the bathroom!" She yelled.

"Do you need anything?" Aoni asked, without entering the bathroom.

"There's someone here. Two men. They were standing in the doorway," she replied.

"I apologize. That's my brother. He didn't know who you are. I hope he didn't bother you." Aoni shot his brother a threatening glare, who just stood there, grinning sheepishly. Stephanie could hear Aoni speaking harshly in Farsi, and could tell that he was reprimanding his brother.

"My *chador* is torn and I don't have anything to wear," she called out, once the arguing had stopped.

"Wait, I'll try to find something for you." After a moment, Aoni reached his hand into the bathroom and threw in a few pieces of clothing. "There's a shirt and jeans here. I hope it fits." The clothes were big on her, but Stephanie thought nothing of it. She picked up the torn *chador* and took out the flash drive.

When she walked into the living room, she found Aoni lying on the sofa, both men beside him. "I apologize again for my brother, Hosni," Aoni said. "He was sure I brought him a present. I used to bring him that sort of gift... Girls."

She shuddered at the thought of what might have happened if Aoni had not come when he did. "What's next, Aoni?"

"You have to leave Iran as soon as possible. Tomorrow morning, a ship will leave the port. It's owned by an Iranian, but it sails under the Liberian flag. I talked to some people I know."

"Where does it sail to?" she wondered.

"It's a freight ship. The final destination as far as I know is Pakistan, but the first stop is Dubai. There's an American embassy there. I'm sure you'll do fine. The most important thing is for you to get out of here as quickly as possible. You can't imagine how many policemen and soldiers there are out on the streets. It wouldn't be an exaggeration to say they took out an army to catch you. I've never seen so many men."

"Have you heard from Mahmoud?" Stephanie asked with concern.

"No," he replied, miserably. "I have a feeling something happened to him. I spoke to a friend of mine who heard he was arrested. Teheran is one big mess."

The lights of Khorramshahr port glittered in front of Stephanie as she and Aoni waited in his parked car.

"Pretty, right?" she heard Aoni say. "This sight always delights me."

"You were born here, weren't you?"

"Yes. I was born two years before the Iran-Iraq war broke out," he said. "Those were horrible times. The city was bombed for months by the Iraqis. Then, they occupied it and we ran to Isfahan, to our cousins' house. We returned to Khorramshahr only after the war ended. I was a child but I clearly remember the ruins the Iraqis left behind."

"Who are we waiting for?" Stephanie asked, feeling more and more anxious the longer they waited.

"We're waiting for the man I told you about. He's supposed to meet us here at exactly ten. I think there is about ten thousand dollars left in the pack."

Stephanie reached below her and pulled up the black bag. "I didn't count."

Aoni took out the money and counted it quickly. "There's $15,000 here," he said. "I don't intend to give him all the money now. I'll give him half now, and the second half when I get a message from you that you are okay."

"Do you trust him?"

Aoni shrugged. "The truth is I know his younger brother a lot better. We did some stuff together in the past. But this guy knows what will happen to him and his family if I find out something happened to you."

Stephanie didn't hide her concern. "How will he get me on the ship?"

"He told me he has a key to one of the side gates to the port. He says the captain and the others are supposed to board only early in the morning. Besides, none of the crew will ask questions. They're used to officers bringing hookers to their quarters that they picked up in port." Aoni looked at her face and burst out laughing. "To be honest, with this wool hat on your head, they'll think he chose the ugliest hooker around."

Stephanie shot him a look, then let out a slight laugh. Her smile quickly faded as she looked back out at the port. "I have a bad feeling about this," Stephanie said.

"That's what my brother, Hosni, said. Look, I just think this is the best way to leave Iran. You board the ship today, and by tomorrow you'll reach Dubai."

"And there's no alternative?"

Aoni thought for a moment. "This was the best offer I could get under the circumstances. The truth is, Hosni suggested we use his smuggling route to Iraq through Abadan. He says it may be more complicated, but it's safer."

"Will he take me?"

Aoni smiled. "For ten thousand dollars, he'd take you to the US on his back."

"Where is he now?"

Aoni pointed backwards. "300, 400 feet behind us. I asked him to back us up." He could see the worry in her eyes. "This was the best I could do with the whole country looking for you," he reassured her.

His Blackberry rang and he quickly pulled it out of his pocket. Stephanie anxiously studied his facial expressions as he spoke. His tone was nervous and his face showed stress.

"Son of a bitch!" he yelled, and hung up the phone.

"What happened?" Stephanie asked, alarmed.

"That smuggling son of a bitch tricked me," said Aoni furiously. "Hosni says the whole area is full of military and police."

"Let's get out of here." Stephanie said.

"Wait," he muttered, "Wait, and let me think for a second." He began to make another call. Stephanie did not understand anything that was said, but the mention of Hosni's name was enough for her to realize he was speaking to his brother. She felt her muscles harden and her whole body was on edge. "Change of plan. Take the bag," he ordered. "Now pay close attention to what I say. We're going to use the situation in our favor."

"How?" she asked in fear.

"Do you see there, on the right, that tall building? It's a mosque. As soon as I start the car, you run there fast. Don't move from there. When everything quiets down, Hosni and his friend will pick you up."

"Where are you going?" she asked.

"I'll pull them in a different direction. We'll make them run around the city. I know this city better than any of these soldiers and policemen. Take the bag with you. I promised Hosni ten thousand dollars if he and his friend get you out of here. I told him if he doesn't bring you to Basra, he won't see the light of day. I made him swear on our mother's grave. You'll be fine, I promise." Aoni scanned the area before continuing, then looked at Stephanie. "May Allah be with you. I hope someday we can sit and talk about all we went through."

Stephanie felt her heart beating quicker, and instinctively grabbed Aoni and pulled him in for a hug. "Goodbye, Aoni. Thanks for everything." She quickly got out of the car and watched him race away. Stephanie stood frozen, but immediately recovered her focus and started running towards the dark building, which was only a few feet in front of her. She passed half the distance when the night's silence was abruptly torn by the roar of engines.

Stephanie immediately dived onto the ground, watching the cars passing nearby her, one after the other, racing away to chase Aoni. She continued to crawl with great effort and felt the gravel tearing her knees. When she finally reached the stairway that led to the building's entrance, she stood and quickly ran up, careful not to trip in the darkness. The surroundings were lit by flashlights installed on military vehicles. Stephanie felt her stomach cramp. She sat on one of the steps, covered by a wall, eagerly listening to sounds from outside to see if anyone was following her. When she didn't hear anything, she slowly continued up the stairs. At the last step, she stopped. A heavy silence welcomed her and for the moment, she was relieved. She rested her head in her hands, praying, trying to stay calm and preserve her energy.

Suddenly, out of the darkness, she heard an engine roar.

"Stephanie! Stephanie!" she heard someone call her. It was Hosni.

She quickly rose and a few seconds later, she was sitting in the back of a worn down Audi, staring at the two men who, hours before, had been staring at her naked in a bathtub. She realized that her life now depended on these two perverts.

# 19

Hosni and his friend, Ragib, were not exactly the types that Stephanie would have chosen to go out to dinner with, but as far as the current situation went, they were the right men at the right time. For a while, they drove in silence. It was Ragib who, barely uttering a word until now, had broken the ice.

"Do you swim?" he suddenly asked in perfect English.

"Of course, I swim." Stephanie was confused by the question. "Why do you ask?"

"We're about to spend many hours on the water. I sure hope you won't need to practice your swimming today." He saw she was not amused by his attempt at a joke. "I'm sorry about what happened back at the house. You know, we got carried away a bit. I hope you're not mad."

Stephanie did not respond.

"I'm sorry. We had no idea you're a famous American actress."

"I'm an American but not an actress and definitely not a famous one," she corrected him.

There was disappointment on Ragib's face. "We heard you were a famous actress in Hollywood and that's the reason why the entire Iranian Army is looking for you."

"I'm an American. I think that's enough of a reason in Iran to arrest me, don't you think?"

Ragib, a sophomore at the University of Isfahan majoring in Economics, turned out to be an intelligent young man, but also quite a talker, trying to prove his expertise in every subject. That is how, without even having to ask, Stephanie learned that he and Hosni were friends since their school days and that the smuggling business helped provide for university expenses. It also created "a financial basis," as he put it, for the day he graduated.

When he was through talking about himself, Ragib started to lecture on the area they were in, as if he was a tour guide. She heard him, in the background, telling about Abadan Island, and how it is surrounded on one side by the Arvand Roud River, better known as Shatt al-Arab, and on the other side by the Bahmanshir Waterway.

"The Shatt al-Arab is actually the merging of the Tigris and Euphrates Rivers," Ragib's voice chimed in her ears. "The river starts in Iraq and ends here, in what we call the Persian Gulf. The river defines the official border between Iran and Iraq, thus, is the cause of the never-ending friction between the two countries over dominance of the river. The peak, of course, was the Great War, when Iraq conquered the area."

"I understand we have to cross over to the other bank."

"Yes," answered Ragib, "there's an area in the river, more or less midway between Khorramshahr and Abadan, where ships can't cross. Hosni found a swamp that's crossable. He knows the terrain with his eyes closed. Truth is, I became an expert myself."

"Are you telling me we are supposed to cross a swamp by foot?"

"No, no." He almost chuckled. "It can't be crossed by foot. We will cross most of it by boat. We'll go in the water in the swamp area and stay alongside with the boat until we reach the other bank. It's a lot less complicated than it sounds. It's not that bad."

"And what's the distance from there to Basra?"

"I estimate that it's about an hour to an hour and a half to Basra. I never reached Basra but Hosni did get there a few times in the last year or two. He knows quite a few people there. You don't have to worry; he will deliver you to the correct place."

The terrain forced Hosni to slow down. From time to time he would turn on the car lights, throw a quick glance at the surface up front and quickly turn them off again. They stopped in front of an iron gate. Ragib opened the door and leaped out. Stephanie watched him as he hastily removed the lock and opened the gate wide, then drove through. He got back out of the car when they approached a group of buildings.

They entered one of the buildings through a broken wooden door. After Ragib turned the lights on, Stephanie examined the vast warehouse. There were two boats at the edge of the warehouse, a large one painted blue and a smaller one, painted green.

"Here, put this on," said Ragib, handing her a blue wetsuit. "It will protect you from the cold water and all sorts of creatures you don't want to know about. And under no circumstances do you want to take your sneakers off."

Suddenly Stephanie remembered the flash drive concealed in her pocket. She debated what to do with it. Finally, she reached out and retrieved the tiny device from her pants pocket.

"I have to protect this," she told Ragib.

"I'll try and find a plastic bag for you to wrap it in." Hosni said something to Ragib who then quickly translated. "He is asking how important it is to you."

"Important," she said.

Hosni spoke again to Ragib. "Hosni says that if it's that important, you shouldn't take a risk. The suit might tear. It's best if you insert it inside your body." An embarrassed smile appeared on Ragib's face. "Yeah, it may sound a bit crazy, but it's the safest. Trust me," Hosni continued. Stephanie watched Hosni take a small package out of his pocket and tear the wrapping. He quickly handed her the rubber. "Here," he said.

Stephanie backed away at the sight of the condom. Hosni burst out with a giggle. Stephanie looked at both men, and with a sigh, took the condom.

"There's an area for privacy over there," Ragib pointed. "And hey, this is not just Hosni's sick idea. How do you think diamonds are smuggled? How do you think drugs are smuggled into prisons?"

The little motorboat quickly made its way through the water, leaving a trail of white foam behind. Stephanie sat at the stern, not far from Ragib, while Hosni, seated on the ledge, navigated the vessel with a steady hand.

Hosni would stop from time to time, scanning the dark waters and listening. Suddenly, appearing out of the dark, there was a giant, threatening shadow of a ship.

"Hold on," Ragib called out.

Stephanie watched the vast ship slowly making its way past. The waves built and then the small motorboat shook from side to side violently. Clutching on to the boat's railing, Stephanie felt jets of salty water splash her face violently and her stomach turning inside out. She could barely stop herself from throwing up.

The ship glided away and Hosni restarted the boat's engine.

"You're okay?" she heard Ragib ask. She nodded, wiping her stinging eyes. "The oil tankers are the biggest threat to us," said Ragib. "Except, of course, for the Iranian Navy ships."

"Another ship," she heard Hosni's voice call out as she watched a huge shadow appear from the dark. Stephanie gaped at the slowly passing shadow as if she was hypnotized. Their boat shook fiercely and it was only a miracle that kept Stephanie from being overthrown into the turbulent waters of the river.

Suddenly, Stephanie noticed there was water filling up the bottom of the boat, the result of the powerful shaking. The possibility of the boat sinking into the abyss panicked her. She called Ragib, pointing at the water filling the center of the boat. He retrieved a bucket and quickly began tossing the water out.

Stephanie felt terribly sick. The constant tension and movement of the boat finally got to her. She hurried and bent over the railing. A sour stream of vomit gushed out of her throat, and soon another and then another. When she finally sank back heavily into the boat, an extreme fatigue had taken over her body. After a few deep breaths, things started calming down gradually. Luckily, as the ship receded, the shock waves got smaller and smaller. Hosni waited until the ship completely vanished from their range of vision before he started the engine anew.

Ragib sat beside Stephanie breathing heavily. She leaned towards him. "What's the distance to the shore?" she asked.

Ragib smiled at her. "I think we're about halfway."

The little motorboat passed the coming minutes sailing slowly, feeling its way in the calm waters. From time to time, Hosni shut off the engine, waited a while, scouted the area with his eyes and then restarted the engine. Stephanie followed Hosni's actions with great anxiety from where she was seated. The expression on the young man's face was severe.

Suddenly, Hosni silenced the engine and blurted out a curse in Farsi. Stephanie turned to Ragib to see his reaction.

"Quiet," he whispered and pointed towards a tiny dot shining over the now dark water. Stephanie looked at the spot of light with fear, having a hard time making it out.

Ragib quietly swung his legs over the boat's side and slipped into the water. He swam behind the boat and started pushing it forward. A minute passed before Hosni joined him in the water. Positioning himself at the bow, he started pulling the boat. Stephanie's eyes shifted quickly between the tiny spot of light and the two young men in the water.

When the light got closer, Ragib and Hosni ceased their activity. Ragib gestured to her with his hand to lie flat at the bottom of the boat. An engine roar of the approaching boat sounded. She raised her head a little and saw in the distance, about a hundred yards in front of her, a military boat moving with great speed.

The strong beam of light aimed at them penetrated the dark of the night. Immediately burying her head back into the boat, Stephanie felt the ray of light hovering above her. She remained lying there, not moving an inch. The ray of light moved on and the darkness, once again, took over the boat.

"That was close," Ragib said. When she lifted her head, Stephanie could see him climbing heavily back onto the boat. Hosni climbed back in as well, and started the engine.

"That was very close," Ragib stated again. This time, he was seated very close to her. Despite the smile on his face, it was obvious that he was very tired and tense. "That was a military boat. Maybe Iranian, maybe Iraqi. It makes no difference to us."

Now she felt exhausted, even though during the last few days she had proved to herself that she had physical and mental strength beyond belief. Every time it seemed she was safe, another threat materialized.

After a while of uneventful passage, Ragib announced, "We're going in the water." He extended Stephanie his hand. "Come, we're not too far from shore. It's about a half hour deal. One last effort and we're done."

Stephanie passed one leg over the edge of the boat and then the other. She closed her eyes, took a deep breath and slowly slid into the murky waters. She watched Ragib and imitated his actions. She held on to the side of the boat with her left hand, thrusting her body forward while her feet pushed off of the sandy bottom of the waterway.

The journey in the water became more difficult as the area they reached grew more dense with aquatic vegetation of all sorts. From time to time, the boat would get stuck in a cluster of flora and Hosni would quickly thrust it toward him.

As they advanced, the water became more and more shallow, which forced them to deal with the swampy sand under their feet. Time and again, Stephanie found herself losing her balance, sinking and struggling to pull one foot or the other out of the sand.

"Come on, Stephanie," she heard Ragib calling from behind. "We're almost there. Twenty minutes more. One last effort to freedom."

Stephanie needed those encouraging words. She felt her strength dwindling and started feeling the pain in her damaged leg as well. The thought that this would all be over in a few minutes and she would finally get to rest, lifted her spirits up.

Suddenly, the entire area was lit with an enormous ray of light, followed by a burst of gunfire. Stephanie froze, watching the bullets spray the water. She saw Ragib sink underneath. A man's voice was then heard over the loud speaker.

Scared beyond the ability to speak, Stephanie felt her breath stop. She let go of her grip on to the boat's railing for a fraction of a second, lost her balance and started sinking into the swampy sand. She felt dizzy and everything around her blurred.

When Stephanie opened her eyes, she found herself seated on a little wooden stool, her back leaning against the wall, in what looked like a holding cell. Ragib was sitting at her feet and not far from him, near a narrow steel door, lie Hosni, completely motionless.

"Where are we?" asked Stephanie in a whisper, her eyes examining the little dark cell. "What happened?" she asked.

"The Iraqi navy got us," Ragib answered, trying to pull at the zipper on his suit. The upper part of his rubber suit was drenched in blood. She quickly held the little hook and partially opened his zipper.

"What happened to you?"

Ragib shrugged. "Don't know. Looks like ricochet," he quietly mumbled, barely concealing his pain. "I can hardly move my hand. Like it was shattered or something."

"You need a doctor urgently," she answered, kneeling beside him. "Where are we anyway?"

Ragib shrugged again. He sounded angry. "I assume in an Iraqi naval base in Basra…"

"How did we get here? I don't remember anything, apart from the moment we were shot at."

Ragib winced out of pain. "You passed out… the soldiers dragged you. You should've seen their excitement when your hat fell off and they found out you were a woman, and a beautiful one at that."

Hosni got up and groaned in pain. Stephanie looked at his swollen face and flinched. He stooped over Ragib and blurted out a few sentences at him. Ragib responded immediately. Then Hosni turned to Stephanie.

"You must tell them that you're an American and that we only helped you escape from Iran. Otherwise, they will make us disappear. They'll throw us in some prison basement for life and we'll never see the light of day again."

"Now?" Stephanie cut him short.

"The sooner the better," answered Ragib.

Stephanie wondered how much resentment the Iraqis still felt about American involvement in their country, whether she would be able to reason with them at all. The three of them began to yell in order to get the attention of someone.

Finally, the door opened and six soldiers holding rifles stood at the entrance to the holding cell. Stephanie stepped forward.

"I'm an American," she said. "I want to talk to whoever's in charge."

One of the soldiers, a tall and wide-shouldered man, cut her words with a roar and barked, "You! You, out." He stabbed his finger at her.

Stephanie stayed put.

"I want to talk to one of the officers." Stephanie held her ground. "These two men helped me escape from Iran. They are hurt. They need a doctor urgently. Please." She could hardly finish her sentence when two sets of hands grabbed her by her arms and pulled her out of the cell. "I want to talk to your commander," she demanded, desperately trying to struggle free from the soldiers clutching hands. "I'm an American citizen and I want to talk to someone from the American Embassy." Her pleas were ignored.

A fear gripped Stephanie as she was pulled through a long corridor. The memory of the interrogations in the Iranian facility surfaced again in her memory and the thought that she might again be put through physical torture and humiliation caused her extreme panic.

Stephanie found herself in a small windowless room with a table in the center and two chairs on the sides. The familiar sight made her shiver.

"I'm an American," she whispered, pleading. "Please... please... I'm an American citizen... We escaped from Iran."

The soldiers ignored her, quickly exiting the room one by one, leaving Stephanie completely alone and agitated. She felt her heart pounding strongly. After about fifteen minutes, the door opened and two uniformed men came in, walking briskly. Even though she could not identify their rank, it was obvious to her that they were officers.

"Please sit," the man with the moustache said, pointing at one of the chairs. "We have a few questions for you."

She remained standing, shifting her eyes between the two officers.

"I'm an American," she said. "I'm an American citizen. I want to see someone from the American military, please." At this point, she was desperate.

The man with the moustache pointed at the chair and positioned himself on the one opposite of her.

"Please sit." He spoke calmly. "How can we be sure you're an American? Do you have anything to prove it?"

Stephanie sat on the chair heavily. She thought about what she could tell them and what she could not. She finally spoke. "I escaped from Iran. They charged me with a crime I never committed. I came to visit my father. He is a deputy chief of police in Teheran. His name is Amir Motaki."

The second officer cut her off.

"What is your name? How did you get into Iran?" He pulled out a small pad and pen from his shirt pocket. "What is your identity card number or your passport number?" Stephanie considered the situation. She found comfort in the fact that the officer spoke perfect English. She knew that at this point she had nothing to lose.

"My name is Stephanie Simmons," she spoke confidently. "I came to visit my father and his family. I entered Iran with a fake passport. The Iranians arrested me and tortured me. I swear to you this is the truth. You can verify this with the American embassy. My identity card number is 29-56-4750. I live in Los Angeles and work for the Bureau of Immigration. My mother's name is Sharon Simmons. What other details would you like to know?"

The officer was smiling as he wrote down her words. When he stood to leave the room, Stephanie followed him with her eyes until he disappeared behind the door. Her gaze turned to the second officer who remained seated quietly.

"I swear to you I'm not lying," she said quickly toward the mustached officer. "You can't imagine the hell I went through these last few days."

The officer ignored her words and said, "Tell us about the two men you are with. Where did you meet them?"

Stephanie shrugged. "It's a long story. They were just doing me a favor. I was paying them to get me out."

"Who introduced them to you?"

Stephanie contemplated this question for a few moments. "It's complicated. Friends of my father's helped me escape, and one of the guys here is the brother of the person who at one point helped me escape. The other one,

Ragib, is a friend of his. Now, that is the truth and they both need urgent medical help."

"Don't worry. They're being taken care of," the officer responded, almost indifferent. "Who supplied you with the boat? Where did you come from?"

"From Adnam? Adanan? Something like that. I barely even know where I am now," she said. "They told me the names but I just don't remember."

The door opened and the officer who had left a couple of minutes earlier reentered the room. A young woman with a sturdy build, wearing jeans and a shirt in a flower motif, stood behind him. Her light colored hair was tied in a bun and made her look exceptionally young.

Stephanie looked carefully at the woman, having a hard time deciding whether she was part of the Iraqi military or perhaps she was working for the CIA.

"This woman claims she is an American citizen," said the officer to the woman.

Stephanie reacted quickly. "I'm really an American citizen. I'm asking you to check that out. I gave them my—"

The young woman stood, staring hard at her. "We are checking," she said. "It'll take some time. I'd like you to answer a few questions for me."

Stephanie shrugged. "I've already told them," she said. "But that's alright. What else do you want to know?"

"How did you get in to Iran anyway? Why did they arrest you?"

Stephanie told her how she had wanted to meet her father after finding out he was alive. She told her about her mother's warning against travelling to Iran, and how she forged a passport. She told her there were a series of tortures after she was arrested and that she preferred not to go into detail about them.

The young woman seemed to be indifferent throughout the story until the point when Stephanie mentioned the name Mahmoud Srkaawi.

"Wait," the young woman stopped her. "Please repeat the name…"

"Mahmoud Srkaawi," responded Stephanie. "He's a good friend of my father's."

"When did you see him last?"

"I told you, a couple of days ago. He releascd me from prison and took me-"

"I know Mahmoud Srkaawi," the young woman stated. "Only yesterday, we got intel from our people on a shootout in the center of Teheran. The Revolutionary Guard raided some house and he was killed in battle."

Stephanie was speechless. "Who was killed?" she asked, hardly containing the turmoil she felt. "Who told you he was killed? That can't be. I was told he was alive, that he's fine. It just can't be." Tears welled in Stephanie's eyes. "You can't imagine what an amazing man he was. He's been our family friend for years."

The young woman cut her short. "But Mahmoud Srkaawi is a key man in the Iranian security forces. Something is not making sense here."

A cell phone rang at that moment in the young woman's back pocket. She reached in and pulled it out. "Yes, let me have it," she said, quickly.

Stephanie watched her facial expression but could not read her. No muscles moved in the young woman's face.

"Okay, thanks," said the young woman as she ended the conversation. "We got confirmation of your statement. That is to say, there is an American citizen by the name Stephanie Simmons in the Department of Immigration in Los Angeles."

Stephanie sighed. "I told you. May I ask who are you?"

"Deborah," the young woman answered. "I'm a liaison officer with the Iraqi forces in the region. I will take you to our base, not far from here."

"What about my two friends?" Stephanie asked. "They need medical treatment. They were only—"

Deborah interrupted. "I can promise they'll be fine. You don't need to worry about them. If they're not with the Iranian forces, then they have nothing to worry about. They'll keep them a couple of days in detention and then they'll let them go."

Stephanie passed by the two Iraqi officers without a word and followed the young woman.

# 20

From the moment Stephanie set foot in the United States, she was confined to a spacious villa in a Los Angeles suburb that belonged to the American intelligence. She had no contact with the world outside, and was forced to tell her investigators over and over about her experiences in Iran.

Blondie, the CIA man she had met in Santa Monica prior to leaving for Iran, was in charge of her investigation. He was not alone. The investigators switched, one after the other, each in his own way trying to extract details from her, including her personal life prior to entering Iran.

"Am I under arrest?" she asked Blondie one night, when he joined her table in the small dining room.

Blondie smiled at her, took the pitcher and poured orange juice into a glass. "Hardly. You're not under arrest nor even a suspect. I think you should know the difference between being under arrest and being detained for questioning. You got enough experience," he joked.

"So what exactly am I doing here? I've already told a bunch of you the story of my life, from the moment I was born to—"

"Try to take it easy. We're just trying to figure out the extent of the damage you caused with that little adventure of yours. We also want to examine what to do with you and how to get you out of all the infractions you committed."

"Meaning, you're still considering filing charges against me?" she asked hesitantly.

Blondie's face remained sealed. "Perhaps. Disobeying a federal officer, forging a passport, entering an enemy country; those are severe charges that cannot be overlooked especially as an employee of the Immigration Department; you're considered a federal officer and that has implications."

The deep fear that had followed her overseas gave way to a relaxed and calm atmosphere, despite being detained. Except for questioning, she was free to do as she pleased. Apart from the meals, which she chose to eat alone in the small, blue dining room, she had a vast library, a swimming pool and even a gym at her disposal.

Twice a week, on Mondays and Thursdays, she was allowed to speak briefly with her mother over the phone. Stephanie cried a lot during these conversations and kept apologizing for what she had done.

Sharon calmed her down. "Enough. It'll be fine. You learned your lesson. You've been through a lot. Now, cooperate and it will all work out."

"When do you estimate they'll let me go?" she asked Blondie repeatedly, since she now felt at ease with him.

"Soon," he replied. "A matter of a few days."

Her investigators focused on five issues: her father, Mahmoud, Yasser Ashraf, the data that was on the flash drive, and much to her surprise, the investigators asked her questions about her boss and close friend, Kevin Shepard.

"Tell me how Kevin Shepard came up with the idea for you to specialize in Islamic studies?" asked one of the investigators, a tall man wearing gold-rimmed glasses. "Were you given the option to choose other courses?"

"As far as I can recall, no," she said. "Even before talking to Kevin about it, I spoke to one of the employees in my department and she told me she was going to attend professional training. I realized that after going through this kind of training, there's a raise of a couple of hundred dollars a month. I think she was the first to suggest the idea that I, too, should go for training. In any case, the idea of taking Islamic studies seemed only natural."

"Did you know that Kevin Shepard was a homosexual?"

Stephanie nodded. "Yes, though he did keep it a secret. He told me he was very concerned about being judged about that and also, he knew that the revelation would hurt his family."

"Did he tell you about his romantic activities with other men? Did he mention the names of any of the men?"

"I remember he told me that he had a relationship with a young man."

"Do you remember the name of the guy?"

"Sorry. I don't really remember the details." Stephanie paused. "Wait, I don't get it. Is Kevin Shepard a suspect? Why are you asking me these questions about his love life?"

The investigator did not acknowledge her questions. "Who, apart from you, were Kevin Shepard's friends? Does the name Abdoul Sarjani mean anything to you?"

"Abdoul Sarjani?" Stephanie repeated the name. "Never heard of him."

"Abdoul Sarjani served as the Iranian delegate to the UN for three years. It's odd that as soon as we got the word of your arrest in Iraq, Abdoul and his family disappeared."

"The truth is, Kevin Shepard didn't talk much about himself. I'm sorry. Most of the conversations we had were about me. He was really very good with everybody."

One day, Stephanie dared asking Blondie about the fate of her father and his family.

"We're still trying to find out," he responded. "His wife and daughters are fine. Your father has not been seen since the day you parted company."

"And what about Mahmoud Srkaawi?"

Blondie shook his head. "Mahmoud was killed at a shootout in Teheran. Aoni didn't score any better. He was wounded and taken into custody. I don't predict anything good will come from that. We weren't able to verify Radek's condition."

"And what's happening with Hosni and Ragib?" she asked.

"You mean the two young guys that were arrested with you by the Iraqis? Truth is we didn't even try to find out. If it's important to you, I'm willing to try and find out for you."

"Yes, it is important to me. Like the others, they helped save my life. It would mean a lot to me."

During her stay in the secret facility, Stephanie went through a series of medical examinations. One of them, as was explained to her, was a new test called "a button scan." They were concerned that the Iranians had inserted a tiny chip in her body during her stay in prison. The "button," they explained, was one of the more sophisticated espionage devices, hard to detect due to its miniscule size. The device is usually idle and can be activated by a computer command. Also, the operator can give the order and dissolve it within 36 hours without causing any damage to the carrier.

"The button is usually planted under full anesthesia, in the shoulder area," Blondie added. "A device of this kind can transmit data on the location for many months."

One morning, Blondie came in, accompanied by a short, dark girl of East Indian descent. "Stephanie, I want you to meet Doreen. She is our agent and an expert on India."

The two women shook hands. Blondie pointed Stephanie to a laptop that Doreen was carrying. "You've got a couple of days to learn about India. It's going to be your cover story. We've built you a trip portfolio, including photographs with various friends you supposedly met along the way. We chose popular vacation sites with lots of sea, sun and alcohol."

"Excuse me," Stephanie politely addressed the man called Blondie. "Is your real name Dan?" she asked, smiling.

"Yes. Why do you ask?"

"Dan, I have something personal for you," she said, while handing him the flash drive. "I caused many problems with my actions lately. That is why I want to present you with a gift from the Motaki family. I have no doubt you'll find much use in this gift."

And so, from one investigation to another, Stephanie spent many hours preparing her cover travel story. With Doreen's assistance, she learned everything possible on India and the friends that the agency matched her with. Stephanie loved the Indian accent and language and preferred it over the Iranian accent, and so the two women were soon busily memorizing the material.

One evening, without any prior notice, Blondie knocked on her door. "That's it. I came to tell you that this is your last night in our company. Tomorrow, at noon, you'll be free to resume your life."

Stephanie, lying on her bed in a white sweat suit, looked at him. "Free? That's it?" she asked hesitantly.

"Yes, free. We decided not to charge you. But you won't be able to go back to working for the Immigration Department. You can understand the reasoning to that. But we're very impressed by you. We got detailed data from our sources on the extraordinary perseverance you showed in prison. And, of course, your exemplary behavior during the escape from Iran. We want to keep an eye on you and the best way to do that is to offer you a position. Do you remember TD Strategy and PR in Santa Monica?

Stephanie gave a sigh of relief and a smile broke across her face. "Really?" she asked. "You really knew what I was going through there?"

"Yes, but I have one more important issue to clarify with you," Blondie insisted. She was alarmed by his shift to a serious tone of voice. "I want you to promise me that you're erasing the memory of this period from your mind. You're not to talk about Iran, not about your father, the arrest, the questioning in the military base and most important, not to talk about or even mention the existence of the flash drive. Nothing. To no one. Forever and ever."

"But my mother knows," she meekly mentioned.

"Except your mother. You can tell her almost everything, except of course, the flash drive issue. Not a word. Not even as a hint. I'm warning you."

Blondie sat beside her and took her hands in his. "Even though we will be neighbors at work soon, I want to make perfectly clear, if we find out that you spoke, told or shared even the smallest detail of your 'Iranian experience,' I assure you that I will personally see to it you go to prison for many years. You're lucky to be alive, Stephanie and you're lucky you're not going to jail. Don't even think about ruining that." He let that last thought sink in before he continued. "Now, do you have any questions?"

"No," answered Stephanie, without hesitating.

"Excellent. To end this briefing I'd like to tell you that, one, I will be very happy if you will accept our employment offer."

"Absolutely. And the second thing?"

"I want you to know that thanks to you and thanks to your father, we found out about one of the most elaborate and dangerous espionage operations of these times."

"And?" asked Stephanie with her typical curiosity.

"Thank you for your service to your country." He winked and left the room.

The next day, when Stephanie walked into her apartment, her mother was already there. Stephanie kissed and hugged her right away.

"I'm so happy to see you," she mumbled, allowing herself to release all the tension she had been holding in. The two burst out crying.

"I'm so sorry, Mom," she said repeatedly while holding tight to her mother, "I'm honestly sorry for everything. It's so good to be home."

The two women spent the day together and Stephanie told her much of what she went through in Iran, from the moment she landed at the airport in Teheran until the moment she landed in Los Angeles, accompanied by CIA agents.

In order to spare her mother pain, Stephanie did not mention the torture and the rape she had endured. Stephanie preferred not to tell the truth about that experience, and said that the investigators treated her decently. As she had promised Blondie, she did not mention anything regarding the sensitive issue of the flash drive to her mother.

From time to time, her mother would stop her flowing speech and sneak in a question. The most painful one was when she asked, "And you have no news of Dad?"

Stephanie shook her head. "Absolutely none. Blondie told me they're not getting anywhere."

Sharon was choked up. "It isn't out of the ordinary when people vanish there. We might never know. And it won't be us alone. It is quite likely that his wife and daughters won't ever know either. They will have to live with that question mark for the rest of their lives, without even having a grave to visit."

After being released, Stephanie tried to call her ex-boss, Kevin Shepard several times, but to no avail. Finally, she visited the Department of Immigration.

"What? Didn't you know?" asked one of his secretaries. "He decided to retire. He was given the option of early retirement and he jumped at the opportunity. I was sure you were filled in."

Stephanie was totally surprised. "No, I absolutely had no idea," she said, "When did all this happen?"

"About two weeks ago. Truth is, it happened very fast. From one day to the next."

Seated on one of the tall bar stools, Stephanie examined the women and men that filled up the Mikado Bar. She felt wonderful in the tight black dress she wore and enjoyed the looks that two young men passing by sent her way.

From the corner of her eye, she saw her best friend Vicky walking swiftly toward her.

"I'm sorry I was delayed," Vicky said. "You can't imagine how happy I am to see you. When did you get in?"

"A couple of minutes ago. I didn't have a chance to order."

The bar, located on the first floor of a commercial building in downtown Los Angeles, had opened a couple of months earlier. Since it was still early, the place was not too busy.

"Tell me, tell me how you've been," said Vicky. "I haven't seen you in such a long time. It feels like ages. I thought you'd forgotten me. How was your vacation?"

"Apart from the trip to India, nothing of significance. What can be exciting about a civil servant's work?"

Stephanie was detached from reality for a minute, her mind going back to an extraordinary past. But Vicky's voice brought her back from those memories. "Well, tell me how your vacation was? How was India?"

Stephanie answered with no hesitation. "Amazing. Amazing. I had to get used to the food and odors, but beyond that I just didn't want to come back. The people of India are warm and honest people. That's why I extended my vacation."

"Now, tell me all about this guy. Who's David? I want to hear all the nitty gritty. You promised to reveal it all."

Stephanie took in a deep breath. A tiny grin appeared at the corners of her mouth. She recited the data Doreen had given her. "David is a handsome man, a computer specialist from New York. He moved to India after his divorce, and he was the best thing that happened to me there." Stephanie closed her eyes and smiled. Suddenly, she felt her cell phone vibrating in her handbag. She immediately pulled it out. "Yes," she answered in a loud voice, trying to compensate for the noise around her. "I can't hear. I'm going out to a quieter place." She promised Vicky she would return soon.

Stephanie hurried towards the exit. "Yes, I can hear you now. Who is it?"

"This is Ross Dalian. I'm not sure you remember me."

"Sure, I remember. You were my agent. How are you?"

The voice on the other end was hesitant. "The truth is I only remembered you yesterday. They're casting a small budget, independent film. It's about a girl who wins the lottery but three months, later, she disappears and—"

"Ross," Stephanie answered quickly, "I just got back from a vacation in India. And it completely changed my life." She looked over at Vicky, holding up a finger, indicating she was coming back in moment. "And I have a new job I'm excited about in public relations. But thanks for the call." She hung up before he could reply and happily walked back into the Mikado Bar.